THE RED BOOK OF PRIMROSE HOUSE

An utterly charming English garden murder mystery

MARTY WINGATE

The Potting Shed Mysteries Book 2

JOFFE
BOOKS

Revised edition 2023
Joffe Books, London
www.joffebooks.com

First published by Alibi, Penguin Random House in 2014

This paperback edition was first published
in Great Britain in 2023

Cover art by Sasha Alsberg

ISBN: 978-1-83526-077-7

To Leighton

PROLOGUE

He returned after everyone had left and stood just inside the gate of the walled garden, surveying the scene. They'd made real progress, but now, what a mess. He couldn't believe it had come to this. Now, it was left to him to sort it all out.

He had intended to take care of it. He had promised he would. But the time for negotiating had passed, and he must take action. Checking his watch, he thought he might as well get to work. Clear this up before he began to clear up the other problems. He looked at the mountain of branches, strewn about and in such disarray.

He reached down and gathered up an armful of the greenery. No sense in letting it lie — it would only make more work for them later. God knows they had far too much to do as it was. He walked to the back gate. It wasn't a heavy bundle, although he had to take care not to step in one of the holes made by the boy. He let go the branches and they fell to the ground, making a soft *flump*. He went back for another load while his mind went over what he would say to each of them. His only concern was to make sure she would be all right — other problems took second place.

"Have you done it?"

He had just let go of the second armload of greens and hadn't seen the speaker approach. "You can't expect it to happen so fast," he said.

"You said you would take care of it. It's gone too far now, and I won't give up."

"I said that I would take care of her," he replied, growing short with this same argument.

"You made promises. We agreed, but you've done nothing."

"I will do what needs to be done, and what I do, I do for her — not for you or for a building or for anyone or anything else," he said, pulling his arm away from the hand that tried to stay him.

"It's cost me too much. How could you let it go this far? How could you let this happen?"

The rising frenzy would not sway him. "How could *I* let it happen? You're here only because of what you've done. Too full of yourself by half. You knew better than to start up, I warned you. I'm looking out for her." He started back to the gate.

"*Do you think I'll let you off that easy?*"

He turned to reply, but it was too late. The hatchet sank straight into his chest, and the impact sent him falling, falling backward until he landed on the soft bed of yew branches.

Primrose House

15 December

Dear Pru,

We love what you've done with the boxwood path out from the kitchen door to the yew walk. How clever to think of making the overgrown hedge into its own arbor walk — so much better than those laburnum walks. We wondered if it would be possible to plant daffodils at the base of the box, seeing as how you've already removed all the lower branches. What a glorious sight that would be!

Is it too late to do that now? You know we are more than happy to cover any extra costs for working on weekends. You are a jewel of a head gardener, and we remain thrilled with all your ideas and hard work. American Pru Parke and the famous Humphry Repton, what a pair!

Here's to a fine Christmas for all of us. Just think, soon you'll be moving into your cottage. It's almost ready!

Best,
Davina and Bryan

P.S. Just one thing. We've decided to open the garden here at Primrose House on 30 July. I'm sure you'll have everything ready. It will be a glorious summer party!

CHAPTER 1

"I'd say that'll do for today, will it, Pru?"

"Yes, Ned, that'll do for today."

Ned adjusted his cap and knocked a clod of dirt from his Wellies as he gathered up the short spade and garden fork. Ned kept himself as befitted a widower in his seventies. That is to say, his work clothes were always in good order, but Pru thought he might cut his own hair, as it usually stuck out from under his flat cap in uneven bits, like gray moss hanging off a tree branch.

Half past three on a mid-December afternoon. Pru glanced up at the darkening sky and climbed out of the mud where she had landed after yanking on an ash sapling growing in a sheltered corner of the walled garden. She sighed and reached up to unclip her hair, comb it through, and reclip. One strand escaped again without delay. Her hair had always had a mind of its own, even now as a little more gray had slipped into the brown. In her earlyish fifties, she was still able to carry out the physical work of gardening, although more and more she appreciated an extra pair of hands.

More than a month had passed since she began at Primrose House, an eighteenth-century manor farm near the village of Bells Yew Green and just a few miles from the spa town of Royal Tunbridge Wells. Much of that time had been spent getting to know the land, her new employers — Davina and Bryan Templeton — her crew, and the historic plan laid out in 1806 by the famous landscape gardener Humphry Repton.

The Red Book, the name Repton gave to the leather-bound books he created for potential clients, had been discovered just as the Templetons hired Pru as head gardener. The Earl of Lamerton had come across it in a box in one of the many unused rooms of the castle — Primrose House had been a manor on the estate. Davina had presented the book to Pru in the kitchen, and although it had not been the most formal of occasions, Pru had felt the weight of the centuries on her when she held the thin book.

She had set it down on the farm table and run her hand lightly over the cover. It was not as large as a coffee-table book, more the size of an old-fashioned accountant's ledger. The red Moroccan leather had faded little, and the ornamental gold-stamped border still locked fresh. Opening the book to the title page, she had seen Repton's self-portrait — a small drawing of him surveying a landscape, and the title *Primrose House in Sussex, A Seat of William Michael Hamilton, Earl of Lamerton* written in Repton's careful, scrolly hand. Following a page of introduction came "Situation of the House." Pru had trembled with excitement.

The entire book was in Repton's hand, and interspersed with his watercolors. It was a treatise on his landscape ideals. "To remedy the great defect of Primrose House . . ." he began. Despite what had gone on in the ensuing two hundred years, it felt as if the great landscape gardener himself were telling Pru how to carry on.

Dozens of his Red Books were still in existence, some held by the original properties and others in libraries or museums, but most of the landscapes retained only impressions of Repton's designs, and some had never even been built. The mere possession of a Red Book was noteworthy in the world of eighteenth- and nineteenth-century gardens and architecture, and the hope that remnants of his designs might still exist at Primrose House and would be recreated made the news in a small article that had appeared in the *Tunbridge Wells Courier*.

Now Pru had both a derelict garden to clear, design, and plant as well as a historic landscape to rediscover and restore — by summer, if you please. She saw the calendar in her mind at all times. The number of days until the garden needed to be "finished" for the open day that Davina had planned without Pru's consent decreased rapidly, while the amount of work that still needed to be carried out seemed to increase each day. It didn't help that light was in such short supply as midwinter approached.

And yet, it was her dream job — head gardener of a historic English garden. Be careful what you ask for, she thought, trying to quell the rising panic that set in each late afternoon. An open garden day may be a wonderful summer party to the Templetons, but it would be a day fraught with anxiety for Pru — she imagined every home gardener in England critiquing her plantings and wondering where the tea and cakes were.

She breathed deeply, reminding herself how lucky she was. She'd moved from Dallas and spent a year in London trying to find work. As the year drew to an end and with no permanent job in sight, she had been hired to build a garden in Chelsea. The garden never got made, owing to Pru's discovery of a body in the shed and her subsequent entanglement in a murder enquiry, but the silver lining to that cloud was meeting Detective Chief Inspector Christopher Pearse, who had conducted the investigation.

She could still see him as she had that first time at the scene of the murder — tall with short, dark hair flecked with gray and cutting a fine figure in his dark blue suit. He exuded an inner strength, and although he had seemed stern, Pru learned he was quick to smile and that his penetrating brown eyes could easily melt her on the spot.

With no job, she had been packed up and ready to leave for her old position at the Dallas Arboretum, when

Christopher had asked her to stay at nearly the same moment the job offer came from the Templetons. The stars had indeed aligned for her, although the decision to stay was both exhilarating and frightening, because she knew that it was more than just a physical home that was at stake, but a home for her heart, too. Now, here she was just an hour away from London and Christopher, although for the moment, she measured the distance in weeks, not minutes. Weeks since they'd seen each other, weeks until they would again.

* * *

She brushed a few clumps of leaf litter off her trousers, smearing mud in the process. The Templetons were gone, and she looked forward to a quiet evening alone in the kitchen of Primrose House, after which she could crawl into bed and wait for Christopher's nightly phone call.

"And tomorrow we'll plant those daffs Mrs. Templeton asked for?" Ned asked.

"Tomorrow," she said, coming back to the moment. Bulb-planting season long over, Pru had needed to buy several dozen pots of forced bulbs to plant below the box. And they had to be the small native *Narcissus*, not one of those garish jumbo selections. That was Ned's idea. He seemed to know as much about old plants as he did the old happenings around Bells Yew Green.

"I can dig the holes, Pru, can't I? You promised I could dig the holes." Robbie, at that very moment digging a hole in the middle of one of the square beds, stopped and waited for her answer, holding on to the spade handle with both hands. Robbie, son of Ivy Fox, the cook at Primrose House, was tall, wiry, with arms and legs sticking just a bit too far out of the sleeves of his red fleece jacket and his trouser legs, and he was almost constantly in motion. Although in his early twenties, his mind worked at about the level of a ten-year-old. Even so, he was a pleasant — if occasionally exhausting — companion for them.

"Of course you can, Robbie. Sorry, I wasn't paying attention."

Robbie grinned and said, "Pay attention, Pru, pay attention."

"Yes," she said with a laugh, "pay attention, Pru." She already had used that phrase with him often enough — *Pay attention, Robbie, watch out for the seedlings* or *Pay attention, Robbie, leave the ax where it is, please* — that he had latched on to it and loved repeating it to her. She turned back to Ned. "We'll hold the bulbs until Friday, all right, Ned?"

"You've a kind heart toward the lad, but it mightn't do the garden much good," Ned said as he pulled on his coat and readied to leave.

"He really is a help," she said. "He digs and . . . arranges the pots in the shed, and brings tea down for us." Robbie had gone back to digging. "I don't mind, really."

It was the only thing that kept his attention, digging holes. The only thing she allowed, that is. Early on, she'd discovered Robbie fancied himself as Robin Hood, or occasionally one of his Merry Men, and thought the hatchet made a good stand-in for a broadsword. She had laid down the rule swiftly on that — Robbie was not to touch any of the tools unless Pru said it was all right and she stood there with him. Robbie understood rules, and he knew how to follow them.

So, digging it was. When he dug, he didn't ask Pru the same question three times in five minutes, nor did he make a constant circuit around the walled garden ricocheting off the same spots each time — "What tree was that? Was it an oak?" "That wall's in need of a repair." "What will you make of the yew? Will you make a teapot out of it?"

* * *

"Shall I walk him up to the big house for you?" Ned asked.

"Yes, thanks Ned, that'll give me a chance to clear up."

"All right, Robbie Hood, we're off," Ned called to him, and Robbie leaned his spade against the garden wall, and took up a pretend sword and returned it to its pretend scabbard. Ivy encouraged her son's fascination with Robin Hood, because she thought a good English folk tale so much safer than those modern, violent television shows.

"I'm off to the pub, Pru," Robbie said. "To have a pint with my mates."

On Tuesdays, Ivy allowed him some male-bonding time at the Two Bells, where he could drink one pint before she collected him to go home. "They all know him there," Ivy said, "and Ted behind the bar keeps an eye on him. It's good for him, and I don't mind, really." Pru thought the tight smile Ivy gave when she said that told otherwise.

Out of the corner of her eye, Pru saw the other two members of her work force amble through the open gate — Liam and Fergal Duffy.

"How're the tools?" she asked.

"Were we being punished, Pru, was that it?" Liam asked. "Only I can't imagine a more boring punishment than cleaning garden tools all day long."

Fergal, ever the calm older brother, even though he was just twenty-nine years of age to Liam's twenty-six, said, "All finished. I've repaired the rack for now, and we hung the tools back up. The rack needs rebuilding, but I'm afraid nailing new wood into that old wall would knock the whole shed down."

For every smart-aleck answer from Liam came a reasonable reply from Fergal, but Pru took Liam in stride, especially as they were the brawn of her outfit. There was no mistaking they were brothers or their Irish heritage — both with dark red hair, blue eyes, pale skin, and quick smiles. They'd got off easy today. She'd had them sanding, sharpening, and oiling a collection of fine old, but badly rusted tools. Ned had come across them in the potting shed, which sat under an enormous cedar of Lebanon behind the walled garden. At least the Duffys had been out of the cold.

"We didn't get to it today, so tomorrow, we'll be removing all the buddlejas. I've counted fourteen of them in here, although there are probably seedlings, too," she said.

"We're taking out the buddlejas?" Liam asked. "And what are we doing that for?"

She'd have more patience with his question if he hadn't asked it the day before, too. "Because they don't belong here, Liam, that's why."

"I never heard anyone complain about butterfly bushes before. Don't they grow along the railway with those pretty flowers all summer long and no trouble at all. I don't see why they have to go," he said.

"They don't belong in the walled garden," Pru repeated. "They're coming out."

"I've always liked a buddleja in the garden."

"They're coming out, Liam."

"I don't know what the butterflies will do now," he muttered.

"*Out.*" She took a deep breath and exhaled slowly. "Tomorrow."

CHAPTER 2

The Duffys left, and Pru watched as Ned walked Robbie to the house. After that, the old man would continue home to his own cottage, a mile farther down the lane. She and Ned had a reasonable working relationship, she thought, although a bit of a rough start. They had first met at the end of the day she interviewed for the post. While she stood waiting for her taxi back to the rail station, he had come round the corner of the house and told her that the job had already been offered to someone else. But it turned out Ned had got his wires crossed and the Templetons offered her the job. Davina said nothing of another applicant, and Pru didn't ask.

On her first workday at Primrose House, Ned had shaken her hand and welcomed her, saying "I'm sure you'll do fine," which seemed to leave room for the idea that she might not, as if she were some young whippersnapper, as her dad might've said. But Ned had lived around Bells Yew Green his whole life, treating events that had happened long before he was born as if they had occurred the previous week, and so Pru had accepted his greeting as she had hoped it was meant.

Pru and Ned had what she would call a serviceable relationship. He wasn't a sparkling conversationalist, but he didn't need to be. There was enough talk with Liam and Fergal, and on Robbie's days, the chat level ramped up considerably.

She checked on the tools. For all his lip, Liam was a good worker, and even though they often went round and round, she usually won the day, either because he thought her American accent authoritative or the fact she was twice as old as he was.

Now the spades, hoes, rakes, and a scythe were lined up on Fergal's repaired wooden rack. On the shelf lay an ax, a hatchet, and three pairs of secateurs — what she had called bypass hand pruners in the States — cleaned of the rust and glistening slightly from the oiling the brothers had given them.

She left the shed and walked inside the back entrance of the walled garden to survey the one-acre scene in the failing winter light. Two centuries ago, it had been primarily a kitchen garden, but over the years, as with so many other walled kitchen gardens, it had become a showplace, growing exotic and ornamental plants that thrived in the captured heat of the brick walls. Pru hoped to bring it back into both ornament and production, as she had seen happen at Grenadine Hall's walled garden in the Cotswolds.

Her walled garden here at Primrose House had been in such a state of dereliction that for the first few weeks of work, it was hard to tell they'd even begun. But now, the main entrance to the garden sported a locally crafted wooden gate replete with decorated iron hinges and a scrolled handle set on an ornate plate. The two side gates and the back entrance awaited replacement.

Where she stood at the back gate — against the south wall — a fine Victorian-style, lean-to glasshouse had been installed. She'd acquired a small paraffin heater for the glasshouse, but with no sustained freezes so far that winter, it was stored away in the shed.

Ivy and Robbie had gone for the day by the time Pru made it up to the "big house," as Ned referred to it. Not quite accustomed to that term, Pru still pictured a prison when she heard him use it. She would be alone for the evening, because Davina and Bryan had left that morning for their Paris apartment to do some Christmas shopping. Since they had finished the house restoration, they were like doves let loose from a cage, often spending weekends and other short breaks elsewhere. "We've got you on the garden now, Pru," Davina said, "and we know we have nothing to worry about."

When she was on her own in the house, Pru confined herself most of the time to the enormous kitchen, kept warm by their large, ever-on Aga cooker. Her temporary quarters were through a door on the far side of the room. She would shower first and spend a cozy evening with her paperwork — drawings, plans, the constantly expanding to-do lists, and accounts spread out before her on the farm table.

A note from Ivy lay on the tile counter.

"Pru — I've left you dinner for the next three evenings until I'm back on Friday. There's an almond cake for your afternoon tea — don't let Liam eat it all — and eggs for your breakfast. Robbie says he dug five holes for you today, and he's very happy. Thanks ever so. Love, Ivy."

What a dear Ivy was. She'd cottoned on to the fact that Pru didn't cook, and, as a thanks for letting Robbie work in the garden, Ivy kept her well-fed.

* * *

Pru had been unprepared for Robbie. On her second day in the garden, Davina had walked around with her, chatting about their joint vision of the landscape and asking Pru what she thought they could do with the large oval space formed by the drive that circled in from and back out to the road.

"We don't want to hide the house, of course," Davina had said, "but wouldn't it be lovely to have some stunning tree in the center, one of those stately conifers from America — perhaps something you grew in Texas — and we could . . ." She stopped and said, under her breath, "Oh dear, I forgot."

Pru followed Davina's gaze and saw Ivy Fox, who cooked and cleaned for the Templetons, walking out toward them accompanied by a young man wearing a red fleece jacket. Ivy was about Pru's age, but a few inches shorter and a lot thinner, as if she never had enough time to sit down and eat a proper meal. Her wispy, light brown hair, cut into a severe wedge just above her chin, was salted with gray. She was tugging at a curly end.

Without taking her eyes off the approaching figures, Davina began speaking again, but this time low and quickly, and Pru had difficulty following her. ". . . and Ivy is such a treasure, really I don't know how we could do without her, and he is a lovely boy, but he's slow . . . is that the right thing to say? . . . and Ivy . . . well, we thought that perhaps he could be with you in the garden for a couple of days a week. It would be such a relief to her and . . ."

Davina's voice petered away to nothing as Ivy and the young man arrived in front of them. Pru had met Ivy briefly the day before, up in the kitchen as Pru's workday in the garden and Ivy's workday at Primrose House both ended about the same time, but she didn't know that Ivy had a grown son.

Ivy had smiled at both women as she fiddled with her apron strings, which looked as if they wrapped around her waist two or three times before she tied them. "Mrs. Templeton," she had nodded her head. "Pru, this is my son, Robbie." Robbie, several inches taller than his mother, stood just behind her.

"Hello, Ivy. Hello, Robbie, I'm pleased to meet you," Pru had said.

He had looked at the ground and didn't speak until his mother prompted him. "Robbie."

"Hello," he had said. Ivy looked back at him. "How do you do, Ms. Parke," he added as he took a step forward and smiled tentatively.

Davina had intervened. "Ivy, we were just talking about Robbie helping Pru out in the garden."

For a split second, it seemed as if Ivy and Davina had held their collective breath as they both looked at Pru. What choice did she have? Wouldn't she be the most disagreeable person in the universe to tell this young man that she wouldn't let him near her garden? Pru smiled. "Robbie, I'd love to have you help us." She had heard Ivy and Davina exhale. "How often are you able to be here?"

"Oh, it's just for two days." Ivy's words had rushed out, her face flushed and her smile widening. "If it's all the same, Tuesdays and Fridays would suit, wouldn't it, Robbie?" She had glanced at her son and then back to Pru. "He goes up to Tunbridge Wells on Monday, Wednesday, and Thursday to a lovely care center where he can—"

"I go to Chaffinch's, but they won't let me help in the garden," Robbie had said a sigh.

"That's because you dug up all their brassicas last spring, Robbie," his mother had said, reaching up to mess his thick brown hair and then smooth it down again. "You must be careful in the garden. Only do what Pru tells you."

"Well," Davina had said, "that's all sorted now, isn't it? That's grand."

* * *

In bed, Pru huddled under her cuvet with two extra blankets on top, phone in hand, waiting for Christopher to ring. It had become a nightly ritual since she started work and they had no time to see each other.

The warm Aga on the far side of the kitchen couldn't throw enough heat to make it in the door of her tiny room, which was situated on the north side of the house. It was a prime spot for the pantry, where food would've stayed cool — but as a bedroom, it kept Pru feeling like an ice cube. The heat from her hot shower had long since left her. She wished she could warm up.

Before the end of the first ring, she greeted him. "Good evening."

"How are you, my darling?" Christopher asked. There now, that warmed her up.

"I'm under the covers wearing flannel pajamas and wool socks, and I'm exhausted." She hoped he could tell from the tone of her voice what she really meant was that she had worked hard all day, accomplished great things, and missed him terribly.

"And did you get Liam to dig up the buddleja?"

"That boy would argue with a fence post," she said in exasperation. "And the cheek of him. On Saturday, when I bent over to pick up a trowel, he pinched my bottom."

Pru heard sputtering on the other end of the line. As this soon changed to coughing and laughing, she laughed along with him and asked, "Are you all right?"

"Yes," he said, his choked voice cleared up. "I'm all right. The question is, how is Liam?"

"Oh, he's fine," she said with grim humor. "Although I'd say he wasn't much good on the prowl at the pub that evening, judging from the yelp he gave when my elbow landed in a particular spot as I stood up."

"Good God, remind me never to take such liberties."

"Nonsense," Pru said, "you're allowed."

Neither spoke. Any vague mention of intimacy remained a touchy subject given their current circumstances. One weekend together — one amazing weekend, Pru reminded herself — followed by these weeks of physical separation caused by her living situation and her new job, which ran seven days a week, left no time together.

"How's the cottage coming?"

"They've finished the walls inside, work on the kitchen has commenced, and the front door will be hung tomorrow. Davina has furniture for me. I don't think it'll take too many pieces to fill up the place." Her cottage sat on the other side of the walled garden from the house — near enough to work and the Templetons', but far enough away to feel private.

"I'm flying back just after New Year's," he said. Christopher would accompany his son, Graham, to Dubai over Christmas to see him settled into a year-long internship with a UK engineering consultancy firm. Graham, in his early twenties and recently out of university, was ready to change the world.

She smiled under the covers. "I hope to be settled not long after that."

"I'm sorry I won't be around for Christmas," he said.

"Yes." She couldn't help the disappointment. "I'll be in Hampshire, and you'll be very far away." She would spend Christmas with Harry and Vernona Wilson. It was their Chelsea garden she had been hired to create. After the murder investigation, they had moved back to their old house near Romsey.

After they said good night, Pru settled in, fingering the necklace Christopher had given her and that she never took off. She drifted to sleep as she relived the events that took place after she did not move back to Texas — the moment she considered the official beginning of their relationship — and when she met Graham. She especially enjoyed recalling the weekend she and Christopher spent together just before she began work at Primrose House. It was a memory she visited often.

CHAPTER 3

She had waited on the Wilsons' front step in Chelsea for Christopher to collect her for dinner. It had been only a few days after the resolution of the case, and the Wilsons were packing up to return to Greenoak, their home in Hampshire. Pru would spend two more nights with them in London before she and Christopher would spend the weekend away, after which she would report for her job at Primrose House in Sussex. In the meantime, he had asked her to dinner at his flat to meet his son, Graham, who was visiting. Her unsettled stomach made her believe that meeting your date's son might be scarier than meeting his parents.

The weather had turned cold, and a wind whipped down the street and through the branches of the plane trees in Chartsworth Square, scattering leaves over the road. But chilly weather was nothing to a gardener, so when she got in the car and Christopher said he would've been happy to park and come to the door if she'd given him the chance, she responded by kissing him and just barely slipping her tongue between his lips before saying, "We'd best be off." He gave her a narrow look and smiled.

The atmosphere inside the car, as Christopher drove from Chelsea to Chiswick, was one of quiet joy and nervous anticipation not only for meeting his son, but also for their upcoming weekend. Alone. The first time.

While stopped at a traffic light, he took one of her cold hands and began rubbing it vigorously. "Graham offered to cook for us. I believe we're having shepherd's pie."

"Excellent. I hope this Rioja I have goes well."

They parked in the garage, walked into his building, and pressed the button for the lift. She glanced at him and said, "I'm a little nervous about meeting him."

As the lift doors closed, his fingers lightly caressed the back of her neck. "There's no need for that."

She looked up at him. "You're a little nervous, too, aren't you?"

He smiled and pressed his lips to her forehead. "Yes, a bit."

But there was no need for nerves, because she and Graham, a talkative, engaging young man, got on famously. He stood several inches shorter than his father, and his hair, which just reached his collar, was blond like his mother's. Pru had met her only once.

The three of them chatted about the countryside, gardens, and Graham's recently finished course of study in environmental sciences. As the evening progressed, she began a long discussion with him about the quality of urban soils. Pru looked over at Christopher. They had taken their coffee in the living room after an apple crumble for pudding. He had leaned back in his chair and stretched out his legs and had a smile on his face and such a look of contentment as she had not seen before.

When the evening was over, she insisted on taking a taxi back to the Wilsons' instead of dragging Christopher out to drive again.

"I'm glad to have met you," Graham said as Christopher helped her on with her coat. "Dad was in a right state when he thought you were headed back to Texas. I wouldn't be surprised if he didn't bite a few heads off at the station." He had that same smile playing about his lips as his father. "You don't mind me saying that, do you, Dad?"

"No, son, I don't mind."

"Good night, Graham. It was a wonderful meal, thanks so much," Pru said as she gave him a peck on the cheek. He blushed.

In the hall as they stood waiting for the lift, Graham stuck his head out the door. "Oh, there you are. Pru, would you like me to email you that article on the depth of substrate needed for the new building codes?"

"I'd love to read it, yes, thanks. You'll get my address from your dad."

"Right, then. Well, carry on. Cheers." He closed the door of the flat just as the lift doors slid open.

Pru laughed. "I don't know what he thinks we're going to get up to in a lift."

Christopher raised his eyebrows. "You never know," he said.

"He's a lovely young man. You should be very proud."

"I didn't have much to do with that." Christopher had been divorced from Phyl since Graham was a boy.

"Of course you did," she insisted. "I can see you in him. Such a sense of purpose, and a good sense of humor, too."

He responded to that by pulling her closer. In the middle of a long and involved kiss, they didn't notice the lift doors open until they heard a small cough. A well-dressed elderly woman with a cane smiled and said, "Hello, Christopher."

They exchanged places with her, as Christopher, still holding Pru around the waist, smiled back. "Mrs. Miller, how was your evening?"

As the doors slid closed, she said, "It was lovely, but probably not as good as yours."

They stood at the curb as he hailed a taxi. He opened the door for her, and after she was settled, he leaned in and whispered in her ear, "I'll see you at the weekend. I can't wait to get you alone."

Her face flushed and she laughed as the cab pulled away. She was glad it was dark.

* * *

20

Most of Pru's belongings, such as they were, had been sent down to Primrose House and on her last day in London, her friend Jo had come round to say goodbye and help her throw the few remaining things in a weekend bag. Christopher had booked a country hotel for the weekend and Pru would meet him there. But as she took stock of her wardrobe — one nice sweater amid sturdy canvas trousers and woolly jumpers — she regretted not having something special to wear.

Jo rummaged through Pru's bag as if assessing its pitiful contents. Pru had never been much of a fashion statement, but Jo always looked well put together in her well-cut business suits and heels that raised her just barely over the five-foot-high mark. Pru admired her fashion sense, but a gardener's clothing requirements were different.

Jo pulled something from her own bag and held up a parcel wrapped in gold tissue paper and tied with red ribbon. "Wear it this evening," she said with authority.

"Wear what?" Pru said with alarm, picturing a lacy black nightie inside the package.

"It's a dress," Jo said, laughing. "For dinner. I didn't think you'd need help with anything else."

Pru wasn't sure which alarmed her more — the thought that the parcel contained a black nightie or that it held a dress. She blushed. "Thanks, Jo," she said and gave her a hug.

* * *

Pru drove her new-to-her Mini Cooper down the lanes to the hotel Christopher had booked for them in the Kent countryside. She passed the turnoff to Sissinghurst Castle and gardens and craned her neck to look down the lane. It was every gardener's mecca, and she hoped to spend time there in the spring. Soon she turned into the long drive up to the expansive old hotel set in the middle of acres of neatly cut grass.

The lobby was huge but warm with dark, polished wood paneling and pillars. She could see a fire going in an adjoining room. Christopher sat on a sofa in an alcove just to the side of the reception desk with a pot of tea on the low table in front of him. He had his eye on the door, and was up and to her before she got halfway to him. They met just behind a large parlor palm.

Well, isn't this silly, she thought. *How can I feel nervous after we've spent the last few weeks unable to keep our hands off each other?* She set her bag down and gave him a small kiss. He stood close.

"Did you have a good drive?" he asked.

Pru nodded and glanced around the lobby. "This is lovely."

He took hold of her left hand. "Would you like a drink?"

Her nervousness vanished, replaced with the desire to ravish him on the spot. She murmured, "Mmm, later."

His fingers, barely touching the palm of her hand, began tracing a circle. "Would you like to have a look around the place?"

"Not right now," she said, barely breathing.

She could see that ghost of a smile. "Are you hungry?"

She cut her eyes around the lobby, looked back at him, and whispered, "Yes."

He squeezed her hand, picked up her bag, and said, "Come with me," as he led her to the lift.

* * *

"Covers," she said, "I need covers." Finally cooled off, she sat up to draw the duvet over them.

Christopher pulled her back down, put his arm around her, and buried his face in her neck. "I was beginning to think this would never happen."

"Events trying to get the better of us?"

"That wasn't what I meant," he said.

She nestled her head into his shoulder. "I know it wasn't," she whispered.

They were quiet for a moment. "I've booked a table for us at half past eight," he said.

"Half past eight? Somehow you knew I wouldn't want an early dinner upon my arrival. How prescient of you."

"I knew *I* wouldn't want dinner when you first arrived."

She sighed deeply, ran her finger down his arm, and closed her eyes for a moment. "What time is it now?"

He reached over her to the nightstand and picked up his phone. "It's eight. I suppose we should be up and busy."

Looking over at his phone, she said, "You won't get anyone ringing you about a case this weekend, will you?"

Without replying, he switched it off. "I'll get dressed and go down to check on our table."

How chivalrous. After he left, she got out of bed, repaired her hair and the dab of makeup she wore, and pulled out the package from Jo, which turned out to be a beautiful, long-sleeved, maroon dress of thin, soft wool with a very wide and deep neckline. She eyed the dress cautiously. It looked as if there would be no pushing up and creating cleavage, so that was a good thing. Still, dresses — let alone dresses with deep necklines — were not Pru's usual forte. *But Jo said to wear it and so I will.* She pulled it on and looked in the mirror.

The fit and the color were perfect, but the amount of exposed skin shocked her. She began tugging at the neckline, trying to pull it higher. "My God, what was Jo thinking?"

"You look beautiful." Christopher had come in without her noticing, and stood across the room.

She whirled around, laughing, and put her hand on her chest. "I feel bare." She needed another layer or she'd spend the night embarrassed. "I have a scarf — I'll wear that over my shoulders."

He smiled at her as he walked over and held out a flat, square leather box. "I have something for you. Maybe it will help."

She opened the box and its contents took her breath away — a gold filigreed, fan-shaped pendant on a gold chain made of etched oval links. Her eyes filled with tears. "It's gorgeous. Thank you. It looks old — art deco?" She picked it up and let the gold chain slide through her fingers.

"Yes, from the 1930s, so they told me." He lifted her chin and watched her for a moment. "I don't know the right time or place for this."

"To give me a beautiful gift?" she asked.

"To tell you that I love you."

"Oh," she said, her breath taken away once again. In Texas, she had kept her relationships at an emotional arm's length, unwilling to make a commitment that would tie her down to a place she didn't want to call home. But now she found her heart as close to him as they were standing.

She laughed. "That's amazing."

"Is it?" he asked with a quizzical look on his face. His arms went round her waist.

"Yes, because I love you," she said, running her fingers through his short hair. She slipped her arms round his neck, and they gazed into each other's eyes.

He kissed her and said, "Dinner."

"Would you help me with my necklace?" She handed it to him, lifted up her hair, and turned around so that he could do the clasp.

He kissed her bare shoulder, and then she heard him patting his pockets. "Hang on a tick — I've left my glasses in my other jacket."

She went to dinner wearing no scarf, not with her necklace to show off. They sat quietly, stealing glances and sharing small smiles while the waiter described the specials for the evening, opened the wine, and served their first courses. They were so obnoxiously in love and still wrapped in that afterglow of sex that Pru wouldn't have been surprised if the waiter had made fake gagging sounds when he walked back in the kitchen. She didn't care.

* * *

It was breakfast before they had time to catch up with news.

"You'll be living in the pantry at Primrose House?" Christopher asked, a forkful of scrambled eggs halfway to his mouth.

24

Pru sniggered. "Former pantry. Just until the cottage conversion is complete. It's en suite." They could put her up in the coat closet, as far as she was concerned — nothing could dampen her good spirits. "It's where Davina and Bryan slept for five years during the house restoration, so I can hardly complain. And it'll make my cottage seem huge."

She effused on Humphry Repton and the Red Book, and told him about the small article in the *Courier*.

"It's just as well that it didn't mention my name," she said. "I don't really have anything to say about it." He glanced up from buttering a piece of toast, and she added, "At the moment."

* * *

The weekend went by far too quickly, as they knew it would. They took a long walk on Saturday, following a path out the back of the hotel that ended in a patch of trees, mostly beeches with their leaves turning gold, and a few oaks warming up to mahogany. On the other side of the trees, the path opened to a meadow with tall, tawny brown grass, beginning to break down in the late-autumn weather. They stood without speaking, their breaths creating clouds of fog in the air. Pru contemplated the view to the east, but she noticed Christopher looking around the clearing.

"What are you thinking about?" she asked.

"I'm wishing it was a warm summer's day and we had a blanket." He looked over at her and smiled. "I'm wishing you didn't have so many clothes on."

She burrowed her face inside the collar of his jacket until her cold nose touched his neck, and gave him a kiss. "Take me back to the room, and at least one of those wishes will come true."

Too early for the Christmas trade, the hotel had few guests, and so they began to lay claim to the sofa in front of the fire on the far side of the lobby in a quiet nook. Typical of English country hotels, on Sunday after the midday meal was served the kitchen closed, with only the bar remaining open and offering a few packaged snacks in the evening. Late in the afternoon as they read the Sunday *Guardian* in front of the fire, the barman approached.

"Excuse me, sir," he said. "Would you and the lady like me to send up a plate of sandwiches to your room this evening? It's just, there's a coachload of Germans arriving later, and you might prefer a quieter place." He cleared his throat.

Pru peered over the top of the paper as she felt her face grow warm. They had been rather obviously preoccupied with each other. Christopher answered with aplomb, although she noticed the tips of his ears turn pink. "Thanks, yes, that would be fine. And a bottle of that cab franc we had last night?"

* * *

Friday evening had been sweet and tender. Saturday, laughter filled the long, lovely dinner. But by Sunday evening, sitting on the floor and eating off the coffee table in their room, an ever-so-slight note of melancholy had crept in.

"We won't have this again for a while, will we?" Pru asked.

"Still," Christopher said, "it's better than it might have been. I was afraid I'd never see you again if you had left."

"I was afraid, too." Looking back, she wondered what she had been thinking, about to go off to Texas.

He fixed her with one of his penetrating looks. "I'd started looking into flights to Dallas."

Her eyes widened in delight, and she reached across the table for his hand. "You were going to come after me? How romantic."

"I didn't want to lose you."

"You haven't lost me — I'm right here. And I'll be just an hour away."

As she fingered the gold necklace, which she now refused to take off except when showering, she swept thoughts of no home of her own and a seven-day workweek under the rug, so that she could fully enjoy the moment.

On Monday morning, they said goodbye in the car park. Christopher promised to visit as soon as she'd moved into her cottage and Pru promised that it would be soon.

Primrose House

22 December

Dear Pru,

Just a thought as we pack up for Christmas. Shouldn't a Humphry Repton landscape have a water feature? We thought that a lovely fountain in the large oval out front would be a magnificent way to greet guests — something three-tiered and Italian, perhaps? We'll let you think about this, and settle on a design in the New Year.

Happy Christmas!
Davina

CHAPTER 4

Pru thought a three-tiered Italianate fountain would be in dreadful taste, but hoped she wouldn't have to go into detail with her employer, who seemed to land on a new idea for that space every few days. Pru wouldn't be surprised if Davina seized on a fairy garden or a collection of gnomes next.

On Christmas Eve morning, Pru left for Hampshire. She spent the holiday catching up with the Wilsons, eating wonderful food prepared by Evelyn, their cook, and taking their terrier, Toffee Woof-Woof, for walks. They exchanged modest gifts. Pru gave Mr. Wilson a book on the Alamo, Mrs. Wilson, a book of stitchery patterns based on Roman mosaics, and Toffee, a box of rat-shaped dog biscuits. They gave her a sturdy hand-knitted sweater made by someone in Mrs. Wilson's Women's Institute chapter, a book of parterre and knot garden designs, and an Aga cookery book. They hit the mark in two out of three, so not too bad.

On Christmas evening, Pru retired to her bedroom to wait for the video call from Dubai she'd arranged with Christopher. Actually, Graham had set it up.

"Are you there, Pru?"

"Yes, hello Graham, happy Christmas."

"You, too." She could see Graham looking over Christopher's shoulder and pointing to the keyboard and the screen. "Right, now, Dad, don't move much or she won't be able to see you, and when you want to ring off, just click—"

"Yes, son, thanks, I think I've got it," Christopher said, a bit of impatience in his voice. "I can take it from here."

"Right, that's me away, Pru. Cheers, bye."

"Bye, Graham."

She and Christopher looked at each other's image, until she saw the door behind him close.

"Happy Christmas, my darling."

She touched his face on the screen. "Happy Christmas. How was the day?"

"The company put on a dinner for all its UK employees and their families here, Christmas crackers and all. And how is everyone there?"

"The Wilsons send their regards. They're settled in and are enjoying being back in Hampshire. They hope that you'll come down, too, next visit."

"I wish I had my arms around you right now," he said.

She produced a small sound somewhere between a squeak and a sigh and left it at that.

* * *

As dear as the Wilsons were to her, she really focused on Boxing Day, the day after Christmas, when she would meet their gardener who shared her surname, Simon Parke. Pru had looked forward to it since she'd first heard of him, when she worked for the Wilsons in London. Simon had been the Wilsons' gardener for many years and, knowing of Pru's interest, Mrs. Wilson had asked Simon over for tea. Pru hoped to discover that he was a distant relative. Her English mother, Jenny Parke, had been an only child, as was Pru herself, but her longing for some family relation in England had led her to dream up all sorts of connections, even though since her arrival the year before, she'd had no time to carry out any actual research. Simon might hold the key.

Boxing Day broke clear and mild. After lunch, Mrs. Wilson noticed Simon out in the garden, and Pru said she'd go out to meet him.

The afternoon sun, low in the midwinter sky, was in her eyes as she walked the path out to the terrace garden. She squinted, put her hand up to her forehead, and saw a figure ahead of her. He appeared as a silhouette, kneeling in the path, one knee up with his elbow resting on it as he took a close look at something. Pru got the queerest feeling, a wave of cold that spread from the top of her head and down over her shoulders. He must've heard her approach, because he stood up and turned to her, and the queer feeling vanished.

"Hello — Simon? I'm Pru," she held out her hand.

He shook it firmly, with a good gardener's grip. He wore a sheepskin coat against the cold. She moved slightly and with her eyes out of the sun, could see that he was older than she by several years and just barely taller. She searched his face, looking for a reminder of her mother, but couldn't say if she saw anything or not.

"Hello Pru, I'm happy to meet you. Vernona and Harry told me all about you and what happened in London."

"They've told me a great deal about Greenoak and the garden. Even in winter, I can see it will be wonderful when the season starts."

They chatted about the garden and looked at the tips of grassy crocus leaves and spears of daffodils already shooting out of the ground. She asked him a few questions about clipping yew for topiary — a task she would be taking up at Primrose House. It was easy to talk with him. It was always easy gardener to gardener, she thought. As they talked, she kept trying to steal glances at him, and a time or two felt him do the same to her.

They walked past several large, fragrant witch hazels, and Pru inhaled deeply. "Oh, they're lovely." Carpeting the ground below the leafless shrubs were hundreds of hardy cyclamens, just four inches high, blooming in white and shades of pink.

"They naturalize quite easily. Do you not have any at Primrose House?" he asked.

"I haven't seen any," she replied. "We don't even have any primroses. Yet, at least."

"Before you go today, we'll dig up a clump for you to take back. We've loads here, more than enough to share. And snowdrops — do you need any of those?" He looked back at the house. "I'd say Vernona will have tea ready soon. Shall we go in?"

They walked into the sitting room together, as Mrs. Wilson put the tea things down on a low table between two short sofas. She brushed off her skirt and said, "There now" but stopped when she looked up at them, but after a moment she continued. "Simon, Evelyn has made shortbread for you."

Mr. Wilson stood in the arched entry to the room and looked from Pru to Simon and back again. "Vernona?" he asked.

"Harry, come sit down," his wife said.

Pru and Simon sat on the same sofa, across from the Wilsons. Toffee took up residence beside Simon, and when tea was poured and Simon had a plateful of shortbread, he broke a piece off and gave it to the dog. Toffee took it out of his fingers gingerly and crunched it down, after which he went over to Pru and sat down. She did the same. "Well," she said, "he's got our number, hasn't he?" and Simon laughed.

"Let's have a photo of the two of you," Mrs. Wilson said, "our Chelsea gardener Parke and our Hampshire gardener Parke."

"Oh, I don't believe you can really call me your gardener," said Pru, her face ablaze. "I didn't have the chance to do anything." As Mr. Wilson wandered off to find the camera, Pru said, "Simon, Mrs. Wilson probably told you about my mother, Jenny Parke. That she was English?"

"You have the same name as your mother?" he asked.

"It is confusing, I know. My dad's last name was Walker. I use my mother's name. I wanted to strengthen my connection over here, and I thought that would help."

"Vernona did mention your mother to Birdie, but I don't believe I'm a Parke relative," he said. He didn't look at her, but reached over for another piece of shortbread, which he put on his plate and then put his plate on the table. "My Aunt Birdie and Uncle George Parke brought me up, after my parents died in a car crash just after the end of the war. It was not long after I was born. My mother was Birdie's sister, you see. Uncle George was the Parke so, he might've been the relative, if there is one. But he's long dead now, and they had no children of their own. Birdie's still alive, though."

"Birdie might know something about your mother, Pru," Mrs. Wilson said. "Weren't your parents from Ibsley, Simon?"

"Is that where your mother was from?" he asked Pru.

Pru had followed their exchange, but the disappointment that rose up inside threatened to overcome her and she didn't speak, but only nodded. She had got her hopes up and now they were dashed. Simon was no relative. Perhaps he was related to someone who might have known her mother, but he wasn't directly family. She smiled at him. "Thanks for coming over today, Simon, during the holidays and all. It must've taken you away from your family. You have a family?"

"My wife, Polly, and two girls. They're grown now, but they don't live far, and so they're home for Christmas."

Mr. Wilson reappeared with a camera, and with a kind but reproachful look at his wife said, "Vernona, I found it in your box of knitting patterns." He turned the camera on and aimed it at Simon and Pru. "There now, big smiles from the gardeners. Right, I'll email you a copy, how's that, Pru?"

From: DavinaPrimrose@bt.com
To: PruParke50@bt.com
25 December

Dear Pru,

We are so pleased with the progress you are making in the garden, and we know that the open day in July will be a huge success.

I wanted to dash off this quick email to you while it was still fresh in my mind. You are becoming quite the Repton expert, and so I know you won't mind investigating this one little thing. You know that large beech at the far corner of the terrace? It's so enormous, I wonder if this wasn't the one that Repton planted to hide the view of the village pub. Of course, the only way we would know that now is to look for the pub from the very top of the tree as it stands. Would you mind climbing up for us to see what you can see?

Best wishes,
Davina

CHAPTER 5

Pru had emailed Davina back immediately, saying she couldn't possibly climb the beech — eighty feet high if it was an inch — citing health and safety regulations, and not her fear of heights.

Returning to Primrose House the day after Boxing Day, Pru first turned off the lane and onto the gravel drive to her cottage — not as grand an entrance as the approach to the big house, but entirely her own. The workers were off now until after New Year's. Through the kitchen window she could see the small dark blue, previously used Aga cooker that Davina had found for her. Still partially assembled, the cast-iron enamel pieces were scattered about and rock wool, used as insulation, erupted from the top. She laughed to herself. Did Davina think Pru cooked? Still, it would be a great source of heat for the cottage.

She turned her Mini back out onto the lane and up to the drive for Primrose House. The Templetons would return later that evening from the Seychelles, and Ivy and Robbie had gone off to Bristol to stay with her sister, so Pru was surprised to see a car parked at the side of the house and a man standing beside it, looking around as if appraising the view. Pru parked just past his car and got out.

"Hello, are you looking for the Templetons?" she asked.

"Are they at home?" He walked to Pru holding out his hand. "Sorry, I'm Jamie Tanner. Are you the gardener?"

"Yes, I'm Pru Parke." She looked down at her hands, still grimy from digging up the cyclamen and the snowdrops that Simon gave her. "Sorry about that." She held up her hands to him.

He laughed and held up his own. "Snap," he said. It looked as if he'd had his hands in the dirt, and she also noticed a couple of raised scars on his left thumb.

"You're a gardener, too?" Pru asked.

"Ned's told me all about you," he said, smiling. "Sounds like you've got things well in hand round here. Can't be easy, restoring an historic garden." He looked out at the wood below the sloped lawn. "You'll be carrying out the tree work?" he asked.

"*I* won't be doing any of it," Pru said with a small laugh. "I don't do well with heights. I've already told Davina we'll need to hire an arborist."

His mention of Ned eased Pru's mind. She knew few people in the area as yet and thought it was high time to become acquainted. But even more than that — Jamie could be her first connection into the garden world in Kent and Sussex. "Bryan and Davina are due back this evening. Would you like me to give them a message?"

"No, no," he said, "there's no need. I can give them a ring when they return. I only wanted to see how it was all going." He gave a small shrug and stuck his hands in his jacket. "I . . . well, I applied for the post here, too."

"Oh." Pru, acutely aware of how it felt not to get a job, tried to think of something to say that didn't sound trite. "Well, I'm . . . sorry that you . . ."

But he laughed in an easy way and said, "Don't worry about it. You're the one with the better qualifications, and so you were chosen. I've no hard feelings. I work for the Council, doing the landscaping around town." He glanced up at the walls of the house. "So, will you replant in front — a few roses, perhaps?"

"Yes," she said, and walked around to the corner of the house, so they could look at the bare expanse of bricks. "I haven't chosen anything yet. We've been starting on the walled garden first."

"There's a job for you now. I hope you've got enough help." He raised his eyebrows. "I'm not looking for work — I don't want you to think that. I've enough to do, and my wife would have my head if I added another job on top of everything else."

"You're married," Pru said. "Do you live nearby?"

"Near enough," he said, running his hand through his blond hair — long on top and short underneath. It fell back immediately into his face.

"What does your wife do?" Pru asked.

"Do?"

"I mean does she work outside the home?"

"She's her hands full enough as it is, believe me. Right, well I'll be off. Good luck with Primrose House." He walked back to his car, hesitated, and said, "Say, I've a friend who grows roses. He's over near Staplehurst. He's got a few large Maigold he'd let you have. I'd say they're already about eight feet, pot-grown, so they've got good roots. I know you can get a rate at the big nurseries, but I don't think you'll find anything this size. As long as you don't mind digging big holes."

"Oh, we can dig holes," Pru said. The climbing rose Maigold, an early bloomer, would be a good way to begin planting at the front of the house. Its golden blooms would be set off well by the red brick. And at that size, how could she resist? "Thanks, that would be great. Should I ring him?"

"I tell you what," he said, "why don't I collect them for you and drop them off?"

"No, I don't want to put you out," Pru said.

"It's no trouble. We've no work before next week. I won't bother you. I'll just leave them here at the front. You can settle up with Michael directly, there's no worry about that. You'll give Davina and Bryan my best?"

Pru thanked him again and watched him drive away. Creeping under her sense of gratitude came a tinge of guilt. He seemed a nice enough fellow, eager to help her feel comfortable in her new situation. But she wondered if he had counted on this job. He had a wife, perhaps young children. Did the head gardener post at Primrose House pay better than a Council job? Had she stolen food out of a baby's mouth?

* * *

She sat at the kitchen table reading when Davina and Bryan returned late that evening. They'd had a lovely time on the beach in the Seychelles, but, as Bryan put it, "There's nothing like a roaring fire on a cold English night," and he went off to light one in the library.

Davina poured them all brandies and sat down at the table, giving Pru the opportunity she needed.

"I want to thank you again for choosing me for this job," she began. "I'm sure you had many others apply, and probably you had a few local gardeners who thought the job was right for them."

Davina tossed her head back, sweeping her gray bobbed hair out of her face, and adjusted a few of the many thin layers of fabric that made up her outfit. Her face lost its color and her reply was sharp. "So, Ned's been talking, has he?"

"Ned?"

"I will not be bullied," Davina said.

Pru had lost the thread of the conversation. "Ned is trying to bully you?"

Davina sniffed. "He's a gossipy old man, Pru," she said, "and you should not pay him any mind."

"But I didn't talk to Ned. I met Jamie Tanner."

"Oh Jamie," Davina said, exhaling with a sympathetic cluck. "How is he? Where did you meet him?"

"He was standing outside when I got back this afternoon. He sends his regards."

Davina was quiet for a moment, as if assembling her thoughts. "Pru, has Ned spoken to you about the head gardener post? That is, how we chose you as the best candidate?"

"No," Pru said. *At least not since the day I interviewed, and Ned told me I didn't get the job*, she thought. But Davina's comments confirmed what Pru had suspected — Ned had been talking about Jamie when he said someone else had been chosen already.

"If he does," Davina said, looking down into her brandy as she swirled it around in the glass, "I don't want you to worry a bit about what he says. He isn't the boss around here."

Ned had yet to try to boss Pru. He wasn't the most talkative or congenial of workers, but for his age, he worked hard and she had no complaints. "Is there a problem with Ned? You hired him to work on the grounds."

Davina picked up Bryan's brandy and walked out of the kitchen as she said, "It isn't as if we had a choice."

Primrose House

29 December

Dear Pru,

We've had the most amazing offer! Hugo Jenkins, a young reporter from the Courier has asked if he could follow the garden restoration with a blog. Posts would appear every week online, all about Primrose House, Repton, and you. Isn't this exciting?

Of course, it's entirely up to you to say yes or no. I wanted you to make the decision, although I'm sure you are as thrilled as we are to be able to share this story with the world. Just give Hugo a ring when you're ready.

Best,
Davina

P.S. I had a sudden thought last night. We could create a "ruin" in the oval bed with broken castle walls and maybe even a tiny moat. Wouldn't that be charming?

CHAPTER 6

Pru found the note on the kitchen table the next morning
— Davina's usual MO, dropping something in Pru's lap and
then leaving town. The Templetons had gone up to London
for New Year's. Pru thought it safe to dismiss any thought of
a ruined castle. She said yes to the blog, even though the idea
of being interviewed about a Humphry Repton landscape
for which she was now responsible seemed audacious. But
when she talked with Hugo, she found it easy to extol the
virtues of a historic garden while also explaining that so much
had happened in the ensuing two hundred or so years that
it wouldn't be possible to put it back exactly as it had been.

* * *

The day after Bryan and Davina left, six large Maigold roses
appeared at the house, lined up just where they should be
planted, spaced out three on each side of the front door.
They would require large planting holes — wouldn't Robbie
be delighted — and copious amounts of manure, which
wouldn't be delivered for a couple of weeks.

A note had been pushed through the letter slot in the
door, but not all the way and so she took it out, telling herself
that it could just as easily be for her as Davina and Bryan

because, after all, she lived there, too, albeit temporarily. Despite her reasoning, she felt a pang of guilt as she read the brief note from Jamie Tanner to the Templetons, which said he hoped that they would enjoy the roses he had found for them. Not exactly subtle, Pru thought. The pang of guilt dissolved. Well, let him try to butter them up all he wants — she was the one with the head-gardener post.

While her crew was off between the holidays, she continued to work. She spent most evenings going over pages of the Red Book and then searching for clues in the landscape. She poked around at the end of the drive, looking for remnants of the magnificent gateposts Repton had recommended. She dug around at the base of the house. He hadn't cared for red brick and often recommended that stucco be applied over it. "I have shewn the effect of changing the house to a stone color," he had written. Perhaps the bricks of Primrose House had been covered with stucco once, but no sign remained now.

She began to come up with a few ideas of her own, too. The broad balustrade stone terrace that ran along the back of the house gave way to a steep lawn-covered slope, ending abruptly at the bottom as it ran into the overgrown yew walk. On the other side of the yew was a clearing beside the wood. Pru hoped the Templetons would eventually terrace the lawn, providing several levels for planting beds. Repton hadn't specifically advised it but did make mention that ". . . the stile and character of the house requires a certain space of dressed lawn or pleasure ground." A stone staircase and stone-edged beds cut into the slope could give way to the more informal landscape below.

Dreams were fine, but more practical tasks made the restoration real. Pru planted the cyclamen and snowdrops that Simon gave her, and she bought ten flats of primroses and cowslips — grown from locally collected seed — and left the flats in the unheated glasshouse to grow on. They would be planted in another month, and Primrose House would have primroses at last.

* * *

Tuesday, the first day they were all back at work, was one of Robbie's days, and he had the only face with a smile on it. A fine, cold drizzle fell. Pru handed out assignments and was met with rebellion.

"Liam, go with Ned, please, and finish clearing out the back two beds, then we'll work our way forward and be ready for the manure when it arrives. And Fergal, would you go up and help Robbie on the holes for the roses?"

"I'll help Robbie," Liam said. He stood a little apart from the rest of them, holding the handle of a shovel and resting his foot on its blade.

Liam seldom had the patience for Robbie, and Pru had soon learned to keep them from working on the same task. "Liam, I'd rather you go with Ned today."

"I won't," he said, and she could see the red creeping up his face and the muscles on his neck stand out. "I'll go with Robbie."

"Liam—" Fergal began.

"*I won't do it,*" Liam shouted.

Ned stood silent, looking back out at the road, as if observing something of great interest. "I'll help the boy," he said quietly. "We'll get started on those holes, will we, Robbie?"

Robbie could pick up a tense tone in the air as well as anyone, and she could see the confusion on his face.

"Liam and I'll clear out the beds, Pru," Fergal said. "We'll do the back four, not just two." Each bed was a large thirty-two-square-foot space chock-full of perennial and woody weeds. To dig out and carry off all the material down to their designated brush pile would take the entire day, as short as daylight was.

Pru felt a mutiny on her hands, and, unprepared for it, decided to go with the flow. "Yes, sure, Fergal, thanks." She took a deep breath. "Well, then, are we all sorted now? Everyone happy?" She looked directly at Liam, who looked away.

They got through the day, although the best thing that could be said about it was that it stopped raining. Ned and

Robbie returned for lunch, which they usually took together, sitting along the warmest wall in the garden, but Liam said he had an errand and returned only when it was time to get back to work.

Tension remained high in the following days, with glaring looks from Liam and sullen silence from Ned, and all Pru could do was to make sure they were nowhere near each other. She gave Liam jobs to do on his own, which he did well and with no objection. She noticed that Fergal kept an eye on him, and once she saw the two of them deep in conversation, Liam's face contorted with anger, while Fergal put his hands in the air, palms out, as if to calm his brother down. She tried to ask Liam what was wrong, but he stomped away, and, as usual, left Fergal to make excuses for him.

"Sorry, Pru, he has a lot on his mind right now." The brothers' lives appeared fairly simple to Pru. Their parents had retired from local jobs and moved back to County Mayo in Ireland, but as Liam and Fergal had spent their entire lives in England, they decided to stay. They had bought a decrepit cottage that they lived in and worked to restore the days they weren't at Primrose House. They hoped to sell the cottage, buy another, and do the same. They were handy lads and didn't seem attached to anything in particular. Liam's exploits with the ladies were common knowledge — mostly because Liam himself talked about them — but Fergal had a steady girlfriend who worked in the freight transit authority office in Tunbridge Wells.

Fergal's excuse for Liam did little to explain the problem, but as long as they made progress, and Pru could keep Ned and Liam apart, perhaps she could ignore it. She did, after all, have other things on her mind, at once more pleasant and more stimulating. Christopher rang when he arrived back from Dubai. They spoke about his flight, Graham's job, and the *Courier*'s blog, but the volume of their unspoken conversation drowned it all out: "When will I see you?"

* * *

On Wednesday morning, she gave herself extra time to check the *Courier*'s website, as the first blog post was scheduled to appear. When she called up the page, the headline screamed at her: *American Takes the Reins at Historic Garden. "It isn't all Humphry Repton, you know."*

Pru jumped back as if she'd been bitten. *Oh my God*, she thought, *how crass, how presumptuous, how arrogant.* Had she said that? She thought back to her conversation with Hugo. Yes, those had been her words, but she had been trying to explain that many others had a hand in the gardens in the ensuing two hundred years.

Half afraid to look, she turned her face away from the screen while she scrolled down and saw that there were already forty-two comments, many of them along the lines of "Leave it to some know-it-all Yank to take over one of our gardens."

She wouldn't read any more now. She couldn't let it get to her — there was too much work to do. Jo rang to provide a few encouraging words. Pru had told both Jo and Christopher about the blog, so she wasn't surprised when Christopher was next to ring.

"I think you shouldn't let it worry you," he said.

She took a deep breath. "Yes. But I will have a word with Hugo. If he wants this to continue, then he needs to be fair."

That's all she asked, for him to be fair. She rang him as she walked out to the walled garden — better to get this out of the way and get to work. Hugo had an entirely different take. "It's fantastic, isn't it, Pru? You're getting the attention now. It's started a real conversation online. Did you see that someone from the National Trust posted a comment?"

This news did not make her feel better. "What did it say? That I should mind my own business and go back to Texas?"

"Certainly not." Hugo sounded as if he were pumping her up for the big game. "It said they look forward to seeing how you will restore the garden. Davina tells me there will be an open garden day in July. Has she mentioned that?"

"I'm not sure that would be entirely appropriate this year." Could she not quell this preposterous idea? "You won't encourage it, will you, Hugo?"

"You're too hard on yourself, but don't worry, I won't encourage her. Next week will be about the tools you found in the shed. Old tools are fascinating."

"I like that idea," Pru said, thinking how that would move her out of the spotlight. "You should talk to Ned Bobbins about the old tools, because he's the one that discovered them and I'm sure he'd like to tell you the story."

Hugo muttered something that sounded to Pru like, "I'll just bet he would."

"Sorry?" she asked.

"Didn't the brothers get them back into working order for you?" Hugo asked.

"Yes, Liam and Fergal. Talk to them if you like." She imagined Liam would love to have his name in the news.

* * *

As soon as she pushed in the heavy wooden gate, she could see the glasshouse door standing open, and the flats of primroses and cowslips upturned and scattered. She ran to the mess and stared in disbelief at the tender young plants now lying broken in heaps of potting soil. She looked round as if she could catch the culprit in flight. *Rabbits?* she asked herself. No, rabbits may nibble the plants down to nothing, but they would create such upheaval.

She phoned Davina to let her know — the Templetons did so love daily updates — and Davina went on the offensive.

"I'm ringing the police right now, and I'll have someone out to see what's happened."

Pru dropped the empty flat in her hand. "Do you think that's necessary? I wouldn't want to waste their time."

"It's probably some local vandals, trying to cause trouble," Davina said. "There are people who don't like to see success, and we must take a stand to let them know they can't get away with it."

Detective Sergeant David Hobbes, a congenial young man with hair that might've been strawberry blond if it had a chance to grow, arrived while they were busy with garden tasks. Pru hadn't cleaned up the mess yet — she knew better than to disturb a crime scene — and DS Hobbes spent a moment staring at the wreckage. But it was a brief interview. He, too, thought it might be vandals, but said he would get back to the Templetons with anything he found.

* * *

Pru filled her weekend with odd jobs around the garden, hoping that an accumulation of tiny steps might result in a sense of accomplishment. Anything to ease the nagging anxiety about opening the garden to the public in only six-month's time. That thought lurked in her subconsciousness.

Sunday afternoon, she stood on the sloped lawn, looking up at the house and sketching out a possible plan for terraced beds and wisteria running along the balustrade. The fragrant purple flowers would scent the air in May — just not this May, she thought. A garden takes time, she kept telling Davina and Bryan. She repeated it so often she was afraid she'd start grabbing strangers on the streets of Tunbridge Wells and telling them, too.

While she sketched, she heard a vehicle pull up on the drive, and soon after, Jamie Tanner came round the corner of the house, his eyes scanning the landscape. Pru called and waved to him, and he came down the slope.

"Thanks for delivering the roses," she said. "They're perfect for the front of the house."

"I'm happy to help." He looked over her shoulder at the rough drawing, more penciled impressionism than a realistic rendering. "Grapes?"

Pru laughed. "That's why I could never be an artist," she said. "It's wisteria."

Jamie's small smile turned to a tiny frown, and he sighed. "Look," he said, "Ned told me about what happened with your primroses. Do you know who did it?"

Pru shook her head. "I was hoping it might be rabbits, but Davina called out the police. A few plants lost doesn't seem like a big deal to most people, but they were important to the garden."

Jamie nodded. "Oh, I know what you mean. That sort of mindless destruction strikes us hard. Look, I hope you don't think I'm interfering, but I wasn't sure if you knew enough people in the area yet, so I asked around and found some replacements."

"You found more primroses?"

"And cowslips. Just a couple flats of each, but maybe that will help replace what was lost. I know a fellow who works with native plants, restoring meadows and the like. He's happy to let you have them" — he laughed — "not free, of course, but for a pretty good price. I went ahead and brought them over, if that's all right."

"Yes, that's great."

"I've left them up in the walled garden. I'll ring Davina and let her know." He grinned. "Don't let the rabbits at them."

Pru laughed and thanked him. She was lucky that Jamie was willing to help even if she did suspect that at least part of his reason might be to butter up the people who didn't give him the job.

* * *

By the following week, she'd almost grown accustomed to the new atmosphere among her crew — tense but workable. She distracted herself with thoughts of moving into her cottage and about Christopher's visit at the weekend. On Tuesday, she saw a short parade of furniture — chesterfield sofa, table and chairs, bed, wardrobe — being carried out from the back of a lorry and into the cottage. She stopped to watch and saw that Robbie, Ned, Liam, and Fergal watched, too.

"There now," Ned nodded toward the activity, "you've a proper home."

"No more late nights in the Templetons' pantry," Fergal said with a smile.

"It's a bit small for a party, Pru," Liam observed.

The Duffys helped her move her belongings. That first evening, with the furniture in, the Aga warming up, and a fire going — Bryan not only set it, but showed her the finer points so that she could do it herself next time — she sat quietly on the sofa, glass of wine in hand, and cried. She wished her mother could see it. For Pru's whole life growing up in Texas, she had lived in her mother's stories of England, and now the setting for those stories was all round her. She rang Christopher.

"I'm sitting in my cottage," she said. She sniffed and cleared her throat. "I'm all moved in, and I have a fire going."

"How does it look?" he asked.

She walked to the front door. "Right, here's your audio tour. There's a small entry. Okay, probably not really an entry, more like one flagstone to stand on and two coat hooks on the wall just inside the door." She didn't move. "And from here you can see . . . everything. The kitchen is to the left with a table and chairs, the sitting room straight ahead — well, I'm standing in it. The fireplace is in a partial wall that's sort of between the two. You'll be surprised when you see the kitchen," she said as she walked past the Aga. "Now, through the kitchen to the bedroom, which is a large room, considering."

"How big is the bed?" he interrupted.

"Big enough." She stared at it and sighed heavily. "There's just room for a wardrobe, but the bathroom seems enormous. A shower, but there wasn't room for a tub, because they've put a small stacked washer and dryer in there, too. All mod cons."

"I'll be there as soon as I can get away on Friday."

* * *

That Wednesday's blog post, "New Life for Old Tools," chronicled the story of their discovery without mentioning Ned, Pru was annoyed to see. Great detail went into the description of the Duffys' careful restoration. That generated a good number of mild comments, mostly memories of the treasures found in Granddad's garden shed, but a couple were pointed comments about Liam and his tools — obviously not the garden variety, and the comments, Pru thought, mostly likely written by women. She expected he would have a few comments of his own at work that morning.

But Liam's comments were lost when they all gathered at the front gate of the walled garden, and Ned noticed a trail of smoke outside the far wall coming from cracks in the potting shed. It was on fire. They all ran to its rescue. Pru pulled open the door, while Fergal and Liam went for water. As it turned out, it was more smoke than fire, and even before the fire brigade arrived, they had made short work of it with a relay of buckets from the nearest hosepipe bib. Even the tools escaped damage.

Stunned by the suddenness of it all, they didn't speak, but watched firemen finish up by carrying out the paraffin heater, the source of the fire. It had been lit and damp burlap set on top.

Not an accident, and so Detective Sergeant Hobbes made a return visit. He and another officer investigated the site, circled the shed in blue-and-white police tape, and told Pru that he would report back to her late on Friday afternoon, stopping by her cottage on his way home, if that was all right.

Pru had plans for late Friday afternoon, and none of them involved a visit by a police officer. Well, now that she thought about it, her plans did involve a visit by a police officer, just not this one. "Yes, sure, I'll look forward to your report," she said.

Primrose House

Friday morning

Dear Pru,

Your level head saved what could've been an enormous disaster. We will not let these vandals deter us from our task! Did you see Ned anywhere early that morning? DS Hobbes seems a competent sort, but we will all need to keep a sharp eye out on the garden.

We'll talk next week.

Best,
Davina

P.S. Couldn't we build a rock garden in the oval garden space? Wouldn't that be lovely?

P.P.S. The stonemason will be there on Monday to start repairing the walls. Do try to move everything out of his way before he arrives.

CHAPTER 7

The pile of fresh dairy manure steamed in the cold air. It stood as tall as the 12-foot-high wall and, unfortunately, rested against it. Pru had hoped they could start spreading the manure next week, covering the large square beds and using it to plant the Maigold roses up at the house. Instead, they would spend today, Friday, shifting a great deal of it to clear the way for the stonemason. It was not the activity she'd hoped for on the day that Christopher was to arrive, but there was nothing else for it.

They all worked on the same task, and Pru kept a sharp eye and ear out. Just let Liam dare to make trouble today because he had to work next to Ned. But work proceeded apace and without incident, and by lunch she saw that they would indeed be able to reduce the pile sufficiently to finish early. She had no intention of telling them why. It was information she did not want in the hands of Liam Duffy.

"Right," she said as they sat against the warmed wall of the garden finishing their sandwiches. "We'll work for another hour, and then we'll finish early today."

"Why?" Liam asked.

"Because we've cleared enough space by the wall for the stonemason to start," Pru said, "and we've all worked very hard to do it."

"Do you have someplace to go?" Liam again.

"No, Liam, I have no place to go. I'm giving you a couple of extra hours — for which you'll be paid — and I think you should be grateful."

"The mason will have plenty to do," Fergal said. "There are gaps all round the garden."

She breathed a sigh of relief at his change of subject. "We'll be working alongside him for a while, most likely," she replied.

"You never let us go early," Liam continued, eyeing her suspiciously. He raised his eyebrows. "Do you have a visitor coming, is that it?"

"I'd say you should be happy for more free time on a Friday," she said, not looking at him.

"Ah, so it is a visitor." Liam was like a dog with a bone. "Have you a girlfriend coming over for tea, Pru?" He shook his head. "No, that wouldn't be it, not on a Friday." He continued to watch her as she brushed a few breadcrumbs off her lap. "It's a man, isn't it? That's right, you've a fellow coming round."

"If you keep talking," she said, as she felt the color creep up into her face, "perhaps we will continue working another few hours, Liam, since you're so eager for it."

"Oh, I don't know, Pru, you wouldn't want your fellow to show up here with you standing in a pile of—"

"Liam," Fergal stopped him, laughing. Liam grinned at her, and even Ned chuckled. She wiped her face on her sleeve to cover up her own smile, while Robbie picked up on the topic.

"Do you have a fellow coming, Pru? Is that who it is?"

"Back to work," she said, and refused to meet any of their gazes.

* * *

At three o'clock, she dismissed her team. She didn't believe that Christopher could arrive this early, and so she'd have plenty of time to shower, but why today, of all days, did she have to be covered in crap?

She rushed around the corner of her cottage, and almost ran right into him. Slightly out of breath, all she could manage was, "Hi. I'm sorry I wasn't at home. Have you been here long?"

"No, I drove up two minutes ago."

She took a breath, and they smiled at each other. "I'm so happy to see you." He took a step toward her, and she shouted, "Don't come near me!"

He stopped short, and she laughed. "I'm sorry, it's just that I've been shoveling manure all day and I reek. I wanted to get a shower before you saw me."

"You look beautiful."

She rolled her eyes and looked down at her clothes, streaked with brown. "You say that at twenty feet, but if you came any closer, you'd change your tune. I'm going straight in to—"

Ned walked around the corner. "Pru, did you want me to — Oh, sorry, I didn't realize you were busy."

She gave him a narrow look. "Christopher, I'd like you to meet Ned Bobbins. Ned, this is Christopher Pearse."

"How do you do." Ned reached up to tug on his cap. "I won't shake your hand, sir, not today."

"Ned," Christopher said. "Pru tells me you're something of a local historian."

Ned brightened. "Well, I've picked up a story or two through the years."

"I'd like to hear what you know about the railways round here some time."

"Let me see, it was 1866 when the . . ." Ned glanced at Pru. "Perhaps we could talk another time. I'd best better be off now. Good to meet you," he nodded at Christopher and walked back the way he came.

"I'm afraid the news of your arrival has been broadcast near and far." She sighed as Liam and Fergal came around the corner next.

53

"Pru," Liam began, "we were just wondering when we should . . ." He looked at Christopher in what Pru thought was poorly feigned surprise. "Oh, are we interrupting something?"

"Christopher, I'd like you to meet Fergal and Liam Duffy. Fellows, this is Christopher Pearse." Liam reached out his hand as both Pru and Fergal said, "Liam, no."

He rubbed his hand on his sweater. "Sorry, forgot myself. It's very good to meet you, sir. Are you from around here?"

Oh God, thought Pru.

"I live in London," Christopher said, and smiled at her. "Just down for the weekend."

"The whole weekend?" Liam asked.

Before he could go any further, Pru said, "Right, lovely of you to stop by. Now, I'll see the both of you Monday morning at eight."

"Eight o'clock?" Liam asked. "Oh, I don't know, Pru, will you be able for eight o'clock Monday morning after this weekend?"

She could see out of the corner of her eye that Christopher was enjoying this. "Liam," she said sweetly, "perhaps we'll see you in the pub this evening."

Liam's face fell. "Ah, Pru, that's not fair."

"Let's go." Fergal nudged his brother. "Good to meet you."

As they walked away, Pru said to Christopher, "I stopped into the pub last Saturday, and Liam said I threw him off his game — he felt like his mother was watching him." She looked down the drive. "We might as well wait for it."

Ivy pulled in and drove up beside them. Robbie sat behind her, his red fleece jacket smeared with manure. Ivy had all the windows down. "Oh Pru, the smell of him — but I see you're the same, now aren't you?"

Pru made the last introductions. Robbie stuck his head out the window and said to Christopher, "You aren't Pru's husband, you're Pru's boyfriend."

"Robbie," his mother whispered harshly.

Pru laughed. "It's all right, Ivy."

"Well now, it's lovely to meet you, Mr. Pearse. Here, I'd best hand this over to you." She gave Christopher a foil-wrapped loaf. "Just something to have with your cuppa. Bye now."

"Thanks, Ivy. Bye, Robbie. See you Monday." She watched him closely.

"See you . . . No, Pru, not Monday. Tuesday is my garden day."

"Oh, that's right. Tuesday "

As his mother drove off, she could hear him calling out the window, "Pay attention, Pru, pay attention."

Pru turned to Christopher and spread her arms out. "And there you have it," she said. "You've met my whole crew."

"Quite impressive." He eyed her closely. "Now, are you going in for that shower, or am I coming over there to kiss you?"

That got her moving. She took her boots off and shook her socks out before darting in the door, saying over her shoulder, "Have a look round. That won't take you long so, pour yourself a drink and make yourself at home." She gave him a quick smile and ran into the bathroom.

Into the tiny washer went her smelly clothes. She carefully hung her necklace on the mirror away from the sink drain, and after a thorough shower and two rounds of shampoo, she dried her hair as best she could and put her necklace back on. That was when she looked around and realized she'd forgotten to bring clean clothes in with her.

The door to the bedroom stood open a couple of inches — evidence of the difficulty with converting a two-hundred-and-fifty-year-old cowshed — but she saw no movement outside. She wrapped the towel around herself and wondered if she should make a dash for it.

"Christopher?" she asked in a quiet voice, just to see if he were close enough to hear.

"Yes?" His voice came from just the other side of the door.

She laughed. "I forgot to bring clean clothes in with me."

"Do you need clothes right now?"

"Well, now that you mention it," she said, "I don't suppose I do."

* * *

She lifted her head up off the pillow and gave him a serious look. "Do I smell like manure?" she asked.

He laughed and buried his face in her hair. "No, you smell like Pru."

She sighed and relaxed again. Christopher traced the chain of her necklace against her skin.

She put her hand up to caress the pendant and answered his unspoken question. "Always. I always have it on." Then, she sat up. "Oops. I think that nice young detective sergeant will be dropping by soon."

Christopher sat up, too. "Sergeant? What's happened?"

She talked fast as she got dressed. "Well, first it was the rabbits — at least, I initially thought it was rabbits — that got into the glasshouse and upset all the flats. But Davina didn't think it was rabbits and rang the police. I told you about that, didn't I?" She hopped on one foot as she pulled up a sock. "Yesterday, there was a small fire in the shed. Someone had lit one of the wicks on the paraffin heater and set some damp burlap on top. It didn't do much damage, mostly it smoked, and we caught it in time, but fire and rescue came, of course and that's much more serious than rabbits, and so we rang the police again, and now we have an investigation of sorts. The sergeant is stopping by to give me a report." All dressed, she looked down at him. "You should probably put on some clothes."

CHAPTER 8

They'd had enough time to look casual. Pru put the kettle on. Christopher lit a fire — a practice he said he loved, and which Pru was happy to relinquish, having smoked up the cottage on her first try — and had just walked back into the bedroom to unpack his case when Pru heard car tires on the gravel. She opened the door.

"Hello, Ms. Parke."

"Sergeant Hobbes, come in." Christopher walked out of the bedroom, and Pru said, "Christopher, this is . . ."

"David?" Christopher asked.

"Inspector Pearse? Is that you? Well, what a surprise." The two men shook hands.

"I'd forgotten that you were in Tunbridge Wells. How's the job?"

"It's fine, sir, I'm really enjoying it. Are you . . . here on official business?" He looked from Christopher to Pru.

"No, not at all. I'm only visiting." To Pru he said, "DS Hobbes was in uniform in London, until he got this promotion. David, who are you under?"

"Inspector Tatt, sir."

"God," Christopher said.

"Yes, well." Hobbes glanced at the floor and gave a little cough.

"Would you like tea?" Pru asked.

The two men sat at the kitchen table and talked while Pru poured. She stepped behind the DS — it was just a bit tight in there — and bent down to get milk out of the half-sized fridge. The fridge was full of a brown paper bag, neatly folded over with a note taped to it: "For Pru from Gasparetti's — compliments of Riccardo." Gasparetti's, her favorite Italian café in London and site of the first dinner she and Christopher had together. She clutched the milk carton to her chest, turned to him, and smiled while Hobbes told a story about the theft of shopping trolleys from the local Sainsbury's. Christopher caught her smile and gave a tiny nod.

"Ms. Parke," DS Hobbes said.

"Please call me Pru."

"Pru. We've found nothing conclusive in the shed. We're asking your workers to come down to give their fingerprints, just so we can check against any that we find. Would you mind doing that yourself?"

"My fingerprints are on file in London. Can you get them from there?"

Christopher said, "Pru was a witness on a case of mine in the autumn in Chelsea, and she had her prints taken then."

"That's fine," Hobbes said, making a note. "We couldn't find any clear footprints outside or inside the shed — mostly the ground had been trampled."

"That was probably me," Pru said with a shrug. "Obliterating evidence is one of my specialties." She had done the same thing at the Wilsons' shed when she found the body.

"Unintentionally," Christopher added.

"Well, we had to get the fire out," she said. "And then fire and rescue showed up, so it wasn't all me."

"Both these incidents happened right after a post went up on the *Courier*'s blog about you and the garden. Mrs. Templeton pointed that out to me," Hobbes said.

Christopher frowned. "Do you know of a connection?" he asked Pru. "Someone who might not like the blog? Someone who could act out of spite or to show the Templetons up?" And then he caught himself. "Sorry, David."

"I don't mind, sir. I'm happy to have you around, you know, to keep an eye out. You might see something we miss."

Pru hoped that Christopher would not start worrying about her well-being from afar. "Kids," she said dismissively. "It was probably kids. Davina and I talked about it, and most likely it's just some local children trying to stir something up. They'll get tired of it soon and stop." She made sure to avoid the subject for the rest of the evening.

* * *

On Saturday, she gave Christopher a tour of the grounds, beginning with a walk through the walled garden.

"We've done most of our work here so far," she explained, glancing around at the barren landscape within the walls. "And most of that work has been clearing away, except for the four yews that had grown together in the middle bed. We'll save them until spring, and then shear them just enough to separate the four plants."

"Will you have time to replant before the open garden day?"

"We'll have time to plant them," she replied, "but the plants won't have much time to grow." Pru stared at the empty beds and the blank brick walls, with only the buttresses for decoration. "Antique apple varieties all along the walls," she said, gesturing as they walked up and around the paths. "We've ordered bare-root and need to start marking where they'll be planted and decide on the shapes they'll be trained. But no fruit the first year, we can't allow that. The trees need to get established."

She told Christopher her ideas for color and form, and how she wanted each bed tied to the next visually with a snaking, low hedge of boxwood and some Victorian flamboyance in the middle — probably cannas.

By the time they left the walled garden and walked up to the house, plans and descriptions were coming fast and furious. They flashed past the front door, where she gave a quick wave — "Roses there, holes all ready" — as she took him around to the broad stone terrace that ran the length of the house.

They stood looking west. That is, Christopher stood, while Pru paced. As she paced, she flung her arms around as if she could conjure the completed garden into being.

"Stone pots, huge ones, and probably twelve of them all along here, with two more on either side of the French doors there" — she gestured toward the entrance to the library then hurried down to point to the doors of the drawing room — "and there."

Back she went, to the other end of the terrace to show him where the wisteria would climb. She waved at the boxwood allée running down to their right and mentioned the daffodils. As she passed him, Christopher reached out and grabbed her hand. "Pru, hold still."

"I can't hold still," she said with a small, high laugh. "There's too much to do." She gave his hand a squeeze and resumed her frenetic tour, rushing over to the balustrade.

From there, after a thirty-foot drop, the land sloped away, until it reached the overgrown yew walk that ran parallel to the house. She pointed to the lawn and told him her idea to have it terraced — later. To the south was the beech copse, mostly bare in winter, but some trees had retained clumps of dried leaves in the interior of the lower branches. It always reminded Pru of an old Amish fellow with a beard growing not on his face but under his chin.

"Over there," she said, "I believe that the beech wood is Repton's." She forgot her fear of heights and stood on tiptoe, leaning out over the stone railing until she saw the ground far below appear to shift. She backed off, bumping into Christopher, who wrapped his arms around her and held tightly.

"I want to hear about the garden, but I don't want you to have a nervous breakdown over it."

She leaned back against him and took a deep breath and let it out slowly. Her heart rate decreased.

"Sorry, I looked down and . . ." She didn't have to add the rest — that she got dizzy when the ground seemed to move of its own accord. He remembered.

"They can't expect you to have it all finished by July," Christopher said. "It's a garden — it has to grow."

She turned her head enough to give him a smile. "Perhaps I could have you come and explain that to them."

"You will have the garden looking its best," he said. "Surely you can describe the history of the place to visitors without needing to restore every bit."

"Yes, I'll memorize the Red Book and recite pages of it to everyone, but only after they've had a few gin and tonics."

He laughed. "Right. Now, I'll hold on, and you tell me what we can see of Humphry Repton."

Her calm restored, her enthusiasm for the garden's history returned. "Repton said that it was best to see deciduous trees with the sun behind them, so the wood was planted south and west of the house."

"So, the trees there are two hundred years old?" he asked, nodding toward the copse.

"Many of them are — beeches, oak, and a few Spanish chestnuts that have survived on the far side. More trees have come up on their own." She stood on her tiptoes again, but remained safely within his arms. "And, here on the north side of the wood, there's a big, dark green meadow of sorts. It's difficult to see with the yew so overgrown. I don't think it started out as a meadow. I believe it's the pond, Repton's water feature, and somewhere along the way it was filled in. He said you should always look down on water, to get a reflection of the trees around. If the water is level with where you stand, all you see reflected is sky."

"Will you dig the pond out?"

She smiled. "Yes. We'll dig it out, and in spring, we'll cut the yew down to a reasonable size, so that we can see the pond."

They stood quietly, Pru daydreaming about the pond and wood while Christopher nuzzled her neck, but had trouble with the fleece collar on her jacket getting in his way.

"Badgers," she said.

He stopped. "Mmm?" His lips vibrated against her skin and tickled.

"Badgers." She laughed. "Come on, I'll show you."

He was a countryman at heart, she knew it, and his eyes brightened at the thought of tramping through the wood and sussing out wildlife. They made their way along a trail below the walled garden and beyond the brush pile to a thin patch of trees with a rocky rise behind them. She'd done a bit of investigating. It looked as if a hole had been dug out of the side of the hill. A few scrubby hollies grew in front.

They stood well away as Christopher peered at the setting. She looked at him with her eyebrows raised.

"Yes," he said, "it's quite possible that's a sett. You haven't seen anything?"

"No. I've come out at dusk once or twice, but it was cold and I didn't wait. You don't think the brush pile is too close?"

"Probably not. They aren't too active in winter. Come spring, we'll see what happens." He put his mouth to her ear. "Wait, see that?"

Her eyes followed where he'd nodded, and she saw a tiny olive-colored bird with a golden stripe on its head, scurrying around the base of a beech. "What is it?" she whispered.

"A goldcrest. You'll want him around your garden. He eats greenfly."

She gave a little gasp. "Aphids — good. I hope he brings all his friends."

They returned to the cottage chilled to the bone, but that didn't last long. Supper consisted of more treasures from Riccardo. Too bad she had such a tiny fridge, she thought, otherwise, she could stock up every time Christopher visited.

That evening they sat with glasses of wine before the fire, Christopher with his feet stretched toward the flames, Pru with her toes tucked under his thigh. She watched him watch the fire until he smiled and looked at her.

"When we first met," she said, "you were a police officer."

He raised his eyebrows. "I'm still a police officer," he said.

"Yes, but not to me. At first, you were doing your job, and I kept interfering."

He took hold of her calf and massaged it. "I didn't want you to be hurt. I needed to keep an eye on you."

"And so you protected me."

He lost a bit of his smile. "I don't know how successful I was at that."

She reached over and traced his lips with her finger. "But now, I don't need protecting, and so I can see you for all the other things you are."

"I reserve the right to protect you if the need arises," he said, as his hand moved up her thigh.

"I might need protecting from Davina's incessant notes. Or possibly from Liam's arguments. Or from Robbie's questions. Can you protect me from those?"

* * *

Sunday afternoon, Pru and Christopher wrapped up against the cold wind and walked to the pub. The Two Bells fulfilled many needs for the locals. In addition to fine ales, the pub had music on the weekends when local DJs took turns at their own playlists, running the gamut from Mel Tormé to Coldplay. They had just claimed a booth when Liam appeared.

"Pru, Christopher," he said quietly, with a glance over his shoulder. "How's the weekend?" He didn't wait for an answer. "Could I . . . would it be all right if I brought someone over for you to meet?"

Pru exchanged looks with Christopher. "Yes, Liam, sure," she said.

He disappeared and returned almost instantly, accompanied by a tall, slender woman with glossy, straight, jet-black hair, a coffee-colored complexion, and a timid smile. "Pru, Christopher," Liam said, "this is Cate."

"Will you join us?" Christopher asked.

"Yeah, that'd be great, thanks," Liam said, sitting next to Christopher while Cate slipped in alongside Pru.

"Cate, do you live round here?" Pru asked.

"Almost my whole life. Ned's my dad," she said, and her smile faded.

"Oh." Pru wasn't as surprised at the difference in appearance — Cate looked like she might be of Indian origin, and so perhaps had been adopted — as she was at the fact that Ned had a daughter. "I didn't know about you." Pru glanced at Liam. He held her gaze for a moment and then looked back at Cate.

"My mum died when I was thirteen," Cate said, "and it was just Dad and me then. Of course, I've been out of the house for ages."

"Cate's a nurse," Liam said.

"Where do you work?" Pru asked.

Cate looked over her shoulder at the door and put her hands on the table, rubbing one on top of the other. "Well, I haven't worked lately. I have a little girl, and she keeps me busy."

"Nanda," Liam said, grinning. "She's a corker."

"Ah, Liam's got a soft spot for her." Cate smiled and looked over her shoulder again. "She's three, and a real handful."

"Shall I get us another round?" Christopher asked.

Liam looked at Cate, who said, "I'd better go. It's been lovely to meet you both. I hope to see you again."

Before they could say anything other than goodbye, Liam spirited her away.

"Well," Pru said, "that was . . ."

"Unusual?" Christopher offered.

"Bizarre," she replied. "On so many levels. Ned has a daughter? Liam — he was polite and kind. Not that he isn't a good person, but he's usually so flippant. I've never seen this side of him."

"She's married — or at least she probably was until recently," Christopher said.

"How do you know that?"

"She was fiddling with her ring finger. There was no ring but a pale mark where one had been."

"Oh, that's right, you're a police officer."

He half-closed his eyes. "Would you like another pint?"

"No, I want to go home with you."

As they walked back on the footpath through a field of stubble and chaff, Pru said, "For the last two weeks, ever since we started back to work after the holidays, Liam has been angry at Ned and made no attempt to hide it." She looked at Christopher, a small frown on her face. "Why would Liam be angry with the father of the woman he was seeing? Although," she remembered, "Cate herself didn't look too happy when she mentioned Ned."

"Who was she married to? Not Liam," he said.

"No, not Liam."

A light mist fell as they walked back, seeping through the layers of clothes. Christopher built a fire — he was an artist in kindling and logs — and they settled on the sofa, soon forgetting everyone's troubles.

* * *

Too early on Monday morning, Christopher drove off into the darkness. Neither of them had been happy about it. They had stood silent in each other's arms before he'd left, until finally he took a deep breath. But Pru spoke first.

"I'm sorry you have to go."

"You'll be busy," he said.

"As will you, I know."

"And I'll be back. But . . ."

"I know we can't do this every weekend," she said. "Still
. . ."

He finished it for her. "It's better than it might have
been. At least you aren't in Texas."

Before getting in his car, he covered her face with kisses.

CHAPTER 9

A pall hung over everyone that morning as they went about their work in the gray light, puffing clouds of fog like steam engines and stamping their feet against the cold ground. Pru couldn't shake the sadness of Christopher leaving. *Really*, she kept telling herself, *he's only gone up to London*. Ned shuffled around, Fergal worked without speaking, even Liam was subdued, and there was no Robbie to brighten the day with talk of Robin Hood. What pale winter sun there was faded after lunch as clouds drew close, and the day darkened even earlier than usual.

Pru had walked to her cottage at lunch and returned by way of the lower path to the back gate of the walled garden. Preoccupied with thoughts of the next big project — the gardens immediately around the house — the loud voices didn't register until she walked in and saw Ned and Liam in each other's face like two rams about to butt heads.

"It's no concern of yours," Ned growled, his hands clenched at his side.

"It bloody well is my concern if you won't do anything," Liam shouted back, jabbing his finger at the old man's chest.

They both stopped when they realized Pru was there and, without a word, turned and walked off in different directions.

Her spirits couldn't have been lower. Here it was, Monday, and the week was already a disaster. Fergal stood near the front gate talking with the mason, and she made her way up to them, longing for some peaceful conversation. The mason had packed up and said he would be back the next day but would have to put off work after that until the following week as he had a job to finish near Lamberhurst.

Ned appeared around one corner, Liam from the other. They stopped about twenty feet from each other, as if their anger created a force field between them. The silence was deafening.

"Let's stop for today, shall we?" Pru said. They had spent the morning spreading more of the manure and had at least made progress. Without comment, Fergal collected the spades and began cleaning them off.

Liam walked toward her, but stopped and turned away when Ned came up first.

Ned looked over his shoulder before saying, "Another day, Pru, perhaps a quieter day, could we have a chat?"

They'd had no quieter day than the one just finished, but she could guess that what he meant was a day without Liam. "Sure, Ned, that would be fine. Do you want to stay today and we can talk?"

"No, not today," he said and lifted his chin. "I've something to do."

"Right, well, any day is fine with me." He made a movement to leave. "Ned," she said as an afterthought, "I met Cate."

She'd never seen such a smile on the man before, revealing a row of too-perfect teeth. "You met my girl? She's her dad's pride and joy. And did you meet the wee one?"

"No," Pru said and smiled, "I haven't met Nanda yet."

"Well, she's a charmer, just like her mum." Ned straightened his shoulders. "I'll see you tomorrow."

Liam didn't approach her again, and they all went their separate ways.

At home, Pru showered and sat at the kitchen table with the Red Book, forgetting her worries as she got lost in Repton's plan. For each of his clients, including Primrose House, he painted watercolor landscape views as they were, and then cut a horizontal strip out of the paper, keeping it attached at one end. Behind the opening he placed another watercolor that showed what his proposed landscape would look like. It was a technique used in children's books, but it suited Repton's purpose perfectly. Here's what you see now, but lift the flap and here's what you'll see if you hire me. He had been quite a salesman.

Tires crunched on the gravel outside, bringing Pru back to the twenty-first century. When she opened the door, there stood Jamie Tanner.

"Pru, hope you don't mind me stopping by like this." He smiled at her as he gave his stubbly chin a scratch.

"Not at all. Come in. Would you like tea?"

"No, no," he said as he fiddled with the zipper on his jacket, "I don't want to be a bother, just thought I'd find out how you're doing. Are you getting to know the place well?"

What was he, the welcome wagon? she thought. "Look, why don't you come in — it's quite cold out there."

"Oh sure, well, if it's no bother." He stepped inside and stood by the kitchen table. "So, have you met some friends?"

She busied herself with the kettle and said over her shoulder, "I haven't had much chance to socialize except to get to know everyone here — the Templetons, Ned, Fergal, and Liam. Robbie and Ivy, too." She heard a chair scrape on the floor, and could've sworn she'd seen him kick it. "Do you know Robbie and Ivy Fox?"

"No," he said, "I don't believe I do. Do you go down to the Two Bells ever? It is your local, after all, and they pour a good pint."

She turned to face him, and leaned back against the rail on the Aga. "Yes, I've been in a few times, usually on the weekends. I've no time during the week. How's your job?"

"My job?" he asked and laughed as if she'd told a joke. "My job is, yeah, good. My job is good." He looked right and left, and then said, "Look, I've got to go. Just wanted to stop and say hello. I'll be seeing you."

She followed him to the door and watched him drive away. He hit the accelerator too hard and showered gravel everywhere. As his car got to the lane and turned out, another car turned in, coming just as quickly as Jamie had left and scattering more gravel when it stopped. Liam got out and slammed the door.

"What's he doing here?" he shouted at Pru. "What the hell is he doing here?"

"What?"

"Are you on his side?" he continued to shout as he walked toward her.

"*Calm down*," she shouted back, "and tell me what you're talking about."

He stopped. His face was blotched, his eyes on fire, and his breathing heavy.

"Come in here and sit down," she said.

She really did feel like his mother now. The kettle had boiled, and she poured up the tea. Liam yanked a chair out, plopped down, crossed his arms, and didn't speak. She cut a few slices of Ivy's tea cake and put the plate, along with mugs, milk, and sugar, on the table. She sat down across from him and said, "There now. What's wrong?"

"Pru, do you not care what he's done? How can you be friendly to a man who would do that?"

"Liam, I do not have a clue what you're on about."

He jerked his thumb toward the road. "He hit her." He stood up again abruptly and walked to the door, as if he could see Jamie through the small frosted window. "She spent years putting up with his yelling and bullying, and then he hit her. And she left."

Pru looked at the door, realization dawning. "Jamie is Cate's husband? I'm sorry, I didn't know. I had no idea." Liam sat back down again and let out a big breath. As she poured the tea, Pru tried to reconcile the image of Jamie that Liam painted of an abusive husband with the image she'd already formed of him — a helpful acquaintance although one who seemed to want her job. "Christopher noticed she'd worn a ring."

"We dated for a while before she met him," Liam said, calming down as he stirred sugar into his tea, "but I wasn't ready to settle down. I'd no real work, and he was older and had a job. She said he was charming." Liam said the last word as if the word left a bad taste in his mouth. "Not too difficult a choice there."

"But maybe now she realizes he might not have been the best choice. Except for Nanda."

That got a grin from him. "I never thought I'd like kids," he said, "but she's something." He reached for a slice of cake and swigged his tea. "I'm only helping out, Pru," he explained. "I only rang her after I'd heard she'd left him. I know she needs time. She and Nanda have moved in with a girlfriend of hers, a flat up closer to town. I'm doing what I can."

He seemed to have grown up remarkably fast, she thought. "But Liam, then why are you so angry with Ned?"

His eyes flashed again as he swallowed a large bite of cake. "Her own dad, and he's the biggest champion of Jamie Tanner. Tells her she needs to stick with her husband, what about her marriage vows. How could he say that to his own daughter after what Tanner did to her?"

Pru had no answer to that, only more questions of her own. Liam quieted down again. "Thanks for talking with us, you know, at the pub."

"She's very sweet."

"Would you . . ." He began as he swirled his tea around in the mug. "It would be great if you might stop in and see her, if you ever had the time."

"I'm sure she has loads of friends to support her," Pru said. She had, after all, spent only ten minutes with Cate.

"Tanner wouldn't let her," Liam said, his color rising again along with his voice. "He wouldn't let her work and he wouldn't let her have any friends. She's lost touch with almost everyone she used to know." He shook his head.

"Then I'd love to stop in and say hello. Why don't you leave me her number, and I'll ring her."

"That would be great, thanks," he said as he scribbled down two numbers. "There's her mobile, and that's the phone number at the flat." He glanced up at her. "She liked meeting you and Christopher." He cleared his throat. "You two, have you been together a long time?"

"No." Pru smiled. Even the description of them as being "together" was still new to her. "We've known each other only a few months."

"Is that right?" he asked as his face brightened. "That's great that you're together, you know, at . . ."

She raised one eyebrow, daring him to say "at your age." He closed his mouth, and then started again. "I could tell that he likes you," Liam said and turned scarlet. "Is he a gardener, too?"

That got a laugh out of her. "No, he's a DCI in London."

Liam dropped his spoon onto the table. "That's a good score."

After three pieces of Ivy's cake and draining the teapot, Liam left much calmer than he arrived. "Thanks, Pru. You're a good boss," he said with a smile. He walked out the door and turned around. "What was he doing here? Tanner."

"Just stopped by," she said. "I've met him a couple of times. He's the one who found the roses and replaced the seedlings that were destroyed." She shrugged. "I just thought he was helpful. I didn't know."

"Look, if he comes round again, and Christopher isn't here, you give me a ring. All right?"

"Thanks, Liam." She smiled at him. "I appreciate that."

* * *

She poured herself a glass of wine, set some of Riccardo's minestrone on to heat, and rang Christopher.

"I had my phone in my hand," he said, "about to give you a ring. How was your day?"

"Weird," she said. "How was yours?"

"Busy, thank God, because every moment I wasn't occupied, I wished I was there with you."

She thought about how far they'd come in the few months they'd known each other. Into her heart had crept the unfamiliar longing for some permanence. Occasional weekends sounded like a gift when they didn't think they'd ever see each other again, but they were not nearly as wonderful examined close up. But for now, occasional weekends were all they had. "Well, here's what you missed."

She filled him in on her two visitors.

"Now we know why she was looking over her shoulder at the door every two seconds," he said. "Can you see that in Ned — why he would want her to stay with an abusive husband?"

"I know so little about Ned," Pru replied. "He's quiet, he works. I don't know why he would tell his own daughter that."

"And what do you think of Tanner?" he asked.

"I know even less of him," she replied. "He's been friendly every time I've seen him." Her mind wandered back. "The first time I met Ned, when I interviewed here, he told me that someone else had been offered the job. After I met Jamie, I thought he was who Ned meant."

"The Templetons never told you that, did they?"

"That I was second choice? No, Davina has never mentioned it. But I could've been."

"Impossible."

"You couldn't be prejudiced, could you?" she asked. She had something else on her mind and wanted to say it while she had the nerve. "Next time you're able to come down — if you wanted to — you could bring some extra clothes and things to leave here. You know, save you packing so much each time."

He was quiet for a moment and then said in a light tone, "Take care, you might find I'll move myself down there for good. What would you say to that?"

"I would say you are very welcome."

CHAPTER 10

Pru barely blinked at the next blog headline "Gardener Intends to Work Magic on Ancient Yew" and she shrugged off the references to druids and witches in the comments section. She had described to the reporter, Hugo Jenkins, what might be done with the overgrown yews in the large middle square of the walled garden. Yew is forgiving, she had said; they could cut it back to old wood and it would break into new growth. Almost like magic, she had said.

A tingle of dread had settled in her stomach when it came time to open the gate to the walled garden. The voice of DS Hobbes echoed in her mind, connecting the blog posts with the vandalism.

She touched the large iron handle lightly, then took hold, pushed the gate, and breathed a sigh of relief: The yew remained intact. It was just another day in the garden.

Apparently, previous events had put Hugo on edge, too, because midmorning, he stopped by.

"Just wanted to check with you about a topic for next week's post," he said, standing inside the gate and eyeing the yew.

"We'll be planting the walls with apples and training them in different shapes. We've chosen cultivars from the

1700s up through late Victorian that are grafted onto disease-resistant stock."

"Antique fruit, I like it," Hugo replied.

"You could talk to Ned about that," Pru nodded to the far end of the walled garden where Ned had appeared. "He's come up with the list and placed all the orders, although the trees won't arrive for another month."

Hugo's eyes followed her nod and his gaze fell upon Ned. He paused a moment and then, with his eyes still on the old man, asked, "What about up at the house? Don't you have big plans for the space in front? Mrs. Templeton mentioned it. Perhaps we'll focus on that for now."

Pru would rather not cast any light on Davina's merry-go-round of design ideas. "Are you sure? Ned would probably love to talk about what he's chosen — he's got a real nose for history,"

"And it's in everyone else's business," Hugo said, almost under his breath.

This was going nowhere, she thought. "Could we talk about it perhaps tomorrow or perhaps Monday?" The reporter didn't answer, but kept watching Ned, who had glanced up at them and then away. "Hugo?"

"Yes," he said, turning back to her. "Sure, Monday."

A full day of work filled her with the confidence that they could get the garden finished by summer. Ned marked the spacing for the apples, which would be espaliered into fans, cordons, candelabra with three trees between each buttress. Liam and Fergal began to clear the path that led from the lower gate of the walled garden to the house. Pru believed the path to be Repton's, and so there should be remnants of a broader walk that curved around to the front gate, too. He preferred things done in a grand style. "At present," he wrote, "the only pleasure ground consists of a long belt connected with the house by an unprotected gravel walk . . . While it is too uniform & too destitute of objects to be beautiful or picturesque; and much too narrow, and too confined, to be in character with the magnificence of the house."

We'll fix that, Humphry. They would re-establish the lower path, and where it diverged and swept up toward the front gate of the walled garden, it would be broad enough for four abreast and coated with flint and stone gravel chippings to match the drive. Beautiful and picturesque it would be.

* * *

Thursday, she stepped out the door after putting on her yellow waterproof jacket over three layers of thin undershirts and two jumpers. *I'm like an onion*, she thought as she walked out to the garden. It had rained through the night, and was still coming down lightly, and when Liam came racing out of the gate, he skidded on the soaked ground as he made the corner and turned toward her, his eyes wide and his face white. "Pru, you haven't been out to see it?"

She didn't answer but ran past him to find Fergal and Ned staring at the yew. Two of them had been hacked to pieces. The plants had been at least twelve feet tall with trunks so wide at the base she couldn't get her arms around one. But now, branches and sprays of foliage lay in heaps. It was not a neat job — the trunks looked as if they'd been hit by lightning and had exploded.

She felt weak and had to take a couple of deep breaths before she built up enough strength to speak. "Did anyone see anything?"

Heads shook. "I got here just ahead of Liam and Fergal," Ned said. "Not ten minutes ago. I saw no one."

"Nobody move, all right? Just stay here." She got out her phone to ring DS Hobbes.

"I could go check the shed," Liam said, "see if the ax is still there. And the hatchet."

"No." She put out her hand to stop him. "We can't disturb anything. There might be evidence." She'd learned that well enough — don't touch. She looked at the ground and waited for Hobbes to answer his phone. The early-morning frost melted in the sun, taking with it any footprints, and their shoes left no impression on the hard ground. Would there be any evidence to find?

The police arrived. DS Hobbes talked with them all in turn, while two uniformed officers scoured the scene. The morning wore on as they took turns telling what they knew, which was precious little. It didn't look like the work of a chain saw, and after all Pru might've heard that, but her cottage was too far away to have heard anything else, plus she'd had BBC Radio 4 on for most of the evening.

"Pru, could you go down and check the tools in the shed. See if anything is missing?" Hobbes asked.

The acrid smell of smoke permeated the shed, but Fergal had tidied up after the fire and laid the tools back out for display, and so she saw immediately the blank space where the ax should have been. Nothing else was missing.

Hobbes took her aside at one point and said, "Will Inspector Pearse be down this weekend?"

"No, he can't make it, and I don't want him to think he needs to be here. It's just the vandals again." She watched his face. "Don't you think?"

"Each time it's been worse," he said.

The DS talked with Ivy. She had arrived at Primrose House later than usual, stopping first to clean for another client. Davina and Bryan had gone up to London early that morning before they flew off to Brussels.

Pru had to give her employers a report by phone. Davina sounded as heartbroken as Pru felt. "Did you see Ned around at all — last evening or early this morning?" Davina asked her.

This is ridiculous, thought Pru. "No," she said. "Why? Do you think he had something to do with it?"

"Oh, Pru, it's such a long story. I'll explain when we're home again next week."

"He wouldn't have been able to do this, Davina," Pru said. "It's too big a job." Not just physically: She didn't believe Ned could have that much rage in him.

In the afternoon, Pru told everyone to go home. Much of the walled garden was off-limits, and they weren't allowed to move any of the debris off the site yet. She would take the paraffin heater up to Tunbridge Wells for repairs — one of the chimneys had cracked when the firemen dragged it out. Before she left, Fergal reminded her that he and Liam would not be at Primrose House on Friday, so she would have only Robbie and Ned.

Reluctant to go back home herself, she wandered through a few shops in town, looking but not seeing. She got a coffee and sat in the café's window seat watching the bustle on the street at the end of a workday. Too many questions were bouncing around in her head, and she needed to sort them out.

Each incident had followed a blog post about the garden, Primrose House, and Pru's work. Did someone want to make her look bad, and if so, why? Was it someone's wish that, if enough of these acts of vandalism occurred, she would quit or be fired from her head gardener post? This trail led her to two people. First Ned. It now seemed long ago that he had told her someone else got the job, but his initial resistance to Pru's securing the post stayed with her. What about Jamie, who had applied for the job? But Ned never acted as if he held anything against her, and Jamie had been nothing if not charming. To her, at least. She thought about what Liam said Tanner had done to his wife. It didn't sound like the same person.

If Jamie showed up at Primrose House the following week with four replacement yews already clipped into peacocks, perhaps she would be more suspicious. He did seem concerned about staying in Davina and Bryan's good graces. Possibly he wanted them to regret their choice of head gardener.

All conjecture. *Just ask him.*

She located the Council parks office and asked where she might find Jamie Tanner.

The girl at the desk sighed heavily as she closed a video she'd been watching about a ten-second haircut technique. "If he's still around," she said, "he'll probably be at the sheds, finishing up for the day. They're round to the back, the other side of the car park."

Pru followed the directions, and stuck her head in a greenhouse that had lockers and a workroom at one end and asked for him.

"I was up at Dunorlan Park with him today," a man with a red ponytail said, as he took off his rubber overalls. "But we were working at opposite ends. He might be up there still. Do you know it?"

Pru knew the park, just outside the city center, but she was losing her nerve as quickly as she was losing the light. "Thanks, I'll find him another day."

As she headed back to her Mini, Jamie pulled in, got out, and walked toward the greenhouse.

"Jamie?"

He stopped just past the pool of light from the security lamp, his face in shadow. "Pru. Are you looking for me?" His voice was quiet, and she walked closer to hear better.

"I'm sorry to bother you at work," she said, wondering what she thought she would say to him. "We've had another problem up at the garden."

"Not more rabbits in the glasshouse?" She couldn't see his face, but could hear a smile in his voice.

"No, it's worse than that. Two of the yews in the walled garden were hacked to pieces this morning. Or last night, I don't know."

He dropped the amused act. "God, that's awful. What's this all about?"

She took a deep breath. "Jamie, did you really want the head gardener post?"

He remained still. "Why do you ask me that?"

"You . . ." Her throat was dry. She swallowed, trying to find her voice again. "You seem to like the place."

"I do like the place, Pru — who wouldn't? But it isn't as if you sneaked in the back door and took something that wasn't yours. And look at the job you're doing. Besides," he said, the humorous tone back, "I've got a job and I certainly couldn't take another on, could I? What would my wife say?"

"Ned . . ." she began.

"And you've got Ned. Ned's a good friend to me, Pru, he always has been. He's helping me sort a few things out."

She had come about the garden, not Jamie's personal issues. "I've got to go. I'm sorry to bother you."

"Come back in daylight and I'll give you a tour of the place," Jamie said.

* * *

A bowl of soup and a half pint at the Duke of York on the Pantiles, the historic section of the town, would do for her supper, but before she went in, she pulled out the paper with Cate's numbers on them.

"This is Pru Parke. Is this Cate? We met at . . ."

"Oh Pru, yes. It's very good to hear from you."

"It was lovely to meet you on Sunday, and I wanted to ring and find out . . ." *If what? If your husband was abusive and is now harassing you?* She didn't know how she was supposed to finish that question.

"We're good, Pru. Nanda and I are doing fine here with Francine." Indeed, Pru could hear little-girl giggles in the background. "We'd love for you to stop by some time."

"Thanks, I will do that. Liam is quite concerned about you." Was that vague enough?

"Liam checks in with us now and then, and he's being very considerate. But really, he shouldn't think he has to fight my battles for me."

* * *

Pru desperately needed some distraction for the evening, and so she sat down to catch up on correspondence. Mr. Wilson's email and photo from Boxing Day had arrived, along with the phone number for Birdie Parke, Simon's aunt. Pru clicked to open the message, and the photo of her seated next to Simon on the Wilsons' sofa popped up on the screen. She frowned and then squinted. She knew they were no relation, but they

80

did seem to look a bit alike. They had the same hair — thick, brownish, and frizzed on the ends, although Simon's had more gray than hers. She reached up to her own, took out the clip, combed through, and reclipped. A knot began to form in her stomach. *Wishful thinking,* she told herself. *We look like two gardeners.* But the knot wouldn't go away. She clicked onto the next email.

From: DavinaPrimrose@bt.com
To: PruParke50@bt.com
Date: 21 January

Pru,

We need to focus on all the wonderful things at Primrose House and not worry about what's happened. We know you will deal with the yew as you see fit. In the meantime, I believe we should concentrate on the gardens directly around the house. We'll begin immediately with your idea of terracing the lawn off the back. As soon as we return, we'll find enough workers to get busy. Can't you just see how popular it would be on our open garden day?

Best,
Davina

Pru rested her forehead in her hand and heaved a sigh. Yes, she wanted the slope terraced — but later, after the summer events, not now when she had so much to do. She reached for her work notebook and added "BUY MORE PLANTS." She went to bed and tossed and turned for what seemed like half the night. Getting up once for a drink of water she returned to bed only half awake, and thought she saw a light through the window bouncing around in the wood behind the walled garden. A car, she thought. A car going down the lane, its headlamps reflecting off wet tree trunks. She yawned, crawled back under the covers, and drifted off.

CHAPTER 11

The next morning, Ivy rang as Pru headed out the door.

"Pru, I've sent Robbie on down. I don't see Ned about. Have you come across Robbie's red fleece jacket anywhere? I haven't seen it for a couple of days, and I don't know where he's left it."

"I don't remember, but I'll have a look round. Have you asked at Chaffinch's? He was there yesterday."

"We couldn't find it when I collected him," Ivy said. "Has it been since Tuesday that I've seen it? Where's my mind? It's just that he said something about leaving it in the garden. I'm sure it'll turn up."

* * *

Robbie stood at the front gate of the walled garden waiting for her. "Where's Ned, Pru?" he asked. "Where's Liam? Where's Fergal? What will we do today?"

"I haven't seen Ned yet," she replied. "Liam and Fergal won't be here today, because they're working on their cottage. So you and Ned and I will do all the garden work ourselves. Are you up for it? Let's walk down to the shed. Maybe Ned is waiting for us there."

"I'll go look. I'll look for Ned." Robbie bounded ahead on the path they'd worn that led around the outside corner of the walled garden. Pru followed, trying to muster half the energy he had. Robbie already had made it to the end and must've come back in through the lower gate, because he popped out of the side entrance. His pale face was even paler than usual, and his eyes wide and dark. "What's wrong with Ned, Pru? Did he have an accident?"

"An accident? Did you see him?"

"He's out there," Robbie pointed out the back gate of the walled garden. "Maybe he fell down. I think he hurt himself. He's bleeding."

She grabbed Robbie's arm to keep him from darting off again. "Wait, let me go see, all right? You stay here." Robbie followed her as she ran through the walled garden to the back gate.

He was lying on a bed of yew branches, which stuck out all around him, as if he was the center of a huge wreath. Legs stretched out, Wellies pointed toes up, and arms flung out to the sides. His eyes were wide open, glassy, unseeing, and his cap had fallen back. Blood formed a pool on his chest. It didn't look liquid, but thick, coagulated, gelatinous. More blood, not bright red, but dark, had soaked into the leaves and dried grass around his jacket.

She recoiled and threw one arm out to stop Robbie from getting any closer. "Robbie, get back. Go back in the garden. I'll go with you — come with me." She hurried him back inside and against the wall.

"What's wrong with Ned, Pru? Did he fall? Can we help him?" Robbie started to resist her, trying to get back to Ned.

"Robbie, come with me. Come with me and we'll ring for help." He was all arms, and she knew she'd never be able to force him anywhere. "Will you help me, Robbie?" She couldn't catch her breath and her stomach was churning, but she knew she needed to focus on getting the boy away.

Little by little she persuaded Robbie to move. Still holding his arm, she got her phone out and rang DS Hobbes, trying to convey the seriousness of the situation without alarming Robbie further. "David, this is Pru. Please come now. It's Ned. Now, David, *now*. You'll need . . . you'll need the medical examiner. I'm in the garden. I have Robbie with me."

Hobbes asked no questions, but rang off immediately.

She concentrated on Robbie to keep the image of Ned's body at bay. "Robbie, let's ring your mum, okay? Is she up at the house? Or did she go somewhere else? Let's ring your mum, all right?"

She rang Ivy's mobile, but got only voice mail. She tried to sound calm as Robbie pulled away, heading for the gate, and she dragged him back. "Ivy, it's Pru. Robbie is fine. Please ring me as soon as you can." She rang the house phone, but there was no answer.

Before long, she heard the sirens that preceded a slew of officers. She pointed out the back gate to show them the way and stayed where she was against the wall at the side entrance to the garden. She couldn't leave, because Robbie wanted to follow them. "It's the police, Pru, it's the police. Is Ned in trouble?" He squirmed as she held both his arms.

"Robbie, we need to stay here, stay with me. That will help the police. Robbie, look at me, pay attention. We need to stay here and wait for your mum." DS Hobbes came back from where Ned lay and approached them, but Pru said, "It's all right, Robbie and I are all right here."

Hobbes returned to the scene and Pru kept talking to Robbie, repeating the same things over and over again, concentrating on calming him and herself at the same time. "Stay with me, Robbie. We'll wait for your mum."

After a while, Robbie stood quietly and watched the show of police parading by. At last, Ivy appeared. Pru saw her at the front gate of the walled garden, stopped by the police. They must've told her what happened, because soon she was running toward Pru and Robbie, grabbing her son in a tight hug, which he attempted unsuccessfully to wriggle out of. DS Hobbes appeared and spoke to her briefly, and

Ivy put a hand on Pru's arm before she took Robbie away. He protested the whole way, insisting that he needed to help Ned and Pru in the garden.

After that, Pru stood unnoticed against the wall, clutching the front of her coat now that she no longer had Robbie to clutch. Hobbes said, "Pru, go back to your cottage. We'll come and talk to you there."

She shook her head. She couldn't go to her warm, safe home where her mind would begin to wander. She needed to be cold and numb with lots of activity around her.

"I rang Inspector Pearse," he said. "I thought he should know. He's on his way."

She wanted to thank him, but couldn't open her mouth, afraid of what might come out. She touched his arm and nodded.

Hobbes went back to the investigation, and she remained against the wall, sucking in deep breaths of cold air through her nose. She made lists in her head, as she shivered. Which annuals will she order? How many flats? Should they have snapdragons or veronica? Time meant nothing — her only concern was to keep her mind busy and her breakfast down. Then she saw him out of the corner of her eye — Christopher flashing his warrant card at an officer before he ran to her, tie flapping over his shoulder, and wrapped her in his arms.

"You're like ice," he said. She shivered, unable to stop.

"She wouldn't leave," Hobbes said as he came over. "After Robbie's mum came, I tried to get her to go indoors, but she wouldn't go."

Christopher searched her face. She looked back at him.

"Inspector Pearse," Hobbes said. "Inspector Tatt will be here soon. Would you like to . . . take a look?"

He hesitated only a moment. "Yes, thanks, David." He looked at Pru. "Is that all right?"

She nodded. He was gone just a few minutes. She occupied herself with trying to identify the dried and broken leaves beneath her feet — oak, ash, beech. When Christopher returned, he said, "Come on, let's go inside." He kept his arm around her as they walked. On the way, he asked, "Do you need to stop?"

She shook her head.

As they reached her cottage she'd pulled her key out and handed it to Christopher. He unlocked the door, saying, "They'll be up here in a few minutes. You should know that Tat—"

She couldn't wait, but broke away from him and ran for the bathroom, making it just in time. She hung her head over the toilet and lost it all — toast, scrambled eggs, tea, and what seemed like much more. When it was over, she rested her forehead against the cold porcelain, breathing heavy, her eyes watering.

After a few minutes, she got up, a bit wobbly, rinsed out her mouth, and splashed water on her face. She seemed to have thrown up most of her energy, too, but at least her stomach was calm.

Christopher had closed both the bathroom and bedroom doors. She had her hand out to open the bedroom door when she heard a commotion and a voice bellow, "Pearse, what are you doing sniffing around my crime scene?"

CHAPTER 12

"Tatt, this isn't an official visit," Christopher said as Pru came out of the bedroom. He put his arm around her shoulders. "Are you all right?" he asked in a quiet voice.

"I'm better," she said. He gave her a squeeze.

"Humph," Tatt said, "so that's it, is it? Name's Tatt. Detective Inspector." He held up his warrant card to Pru. She looked past it to get a look at the man himself — short, stocky, with a florid complexion and a wide face. Five or six strands of hair that grew above his left ear stretched across the vast expanse of his bald head and were plastered down just above his right ear. His free hand was in his trouser pocket, and she could hear the metallic jingling from keys and coins. "Sit down, Ms. Parke," he said, indicating a chair at her kitchen table.

She hesitated for a moment at being commanded to sit in her own house, but then she sat. So did Hobbes, who had followed Tatt in. Christopher had put the kettle on, and he stood leaning against the rail of the Aga with his arms crossed. Tatt plopped himself in a chair across from her.

"DS Hobbes tells me that one of your workers found the body. Fox, is it?" he cocked his head at his sergeant.

"Robbie Fox, sir," Hobbes said.

"Well?" Tatt barked, making Pru jump. "What happened?"

She explained, for the first time piecing together each moment in her mind. When she arrived at Ned's body, she stopped and swallowed.

"The body, Ms. Parke. What did you see?" Tatt asked. She wished he would turn down the volume.

Christopher poured out mugs of tea and sat. Pru took the milk jug, but her hand shook, and so she put the jug back down, and Christopher added it for her, as well as a spoonful of sugar. "Take your time, it's all right," he said.

"It's a straightforward question, Pearse. There's no need to mollycoddle her."

Pru supposed after two kind police officers — Christopher and Sergeant Hobbes — her number was up, and it was time for an annoying one. She took a sip of sweet, milky tea, and described what she saw.

"Where were your workers today?" Tatt asked. "Hobbes says there are two others — Fergal and Liam Duffy," he said, looking down at his notebook.

"They weren't scheduled to work."

"And what do you know about this Fox? Does he cause trouble around here? Get in arguments?"

"Of course not," she replied, her indignation on Robbie's behalf rising to the surface. "He's a fine boy, he's very helpful."

"Boy? Hobbes," he whirled around to his sergeant, "you told me he was twenty-three."

Pru answered first. "He is twenty-three, but mentally he's more about ten. He works hard in the garden, and we like having him here."

"Where are the Templetons?" Tatt asked.

"Oh God," she said, looking at Christopher. "I should ring Davina."

"Do you know when—" Christopher began.

"Ms. Parke, pay attention." Tatt raised his voice another few decibels.

"I *am* paying attention." Anger had replaced nausea, but she wished that, if she did need to throw up again, it could be on Tatt.

"I rang Mrs. Templeton and left a message, sir," Hobbes said.

A knock. "Hobbes," Tatt said, jerking his head toward the door.

The DS got up to answer. Pru got up, too, but kept behind him. A uniformed policeman stood outside with a large clear plastic bag containing something red. Pru backed off a step, but then realized that the red wasn't blood. The bag held a red fleece jacket, and she was close enough to read the name written in black marker on the inside of the collar: R. Fox.

Tatt pushed past her and stepped outside to talk. Pru peered over his shoulder, and noticed that the officer held another bag, too. This one had a hatchet, and its blade was bloody. She felt Christopher's hands on her shoulders.

Tatt turned back inside and saw them clustered around the door. "What's all this? Hobbes, get this Fox to the station for questioning."

"Why? Why do you need Robbie?" Pru asked. "He didn't have anything to do with this."

"And how would you know that? You know very little other than what you saw. You don't even know when the murder occurred, Ms. Parke, now do you?"

"When?" she asked.

"At least eighteen hours ago," the sergeant replied.

"Shut it, Hobbes," Tatt said. "Ms. Parke, that's none of your business. Or yours, Pearse."

Pru felt Christopher's hands tighten on her shoulders. "Robbie's mother has to be there when you question him," Pru said. "And I'll be there, too."

"You will not be there," Tatt replied. "Who do you think you are?"

"I'm his advocate, that's who I am." At least, she thought she could be. Pru had heard Ivy talk about advocates — someone who could help advise and interpret situations. More a friend of the family than licensed professional — certainly Pru could fill that role. At least she didn't believe Tatt could tell her that she couldn't, as long as Ivy approved. "I have a right to be there."

"You have no rights," Tatt's voice got both louder and higher.

Belying the grip he held on her shoulders, Christopher was the picture of calm. "I believe she does."

Tatt glared at them all. "Well, don't try flashing your warrant card around my station, Pearse. I can at least keep you out of that." He stalked away.

Hobbes followed, but before he left, he turned back and said, "I'll ask Ivy to bring Robbie in at three o'clock."

"Thanks," Pru whispered.

"Hobbes!" Tatt shouted over his shoulder. The DS left, closing the door behind him.

Pru stared at the closed door. "What a jerk," she said. She turned to Christopher. "You know him. You know how he works."

"Yes," he said, "and I dislike his methods."

She almost laughed. "Dislike?"

One corner of his mouth turned up. "Intensely."

"Don't get carried away now," she said.

He took her in his arms. "I don't get carried away by anything but you. I love you with all my heart, and I'm so sorry this happened."

It was the permission she needed. She gave a shudder, and the tears burst forth. Christopher didn't speak, just let her get over it, stroking her back. Once she'd sobbed herself quiet again and heaved a couple of heavy sighs, she looked up. "All right," she said, "that's that." He offered his handkerchief and she wiped her cheeks and patted his damp lapel. "You're quite good at soaking up my tears. Now, I'll fix us some sandwiches."

"You'll fix them, will you?" he asked. That got a smile from her — he always had his ear out for her Texas vocabulary.

Christopher brewed another pot of tea, and when they sat down to lunch, Pru found herself alternating between being famished and having no appetite.

But before she could take a bite, Davina rang from Brussels, having heard only the bare minimum from DS Hobbes. Pru kept the horror of her discovery for a later conversation and related the facts as simply as possible.

"Poor Ned. And how are you holding up?"

"I'll be fine." Pru looked across the table and smiled. "Christopher is here with me."

"Thank God you aren't alone. We'll be back first thing Monday," Davina said. "I'm so sorry to leave this with you, but we just can't get away. You have the police ring us with any questions until then."

Pru didn't explain about Tatt, but she wished she could be a fly on the wall — or a bug on the phone — to overhear that conversation.

She backtracked and told Christopher about the yew — obviously not the big news it had been yesterday — and about seeking out Jamie.

"I don't know why I thought I should talk with him," Pru said. "I guess I hoped I could get him to confess to cutting down the yews, even though I cannot imagine how any gardener could be so destructive. By the time I got back, it was well after dark." She looked out the window above the sink, as she remembered. "I thought they had left in the afternoon. We'd finished for the day, although Ned did have a tendency to putter about on his own. I think he wanted to remind me that he had been here longer and knew what had to be done. This morning it looked as if he'd started to take the yew branches down to the brush pile, but when I got back last evening, the place seemed deserted."

Christopher watched her for a moment. "Have you ever seen Robbie angry?"

"No," she said as she shook her head. "Robbie had no part in this. No."

"You said he liked to play with the hatchet as if it were a weapon," he reminded her.

"We have rules, and he follows the rules," she said, her voice wavering. "No."

He took her hand across the table and stroked it for a moment. "Liam has had a grudge against Ned."

She took her hand away, alarmed at the image that sprang into her mind of Liam yelling at the old man. "No, not Liam. I know he has a temper, but he's not violent. He couldn't do it."

Christopher took her hand back again and held it. "Tatt will ask these questions and more, and it won't be pleasant. You have to ask hard questions to get at the truth — there's no way around it. You have to keep asking until you get the answers."

She didn't reply, but waited for him to realize what he'd said.

"Not *you*," he said in a rush. "I didn't mean that *you* should ask the questions." She got up, walked around him, and put the plates in the sink. "Pru, this was a horribly violent act. You can't take any part of the investigation upon yourself. Please don't put yourself in danger, thinking that you need to prove someone's innocence."

He turned round in his chair and she stood between his knees, resting her arms on his shoulders as he sat. "I know Robbie and I know Liam. They aren't capable of this." She kissed him. "You don't have to worry. I won't stick my nose into anything I shouldn't. I'll stay out of trouble."

"Yes, I'm sure you will." His ironic tone was not lost on her. He put his arms around her waist. "You're loyal to your friends."

"Woof." She kissed him again as he slipped his hand under her sweater in back. His phone rang.

"Seems like old times," she said, and turned to the sink as he stood and walked into the sitting room to answer.

"Pearse . . . Yes, I knew it was coming in today . . . Put it on my desk and I'll attend to it on Monday . . . No, it isn't urgent. Monday will be in plenty of time . . . No, I will not be in tomorrow . . . *On my desk*. Right."

He rang off. She leaned against the sink and said, "You weren't supposed to be here this weekend."

He returned to the kitchen and sat on the edge of the table. "I'm grateful that Hobbes rang. I couldn't leave you alone with this."

A vision of Ned's body appeared in her mind, and tears sprang to her eyes. She blinked them away, hoping to sound levelheaded and reasonable. "Is it going to be a problem for you?"

He regarded her in silence. She loved those long, deep looks of his, and could so easily get lost in them. "For a very long time," he said, "I had nothing in my life except work. Evenings and weekends were merely opportunities to file reports, interview suspects, go over evidence. The people I work with grew accustomed to the fact that I was available at any time." He pushed a wisp of hair out of her face. "But now I have you in my life, and I don't want to spend every waking moment as a DCI — nor do I need to. I know that, and I hope that you know that. It'll just take time for the rest of them to figure it out." He smiled. "It isn't a problem. You could never be a problem."

"Really? Never?" She laughed. "I'll remind you of that some time."

CHAPTER 13

They took Christopher's car to the station, and on the drive, Pru asked, "How do you know Tatt? Did you work together?"

"We were up for DCI at the same time a few years ago," Christopher said. "I got it, he didn't. Instead of staying in London with the Met as a detective sergeant, he took this post."

"He's envious of you then," she said. "Has he always been this mean?"

"His manner is probably one of the reasons he didn't make DCI. He may get the job done, but no one likes to watch."

When they arrived at the station, Ivy, with Robbie in tow, stood at the front desk speaking to the sergeant.

"Oh, Pru, did they make you come down, too?" Ivy asked. "I don't know what they expect Robbie to tell them. You told them about Ned, so Robbie shouldn't have to describe what he saw." She kept a firm grip on her son, while he watched police officers come and go.

So, they hadn't told her yet about Robbie's jacket. Perhaps Tatt was hoping for a shocking revelation and confession, Pru thought, her annoyance at the DI continuing to grow. "I said that I would be Robbie's advocate, so they would have to let me be there when they talk with him. With you there, too. Is that all right?'

Ivy grabbed Pru's arm, too. "Thank you, you'll be such a help."

As if he thought Christopher would hijack the interview, Tatt monitored admittance to the interview room, allowing in Robbie, Ivy, and Pru, after which he slammed the door. His theatrics were lost on Christopher, who had already settled in a chair in the lobby.

DS Hobbes was also in the room. He started the recorder and gave the vitals — day, time, those in attendance — after which Tatt took over.

"Robbie my boy," he said, holding up the bag with the red fleece jacket. "Is this your jacket?"

Robbie turned to his mother. "I didn't lose it, Mum, I didn't lose my jacket."

"This jacket," Tatt said to Ivy, his voice ricocheting off the hard surfaces of the room, "with your son's name inked in it, was found buried in a shallow hole behind the brush pile at Primrose House, Ms. Fox. Wrapped in it was the murder weapon."

Ivy gasped and squeezed Robbie's arm, causing him to let out a yelp. "How could that be?" she said in a hoarse whisper. "It was lost, wasn't it, Robbie? Did you forget it at Chaffinch's?"

"It was cold outside, and he needed my jacket," Robbie said.

The room was quiet. "Who needed your jacket, boy?" Tatt asked.

"My mate. I gave it to my mate. He was cold, Mum," Robbie said. "I was sharing."

Relief washed over Ivy's face. "Was it Andrew?" To Tatt she said, "Andrew is Robbie's friend at Chaffinch's. Andrew must've borrowed the jacket."

Tatt ignored her and turned back to Robbie. "You didn't give it to anyone, now did you, Robbie?"

"What do you think he did," Pru said, trying to keep her voice under control, "drive himself down to Primrose House, kill Ned, leave his jacket, and drive back to his care center?"

"If you'd like to remain in this interview, Ms. Parke," Tatt bellowed, "you'll keep quiet."

"Robbie hasn't had his jacket since Tuesday," Pru said. "None of us remember seeing it since then, isn't that right, Ivy? Robbie may have left it in the garden that day. We were all working very hard, and he got warm, took it off, and probably forgot it. Someone else must've found it."

"Well now, isn't that convenient? Just the thing to wrap a hatchet in." Tatt said. "Where were you yesterday afternoon, Robbie my boy?"

"I'm not allowed to touch the hatchet," Robbie said. "Pru says I'm not allowed. 'Don't touch the hatchet. Don't touch the ax.' That's what you said, Pru."

Pru looked at Tatt as she replied. "Yes, Robbie, that's what I said."

Continued questioning brought no other details to light. Pru admired how Robbie kept his good humor, because she came quite near to slapping Tatt and Ivy jumped at any little sound or movement.

Tatt assigned Hobbes to check out Chaffinch's and Andrew. The inspector was reluctant to let them go, but eventually dismissed them with a warning that Robbie could be called back for more questioning at any time — as could Pru.

Christopher met them as they emptied out into the lobby. DS Hobbes came up and asked, "Pru, have you seen this before?" He held out a small plastic bag containing a pocketknife.

"No, it isn't mine. I don't believe I've seen Liam or Fergal with a pocketknife. Or Ned. Although, a pocketknife is always handy in the garden."

"But it isn't specifically a garden tool, is it?" he asked.

"Anything can be a garden tool," Pru said. "I have a friend who weeds with a screwdriver." She took the bag from him. The knife had no initials or other marking that might identify its owner. When she turned it over, she saw a smear of blood, handed the bag back, and wiped her hand on her trouser leg. "Where did you find it?"

"Inspector Pearse spotted it," Hobbes said, giving a quick look over his shoulder. "Just beside the . . . near Ned."

"Doesn't look like it's been there long. You'll check for fingerprints, I suppose?" she asked.

"We'll check against all of yours at the garden — routine, of course. We don't have the Templetons' fingerprints, so they'll need to come in when they arrive back."

As Pru and Christopher walked out to the car park, a dreadful realization hit her. "Cate — I forgot about her."

"They'll have told her by now," Christopher said.

"But I need to tell her, too. I'll ring her now."

Christopher's phone rang, and he walked away to answer. "Pearse . . . No, I won't be in tomorrow . . ."

Pru made her call and Cate answered in a weak voice.

"It's Pru. I'm so sorry about your father."

Cate gave a little sob. "I don't know how this could happen."

Pru responded with a few words meant to comfort. They chatted only a couple of minutes more. Pru could hear voices in the background and so she knew Cate wasn't alone. She rang off just as Christopher returned.

"Shall we stop for a meal in town?" he asked.

Pru wondered where the day had gone. "Yes, we'd better. All I've got is a frozen moussaka from Ivy." On the short drive down to one of the cafés on the Pantiles, she asked the question most important to her, although she was afraid to hear the answer. "Have you been called back to work tomorrow?"

He finished pulling into a parking space before he answered. "I won't leave, at least not until Sunday evening."

The thought of his presence at the cottage and his warm body next to her in bed brought her to the edge of grateful tears. Pru kissed Christopher first on the cheek, and again on the mouth. "Thank you."

After they were seated and served the wine, he asked, "How is Cate?"

"She sounded as if she were trying to be brave." Pru toyed with the stem of her glass. "Cate told me that Tatt will be there tomorrow morning to talk with her. At eleven o'clock." She felt his eyes on her. "I said we'd be there at ten-thirty," she continued with a quick glance up followed by a sip of wine. "You don't have to go. I don't want to assume that—"

Christopher picked up his glass as he said, with a gleam in his eye, "I wouldn't miss it."

"Cate and Nanda have been staying with a friend, but Francine is out this evening," Pru said, and paused, staring at the table. "I heard a man's voice in the background. I think it was Liam." Christopher didn't have time to reply before she took his hand and said, "It's good she isn't alone. Think how unbearable that would be."

"You only think it was Liam or are you sure?"

Pru shrugged. "When I talked with her before, Cate made it sound as if she saw Liam only occasionally, but now, I don't know."

* * *

As they pulled into Pru's drive, she could see the lamp by the cottage's sofa glowing with a warm and cheerful light, unaware of the tragic events of the day.

Once they were inside, Christopher got to work on a fire. Pru ticked the heat up a few degrees and stood by the Aga until there was a blaze going.

They settled on the sofa, brandies in hand, his arms encircling her. She tried to relax, but her thoughts were like jumping beans, and at last she sat up, put the brandy on the floor beside her, and leaned toward the fire.

"This is such a terrible thing," she said. "Cate's lost her father. I can still see Ned lying there and I keep wondering, did he die immediately? Did he hope someone would come?"

Christopher rubbed her back. "You can't think of that now, not tonight."

She glanced back at him, her face hot with guilt. "What I'm really thinking about is — what about the garden? What will happen to it? Will Davina and Bryan chuck it all in?

What about me?" She covered her face with her hands. "Oh God, how could I be so selfish?"

"You're putting so much of yourself into this place — how could you not be concerned? Come here." He reached for her and she willingly went back into his arms. "Life has to go on. This is a tragedy and someone will pay for what happened, but the rest of us have to go on." He kissed her hair. "It's just that it's so fresh in your mind right now, you don't think you'll ever get over it. I don't believe this would deter the Templetons from showing off the garden. Your garden."

She allowed herself to be comforted. "Mmm. My garden." All was quiet except for the hissing and crackling of the logs. Even her mind was stilled as the flames mesmerized her. Eventually, a burned-through log broke apart and fell in a shower of sparks.

"How did you learn to build such fine fires?" she asked.

He didn't answer, but her head was against his cheek, and she could feel him smile. She sat up and saw that he'd turned red, and not from the fire. "I was a Boy Scout."

She laughed as she cupped his cheek in her hand. "Oh," she said, "of course you were a Boy Scout. Did you help little old ladies cross the road?"

"Certainly not," he said, "that's far too dangerous."

"The roads?"

"The old ladies."

She laughed again, leaned in and her lips brushed his as she said, "You're quite good as distracting me."

"I can do better than that if you let me," he whispered.

"I'm all yours."

* * *

Snuggled up against him in bed, she drifted off quickly, but sometime during the night she woke up shouting, "*No, no,*" and flailing her arms as if to ward off an attack.

"Pru, it's all right, you're all right." He held her close and began murmuring quiet, calming words.

"I looked in Ned's face," she said, breathing hard. "His eyes were open, just as I found him. But then he spoke. He said . . . I can't remember the words." She wiped the tears from her face, and said to Christopher. "Why can't I remember the words?"

"Lie back down," he said. He covered them both up and wrapped her tightly in his arms. As dreams do, Ned's face faded from her mind as Christopher talked, soft and low. He started telling her a story about going on a Boy Scout outing to Staffhurst Wood, near Edenbridge, where he grew up. He had been just seven years old. It was the first time he saw a badger. She wanted to listen, to remember this piece of his childhood, but her muscles began to relax and she slipped into that twilight place before drifting off to sleep.

CHAPTER 14

"We should stop by the shops this afternoon," Pru said as they got out of the car. Francine's flat, where Cate and Nanda were staying, took up the ground floor of a house off the Frant Road out of Tunbridge Wells. "Just for a few things." Breakfast had been meager, as she hadn't expected Christopher for the weekend — tea and toast didn't seem enough to offer. At least she'd taken Ivy's moussaka out of the freezer for their dinner. "Buttermilk," she said. "We'll need buttermilk for breakfast."

"We won't drink it, will we?" he asked.

A stout woman had appeared on the front step of the house across the road from the flat and stood watching them. Pru smiled and nodded, and the neighbor did the same, after which she called over her shoulder into the house. "Trevor — come!"

Pru expected either a young boy or a husband to emerge, but instead, out trotted a stout beagle, wagging his tail. The woman attached a leash and walked to her front gate as Pru rang the bell at Francine's.

Cate carried a wadded-up tissue in one hand when she opened the door. She waved wanly at the woman who waved back, and the beagle gave a single yip.

"Mrs. Arabella Sock," Cate explained in a quiet voice. "Nanda and I have been here at Francine's for only three weeks, but I can already tell you that Mrs. Sock keeps an eye on everyone, whether she's asked to or not." She led them into the sitting room and said, "I'm so grateful you're here. Francine is taking Nanda out, and I didn't want to face the police alone."

"You don't want to face one of them alone," Pru said over her shoulder to Christopher, "that's for sure."

A young woman with long auburn hair came out of the hall putting on a coat while she herded a little girl in front of her. Cate introduced Pru and Christopher to Francine Rosse, who said hello, and to Nanda, who said nothing, but stared at them with big blue eyes. Her coloring was midway between Cate's black hair and dark skin, and Jamie's blond features. Her hair, drawn up to the top of her head, shot out of its short ponytail like a palm tree.

Pru knelt down in front of the little girl. "Hello, Nanda." Nanda stared back.

"Right, we're off, Nanda-Panda," Francine said. "Nanda's going to help me buy a new pair of boots, and then . . ."

"I get sweeties," Nanda burst out.

Cate gave her daughter a hug and a kiss. "You be a good girl for Franny."

"Bye, Mummy." Nanda waved at Cate on her way out the door, looked at Pru and Christopher and snatched her hand back.

When Francine opened the door to leave, Pru could see that Mrs. Sock and Trevor had made little progress and seemed to be still in the process of pulling the gate closed.

"Mummy! I see the doggie!" Nanda said, jumping up and down. That caught the attention of Mrs. Sock — who smiled and waved — and Trevor, who yipped and whose tail beat back and forth like a metronome set on presto.

"Off you go with Franny," Cate said to her daughter. "Don't bother Mrs. Sock."

The door closed, and Pru put her arm around Cate, thinking that both Mrs. Sock and Trevor looked as if they'd love to be bothered by Nanda. "If there's anything I can do, you'll let me know, won't you?"

"Thanks," Cate said, dropping the brave face she'd had in front of her daughter. "You . . . you f-f-found him, didn't you?"

Pru had hoped that Cate wouldn't ask for details. She didn't want to think about it. and she didn't think Cate should hear it. "Robbie saw your dad first. You've heard of Robbie?" Cate nodded. "Robbie thought something was wrong and came back to get me. I rang the police immediately, but . . . it was too late."

"Are you going to conduct the investigation, Inspector?" Cate asked.

"Please, call me Christopher," he said. "I've no jurisdiction here. The Met can be called to work on cases outside of London, but only if requested. I wish I could help."

They chatted a few minutes about a service for Ned to be held, Cate hoped, on Thursday, if the police would release the body.

Forewarned is forearmed, Pru thought. "Cate," she said, "the sergeant, David Hobbes, is a good man, very easy to talk with. But the inspector — well, he's sort of loud and—" That was as far as she got before the knock.

When Cate answered the door, Tatt held out his badge, and bellowed, "Cate Tanner? Detective Inspector Tatt." He saw Pru and Christopher standing behind her and shoved his badge back in his pocket as he said, "We need to speak with you about your father — should we come back when you're alone?"

"Is it all right if they stay?" Cate asked. "I'd like to have them here."

"That's just *fine*." Tatt spat out the words as he walked past her, ignoring Pru and Christopher. His DS trailed after him.

"Detective Sergeant Hobbes," he introduced himself to Cate. "I'm very sorry for your loss."

"Shall I start the kettle?" Pru asked.

Cate kept her eye on Tatt, but turned her head to Pru. "Yes, thanks. I've the tray all set up."

After clicking the electric kettle on, Pru returned to the sitting room. All the breathable air seemed to have been sucked up by the cloud of irritation that surrounded the inspector. She sat with Christopher and Cate on the small sofa, while Tatt and Hobbes each took a chair.

"Mrs. Tanner," Tatt began.

"Bobbins," Cate said.

"What?"

"It's Bobbins. I'm taking back my own name. Cate Bobbins."

Hobbes jotted something down in his notebook, while Tatt barked, "Are you married to Jamie Tanner?"

"We're separated." Cate drew herself up straight.

Tatt sighed. "When was the last time you saw or spoke with your father?" he asked.

"He rang on Wednesday. He wanted to see Nanda today, and so we were going for a visit. He . . ." a sob caught in her throat.

"Mrs. Tanner," Tatt began.

"Bobbins, sir," Hobbes said quietly.

Tatt glared at him. "Do you know anyone who might want to harm your father? Someone with a grudge? Someone angry with him?" Each question seemed to hammer Cate farther down into the sofa.

"What do you mean? Someone who would . . . ?" Cate swallowed hard.

"You know what I mean, Mrs. Tanner," Tatt cut in.

Pru couldn't keep still, but as she opened her mouth to object to his manner, Christopher intervened, in a quiet, but firm voice.

"This can't be easy for you, Cate," he said. "Take some time to . . ."

"*Pearse!*" Tatt shouted. "I'd like to see you outside. Now."

Christopher followed Tatt out the front door without looking back. The three of them — Cate, Pru, and DS Hobbes — sat in silence, their attention inexorably drawn to the raised voices on the porch.

"Are you trying to steal this investigation, Pearse?" Tatt's voice was too loud even through the closed door.

"You might get more information if you would show some sympathy for—" Christopher started, not too quiet himself.

"Are you saying I need help in this investigation?" Tatt bellowed.

"Are you *asking* for help?"

"*How dare you!*"

Click. They all three jumped as the electric kettle switched off. Pru stood, eager to get as far away as possible from what sounded like the beginnings of a brawl.

By the time she returned with the tray, Tatt and Christopher were filing back in. Tatt's florid complexion had taken on shades of apoplexy, and Christopher's expression was grim.

Except — Pru took a second look and could see that ghost of a smile around his mouth. She almost dropped the tray and hoped the rattling teacups covered her snort of laughter.

"Ms. — Bobbins," Tatt began, sounding as if someone had hold of his throat, "did your father own a mobile phone?"

"Yes," Cate said, with a small, sad smile. "But he never used it. He would never even turn it on. Just one more thing to carry in his pocket."

"We haven't found one on the body or at his cottage," Tatt said.

Cate's chin quivered. "Are you saying someone did this just to steal his mobile?"

"We are looking for any piece of evidence that could lead us to the murderer, Mrs. Tanner." Tatt turned his head, as if pulling at a too-tight collar. "Ms. Bobbins."

Cate reached for the teapot with a shaky hand, but Pru stopped her. "I'll be mother," she said. As she handed out cups of tea, her eyes met Christopher's for a moment. He should be a teacher, she thought — he's already got Tatt acting more civil.

"Do you know any of Ms. Parke's workers at Primrose House?" Tatt asked Cate. A stillness settled over the room, while a prickly sensation crept up Pru's arms.

"Yes," Cate said.

"Do you know Liam Duffy, Ms. Bobbins?"

"Yes, I know Liam and Fergal. We were in school together, but that was years ago."

"And do you know Robbie, too, and his mother, Ivy? Have you met them?" Pru asked. She didn't like Tatt singling out Liam, making it look as if he suspected Liam of . . . something. "Cate's lived here most of her life. Lives overlap — she knows loads of people in the area."

"Did you see Liam Duffy the day of the murder?" Tatt asked, ignoring Pru with his pen poised over his notebook.

"No," Cate said, her voice on an even pitch and her face calm and quiet. "Why would I see him? What's that got to do with what happened to my dad?"

"Was your flatmate here Thursday evening?" Tatt asked.

"This is Francine's flat; she's been kind enough to let us stay for a while. Francine's the nurse at Chaffinch's, the day care center in town, but she sometimes takes on private work, too. She was with a patient Thursday evening and didn't get home until late. And so, no, she wasn't here."

Tatt stood up. "That'll be all for now. We'll let you know if we need to talk with you further."

Tatt ignored Pru and Christopher as he left, but Hobbes gave them a nod. When the front door opened, Pru noticed Mrs. Sock and Trevor now stood in front of her next-door neighbor's house, chatting with a man on a ladder set up against the chimney.

Cate closed the door, turned to them, and said, "I'm sorry to rush you off, but I've got something I must do. Thanks so much for being here. Pru, I'll ring you as soon as I know about the service." She spoke all this as she swept them into the front hall and out the door. The police car had pulled away. Mrs. Sock remained where she was. As they left, Pru looked back through the single pane of glass in the door and saw Cate pick up the phone.

CHAPTER 15

Pru waited until they were in Sainsbury's shopping for buttermilk before bringing it up. "You enjoyed that, didn't you? Telling Tatt off."

A small smile and a slight shrug. "It isn't my place, I know, but I can't help feeling as if I might be able to . . . guide without carrying any responsibility. But," he said, as he chose a baguette from a tall basket, "Tatt won't put up with too much of that, and so I need to keep my distance. And you cannot be involved."

"I'm not involved," she said, as if the idea never crossed her mind. He raised his eyebrows.

They pulled into the Two Bells on their way home, and once settled with pints, Pru realized she'd left her hair clip in the car, abandoned when she didn't have room to maneuver. "I'll just get it."

She practically had to stand on her head in the footwell of her Mini before she came up with the hair clip, and found herself a bit lightheaded when she stood up again. She shut the door and leaned against the car, pulling her hair back and inserting the clip, then turned to see Jamie Tanner standing a few feet away.

He looked dreadful — crumpled clothes, puffy face, and bloodshot eyes. Cate had moved out weeks ago, had he finally given up hope or only just run out of clean clothes?

"Pru," he said in a hoarse whisper. "You've got to help me." He wiped his eyes on his sleeve.

"Jamie, what's wrong?"

"What am I going to do without Ned?" he asked.

Of course, Pru thought. *Of course he would've heard the news.*

He went on before she could reply. "I've nothing now — no one left."

Ned had been his champion, persuading Cate to stay with her husband. It had incensed Liam.

"What help do you need?" Pru asked.

"I've got to get her back," he said. "Ned was going to help. He knew we should be together, he said he'd tell her that we needed to stay married. But now" — he sobbed — "now what? Ned's gone." And then he was quiet. "You know who did it, don't you?"

Caught between sympathy and repulsion, she chose a businesslike attitude. "Look, Jamie, I'm sure this is difficult for you, but you need to talk with someone — a therapist. I'm in no position to do anything, and—"

He took a step toward her so fast she instinctively backed up, but ran into her car. Just then, a Range Rover pulled in next to them, and four young women got out laughing. That seemed to bring Jamie to his senses. He shook his head at Pru, turned, and left.

She returned to the pub and sat down. She took her clip out, but couldn't keep hold of her clip, dropping it twice under the table until Christopher took hold of her hand and said, "What's wrong?"

"I just saw Jamie Tanner outside."

"What did he do?" Christopher asked as he started out of the booth.

She grabbed his arm. "No, it wasn't that. And he's gone now." Once Christopher settled back down, she said, "He's upset about Ned. I think they were very close. He counted on Ned to persuade Cate to take him back. He's upset."

Christopher rubbed his forehead. "I'll side with Liam on this one. Tanner may seem friendly, but you should be wary.

If he comes by again, ring Hobbes. In fact—" he took out his mobile — "I think we'd better tell him right now."

They learned from Hobbes that Cate had never filed a complaint about Jamie's abuse, and so a report that came second- or even thirdhand, couldn't be acted on, but the DS did have resources available to victims of abuse and immediately sent them to Pru to give to Cate. At least, Christopher said, the DS would now have his radar up.

* * *

After dinner at her cottage, she sought some topic of conversation other than murder, and pulled up the photo that Mr. Wilson had emailed that showed her sitting next to Simon.

Christopher patted his pockets until he found his glasses, then sat at the table. Pru sat across from him, watching his reaction. "Do you think we look alike? That we could be related?"

He stirred, looked at her, and back to the screen. He took his glasses off, reached for her hands across the table, and searched her face. "Yes, I do think so. Can you not see it?"

Pru stood up to look over his shoulder at the photo. "I'm not sure. I suppose I can. Why would Simon say we aren't related if we are?" A thought occurred to her. "Maybe he doesn't know. George and Birdie Parke brought him up. He said that his mother was Birdie's sister, and so he's no relation to George Parke. But perhaps there was a Parke on Birdie's side of the family that she's forgotten to mention."

Christopher stroked her hair. "Perhaps. Will you try to find out?"

"Yes. The Wilsons sent me Birdie's phone number. I'll talk with her. I could even go meet her. Perhaps next week — we may have to steer clear of the walled garden." She felt a spark of hope. "Maybe I do have a relative after all."

* * *

Sunday breakfast was a revelation for Christopher.

"I'm fixing biscuits," Pru declared when he walked out of the bedroom. A cloud of flour rose from the counter.

"American biscuits?" She'd explained to him the difference between English biscuits, which were cookies, and the biscuits her dad had taught her to make.

When she set the steaming plate on the table, she said, "Butter them while they're hot."

"What, all of them?" he asked.

"Yes, butter all of them now, and put them back on the plate. Then have at it. We have marmalade or damson plum jam — Ivy's, of course." She crossed her arms. "I hope you like them."

Pru decided breakfast was a success after Christopher had eaten six biscuits. "My God," he said. "I need a walk. Or a nap."

"Let's start with the walk."

They avoided the walled garden entirely, and headed off in a different direction, skirting around to the far side of Primrose House and down to Repton's wood. As they walked, they began to go over what she knew.

"How did police know to ask Cate about Liam?" she asked. "Who would've told them that?"

"Who had reason to tell them?" Christopher asked.

She nodded. "Jamie, I suppose, out of jealousy. That means someone told him that they were at the Two Bells together. Maybe that's why he was asking me about the pub. But what was Jamie doing even talking with the police?"

"They could've contacted him first, looking for Cate."

That seemed reasonable. They stopped near an enormous beech, the one that Davina had wanted her to climb. "Cate acted as if she's had no contact with Liam at all, but I don't believe that's true."

"Why would she lie about it?" he asked. "Who would that protect?"

"It would protect" — Pru frowned — "her. If Jamie thought she was seeing someone else, he could become violent again."

"What if Cate wasn't lying and she really hadn't seen Liam the day of the murder or after?"

He was leading Pru in a direction she didn't like, creating an unwelcome doubt in her mind about Liam.

Christopher put his arms around her from behind, and held on. "If he wasn't with her on Thursday, he quite possibly doesn't have an alibi. I know you want to think the best of everyone."

She smiled. "Yes, I know. I'm trusting and generous — code words for gullible." He gave her a squeeze. She looked out at the woodland and the fields beyond. "Where are the hedgehogs?" she asked.

"There's a subtle change of topic," he said. "The hedgehogs are hibernating — no sense in spending energy looking for food when its scarce." And he began to tell her about the hedgehog's year as they walked back to the cottage.

It was already dark when he was ready to leave. They stood at her front door. "I'll be fine this evening," she said. She wouldn't, of course, she would long for his company, but couldn't say that when he'd already sacrificed to be there. She picked up his bag. "It's very light."

"When you said I should bring a few things down to leave here, I packed this bag and put it in the boot of my car so I would be all ready. I didn't realize I'd be back so soon. That's all right, isn't it?"

She had walked back into the bedroom before he finished talking and opened the wardrobe. She'd left space and hangers, and one large drawer completely empty just for him. A few shirts and a pair of trousers were hung, and when she pulled the drawer open she saw sweaters and underwear neatly folded.

"I unpacked while you were in the shower this morning. Did I put them in the right place?" He leaned against the doorjamb.

Her eyes glistened as she said, "Who knew that socks could make me cry?" She took his hand, led him back into the kitchen, and took a key out of the top drawer. "Here. You can let yourself in next time."

He took it and turned it over in his palm before putting it in his pocket. "What will you do tomorrow?"

"Talk to Davina. Try to figure out what will happen next." She felt his eyes on her as she looked at her hands. "You know, about the garden. No Liam and Fergal tomorrow, but they'll be back Tuesday. Robbie, too, I suppose, if Ivy doesn't keep him away. Tuesday I'll talk with Liam."

He took her hands and looked into her eyes, a long look that lasted even longer than usual.

"Yes?" she prompted him.

"I find myself in a difficult position," he said at last. "I want you safe. I understand that you know these people, but you may not know everything about them, and I don't want you involved in situations that could put you in danger." She kept quiet, hoping his preamble would lead to permission to snoop around a bit. "I'm not a part of this investigation and neither are you."

She sighed. "I am not a police officer."

"But you'll let me know if you hear anything that might be relevant to the case?"

The words came out so reluctantly that she laughed. "Really?"

He nodded. "Really. You will take care?"

"I will." She stood close, one finger tracing the edge of his ear and down to the base of his throat. He began rubbing that spot low on her back in a slow circle until she took a sharp breath and stepped away, putting her hands behind her back. "Go," she said. "Go now, or I may not let you go at all."

* * *

After he left, Pru paced her tiny cottage, checked email, saw what was left in the fridge, and washed out their tea mugs. She realized what she was missing — being able to sit with her friend Jo and talk about nothing over a glass of wine. They chatted on the phone now and then, but it wasn't the same, and she'd made no close women friends around Bells

Yew Green yet. And now she felt Christopher's absence even more.

Finally, she sought refuge in Repton's Red Book — far, far away from murder, loss, absence. She kept it in her wardrobe, hidden among a stack of sweaters — the spot wasn't safe or secure, but it was dark, cool, and dry. Sort of like storing potatoes for the winter. Christopher had made sure to lay the fire — it looked like a modern-art installation in wood — so she followed his instructions to strike a match and stuff it into the crumpled papers below. As it caught, she sat on the sofa and opened the Red Book up to a random page. She and Repton were becoming good friends, and she thought she had a fair number of passages memorized by now, but the sentence that jumped out at her that moment had echoes of more recent events at Primrose House.

"And in landscape gardening," Repton wrote, "everything may be called a deception by which we endeavor to conceal the agency of art and make our works appear the sole product of nature."

Concealment and deception — it seemed that not even Repton could keep her from dwelling on the murder.

CHAPTER 16

On Monday afternoon, Pru headed for Primrose House. It had become her habit to walk from the cottage to the house by circling around to the bottom of the walled garden and pick up the trail near the brush pile, and her mind was so full of other thoughts that her feet took her this way — she was on peripatetic auto pilot. What would she do with Robbie tomorrow? Was Liam with Cate at Francine's flat on the evening of the murder? What is Davina hiding? Should she order pillar roses for the walled garden or ramblers?

Her questions ceased when she reached the blue-and-white tape. It stretched from the corner of the walled garden out to the potting shed, around the brush pile and to the back gate. In the middle of it all lay the yew branches, and she imagined that she could see a bloody stain.

"Pru?"

She jumped. "Oh, Sergeant Hobbes, you startled me."

"I'm sorry. But you shouldn't be down here."

"Yes, I know. I forgot. Actually, I was thinking about so many things I didn't pay attention to which way I was going." *Pay attention, Pru,* she thought. "Why are you here?"

"I wanted to take a look at this," he said. "Do you use it much?"

He nodded toward their access track. It came off the lane farther down past her cottage, and took a route that snaked between groups of trees and ended near their brush pile.

"Occasionally," she said. "It's a direct shot from the lane, but the ground has a streak of sticky clay. It's the only clay soil we've got in the garden, and it's a real nuisance. I want to bring a load of chippings in to lay on top, but I haven't quite got to it yet." Far too many pressing tasks had pushed this job toward the bottom of her never-ending list. "Why do you ask?"

"It certainly is sticky," Hobbes said. "Sticks well to everything, including tires."

"Yes," she said, laughing, "maybe we should open our own pottery . . ." But then she realized what he'd said. "Sticks to whose tires? Do you think the murderer drove in that way?"

"We're taking samples from everyone's cars," he said, "although the track itself is difficult to read. I doubt we could get a good cast of tire tracks. Who would drive down here?"

She racked her brain trying to think of the last time they used it. "The manure was delivered that way. I don't remember the last time any one of us drove on it. What will you do if you find that clay stuck on someone's tires?"

She knew he wouldn't answer. "Just following a line of enquiry," he said.

* * *

Later, she sat with her elbow on the kitchen table in Primrose House, chin in hand. Davina stood at the Aga, having put the kettle on. Tatt was expected.

"Ned always talked as if he owned the place," Davina said with a sad smile. "I didn't mind, really. He used to work for the earl, you know, up at the castle. He said he'd always hoped someone would take Primrose House. He could be a bit bossy, but always in a quiet way."

115

It's easy to speak well of the dead, Pru thought. "Why did you ask me about Ned after I told you about the yews being cut? Did you think he had something to do with it?"

Davina frowned. "Oh really, Pru, it doesn't matter now, does it? Let's remember him as—"

A knock on the door boomed and echoed down the corridor from the front. The brass knocker, in the shape of a badger's head, had been Pru's introduction to Primrose House — she still remembered stroking its snout for good luck — and she rather enjoyed its rich sound even if this time it heralded the arrival of Inspector Tatt.

He followed Davina back to the kitchen, caught sight of Pru, and said, "My God, must you be everywhere?"

"I beg your pardon," Davina said, turning on him.

"Mrs. Templeton, I don't see the need for your head gardener to sit in on every conversation?"

"*My head gardener,*" Davina cut in, "has every right to be here. Have you not even considered the trauma she's been through? Is this how you treat all your witnesses, Inspector?"

Pru choked down a snicker. She didn't think her employer actually wanted her there — what Davina really wanted was to annoy Tatt, who was already off to a bad start.

Tatt was speechless, but that passed quickly, although when he began again, it was in a subdued tone. "Mrs. Templeton, we are investigating the suspicious death of—"

"It's all right, Davina," Pru said, standing. "I need to get to work." She turned to the door that led out the back, but then stopped, did an about-face, and instead walked toward the front. There was no need for her to stay in the kitchen when she might hear a great deal more if she was out of sight in the corridor. "I'll just go out this way, shall I? I want to see how the roses are doing in the front."

Davina and Tatt both acknowledged her departure with nods and Pru let the swing door swing closed behind her. She sprinted the length of the house on tiptoe, opened the front door, and closed it again, making sure to give it a shove so that the sound echoed all the way to the back of the house.

116

Then she kept to the wall and retraced her steps, walking silently closer to the kitchen to listen. *No danger here,* she told Christopher in her head.

For once, Pru appreciated Tatt's volume, because the voices came through the door loud and clear as Davina apparently felt the need to match him as she went through her whereabouts on the day of Ned's death. She had little to offer, saying that she and Bryan had gone up to London that morning. But she had questions for Tatt.

"Do you have any suspects?"

A pause. "We are following several lines of enquiry." Pru rolled her eyes.

"You have the murder weapon, Inspector," Davina said. "Did you find fingerprints?"

"There was a veritable cornucopia of fingerprints on the handle of the hatchet. Ms. Parke's, both Liam and Fergal Duffy's, even the victim's."

"Well, that seems logical, don't you think? They all work in the garden. You didn't find Robbie Fox's fingerprints?"

"There was a partial print," Tatt said, "but we couldn't identify it. It wasn't from the boy." Pru arched an eyebrow at the disappointment in Tatt's voice.

"I don't believe that Pru allows Robbie to handle those sorts of tools."

"Do you know if the victim had any enemies?" Tatt asked.

"Ned? Ned had no enemies," Davina said. "Even Lord Hamilton knew him — go ahead, you ask him. Ned was the unofficial historian of Bells Yew Green. He took the long view of events." Pru could hear the smile in Davina's voice. "I remember him telling us once about some brickworks that used to be nearby. He said, 'Oh, but that closed back in the '90s.' Except he wasn't talking about the 1990s, he meant the 1890s."

"Mrs. Templeton," Tatt said, "you know of no problems Bobbins had? No one is universally well liked. Had he no business irregularities or family difficulties — someone he could've angered by something he'd said? Had he ever threatened anyone that you know of? Or been threatened by someone?"

"Must you assume the worst? Is that your job?" Davina said. "I'm sorry to disappoint you, but I have no terrible secrets about Ned. I can't imagine anyone would wish him ill."

Pru thought about the many remarks Davina had made about Ned's hold on her and Bryan, but those thoughts vanished when she suddenly heard Tatt's voice from just the other side of the door. "Thank you, Mrs. Templeton, we'll be in touch." Adrenalin rushed through Pru's body and confused her — should she stand and fight or make a run for it?

She'd got only halfway to the front door when Tatt bellowed, "Ms. Parke?"

Her face was hot and she was out of breath, but tried her best for nonchalance, leaning up against the wall. "Oh Davina," she called past Tatt, "I've just looked in on the weeping fig here in the dining room — the one you asked me about. I'm afraid it looks as if it's been overwatered." She feigned surprise. "Oh, Inspector Tatt, I didn't realize you were still here."

"The what?" Davina called, coming to the kitchen door.

"The weeping fig. Here," Pru said, jerking her head toward the dining room. No, Davina hadn't asked her to take a look, but Pru remembered the plant had appeared a bit peaky last time she'd seen it several weeks ago.

"Bryan," Davina said dismissively. "He's always walking around with a watering can." She turned to Tatt. "Anything else, Inspector?"

Tatt glared at Pru, as if to say he didn't believe a word of her cover story. "Good day, Mrs. Templeton," he said, and added as he passed Pru on his way out, "Ms. Parke. I'm sure I'll see you again."

* * *

She got herself ready to ring Birdie that evening. Birdie's importance had mushroomed in Pru's mind. Her mother had lived in Ibsley, and Birdie, George, and Simon had lived in Ibsley. To be this close to someone who might know something about her mother as a young girl in England, someone who might lead her to a distant relative — however precarious that lead — was almost more than Pru could bear. She sat at the kitchen table, staring at her phone for ten minutes, practicing what she would say and trying to think up questions to ask. She wondered if it was too presumptuous to suggest that they meet. She tried to remember the names of people her mother had talked about — had she ever mentioned a Birdie? She wished that she had that small box of photos and letters her mother had saved, but it was still stored at her friend Lydia's in Dallas. She should've had it sent over by now, but it seemed too precious to trust to the vagaries of international shipping.

Finally, she dialed the number, and when, after several rings, an elderly woman answered, Pru took a deep breath.

"Hello, my name is Pru Parke. Vernona Wilson gave me your phone number. I met Simon on Boxing Day. You see" — she had to exhale and inhale again before she could continue — "I'm American." *Oh God,* she thought, *I sound like an idiot. Of course I'm American, she can tell that.* "But my mother was English, and her name was Parke." She felt lightheaded, and paused for a moment, trying to even out her breathing.

"Yes, I was expecting you to ring. Of course I knew Jenny," the woman said in a quiet voice.

That caught Pru off-guard. She hadn't heard anyone say her mother's name in so long. "Oh, that's wonderful. Was she related to your husband? I would love to . . . if you ever had the time to talk with me about her . . ."

"Why don't you come and see me? It would be better to talk in person."

"Thank you, yes, that's so kind of you. I'd love to, Mrs. Parke." *Stop gushing,* she told herself.

"Call me Birdie."

* * *

Pru could go down on Friday. Davina and Bryan would be gone, Ivy could manage with Robbie, and Liam and Fergal had their own work. Birdie lived not far from the Wilsons, and so Pru knew that she could make the two-hour drive to Hampshire, visit, and be home by evening, especially as the Wilsons were not at Greenoak, but in Majorca for a winter holiday. She smiled to herself as she drummed her fingers on the table, and her mind filled with the possibilities of familial discovery.

She rang Christopher with the news of the day. He asked what Davina said about the garden and Pru had replied "We will soldier on, apparently." Then, she explained about Tatt's fingerprint report, skipping over the part where she had eavesdropped. When she told him about visiting Birdie, he said he hoped for the best and would see her late Friday evening.

CHAPTER 17

Primrose House

29 January

Pru,

I'm so sorry Bryan and I will miss Ned's service. Please do give Cate our condolences. We have been thinking about a way to honor Ned and his life here in the village, and I think we've hit upon it. We'll plant a special garden for him in the oval and we'll commission a statue. Can't you just see it? Something quiet and understated, of course. We'll start asking around for marble sources.

Best,
Davina

Pru covered her face with both hands. "Oh my God," she groaned. And then, a vision flashed through her mind — a statue of Ned as Michelangelo's David. She began to giggle, after which a snort of laughter escaped. Soon, she was laughing so hard she could barely breath. When at last her laughter petered out with a hiccup, she felt enormously better.

* * *

Pru cracked the whip on Tuesday. She wanted her crew to stay so busy that they had no time to dwell on what had happened. Busy hands, busy whatever. It was a fine, clear, cold day, and the three of them — Liam, Fergal, and Pru — measured and marked where the new staircase and terraced beds below the house would go, in preparation for the workers to begin. Robbie decided he was Will Scarlet, one of the Merry Men, and spent most of the morning trying to fashion a bow so that he could aim pretend arrows at the Sheriff of Nottingham, but the dry sticks he chose kept snapping.

Finally, Fergal went down to the yew walk, cut off a stiff but pliable branch and stripped it of its needles. "There y'are now, Robbie, that's what Robin Hood would've used, a branch of yew."

"Thanks, Fergal," Robbie said in delight. "Thanks."

"We're mates, aren't we, Robbie?" Fergal asked.

"You're my mate," Robbie said, as he began to tie a length of twine to the branch.

Robbie's words echoed in Pru's mind. His mate. "I gave it to my mate. He was cold" Robbie had said at the police station when asked about his red fleece jacket. *Nonsense,* she thought, *Robbie has lots of mates.*

Pru thought she could get a word with Liam during the day. The first time she tried, she called him over as she ran twine between two stakes marking the lower bed. But she'd no more got out the words, "I wanted to ask you—" than Fergal called from up the slope.

"Liam, I need you to mark that corner for me."

Liam climbed up the slope.

The second time was just before lunch. She walked up to Liam as he began to cut away at the turf at the top of the slope to give them an idea what the steps down the middle of the terraces would look like. Robbie had taken a spade and started digging at the bottom end.

"Listen," Pru said, "were you—" Over Liam's shoulder, she saw Fergal rushing up.

"Liam, come over here with me now so we can shift that piece of timber for the equipment to get in."

Pru frowned. "Fergal, I just wanted a word with him."

"We've got a lot to do here before the end of the day," Fergal said, giving his brother's arm a light jab. "Let's go."

"Yes," she called after them, her face hot. "I know we have a lot to do."

At lunch, Ivy invited them all in the kitchen where she served a thick beef and barley soup with slices of cheddar and an entire loaf of her own bread. Fergal got Robbie to list the names of all of the Merry Men, which took a while as he kept repeating Little John and asking if Marian were a woman and if so, could she even be considered.

When Robbie ran out of steam, Fergal jumped on the subject of the terraces and how the gardens at Primrose House were not just about Humphry Repton. That prompted Pru to give a mini-lecture on what might remain of the Repton landscape. She described his watercolor of the view off the balustrade, which showed the pub off in the distance, until the tab was lifted to reveal his design that included the beech wood covering up the pub and creating a bucolic scene. But many of the landscape elements, she pointed out, were later additions.

"You should put a bit of yourself in the garden," Liam said.

"I could import a few cowboys, would that do?" she asked.

Liam laughed. "Well, it's your garden, too, not just Repton's and not just a load of Victorian flowers. There should be something American."

"I'll see what I can come up with."

* * *

Ivy departed after lunch, taking Robbie with her, but she kept the kitchen open and a currant cake for their tea. Later in the afternoon, Pru put the kettle on while Liam ran the string around the last few stakes. Fergal walked in and stood at the table.

"So," he said. "The police came to see us."

"I imagine they did," she said. "They've questioned all of us."

"It must've been a shock for you — you and Robbie — finding Ned's body."

"I'm not sure Robbie really understood at first."

Glancing out the window at his brother, Fergal said, "They found Robbie's jacket with the hatchet, didn't they?"

"Yes. Obviously someone came across his jacket or took it from him and used it. Someone who thought it would be easy to blame Robbie," Pru said.

Fergal looked down at the floor. "But Robbie . . . if Robbie was accused of the murder, it isn't as if he would go to prison. Right? They wouldn't do that to someone like him."

Pru didn't like the implication. "That doesn't really matter, does it, Fergal — whether or not he would be sent to prison? Would it be fair if Robbie took the blame for something he didn't do just because he might not be punished? That isn't right — to let the real murderer goes free and an innocent young man be blamed?"

"No, that wouldn't be fair," Fergal said in a weak voice. "I'm just saying that maybe sometimes—"

Liam walked in. "Is there tea?"

"Yes, sit down," Pru said, hoping at last for a chat.

Fergal's face grew red. "Liam, come on. Gordon MacKenzie, will be doing the terracing, and Pru has asked him to stop and take a look at the slope before they start to level it. We'd better be out the way for him."

"He isn't here yet," Liam said with a cross look. "We can sit for a minute."

"No," Fergal said, "let's go out, he might be looking for us. Now." He marched out the door and waited.

"*I'm having my tea!*" Liam shouted after his brother. Fergal scowled, then looked down the terrace and broke out in a smile. "Gordon," he called, "come in and have a cup of tea."

It was Pru's turn to scowl. Well, wasn't that convenient, she thought. Fergal seemed bent on preventing his brother from talking to her and so far he had succeeded. Pru poured and they had their cake, discussing the terracing with Gordon, whose crew would start the following week. When they finished, she suggested they call it a day.

"We'll get the tools together before we go," Fergal said.

"You two go on," Liam said to his brother and Gordon. "I'll be along."

"Liam, we should—" Fergal began.

"Go on, Fergal, will you leave me. I won't be long." Fergal hesitated for a moment, but followed Gordon out when his brother didn't move.

Liam continued to stare into his mug. Pru got the impression that he wanted to say something and, at the same time, didn't. After a few silent moments, she asked, "How's Cate?"

"She's . . . sad." He put his hands around the mug, as if to warm them, although there was no tea left. "Her aunt from Norwich is here. There's a service on Thursday."

"Yes," Pru said. "She rang and told me. I'll be there."

They were quiet, Liam still not looking at her. He finally shook his head and said, "He shouldn't have done that. Tell her to stay with Tanner. I don't know how he could say that to his daughter. But he wouldn't listen. Think how that's left her now."

"Liam, were you with Cate at Francine's flat on Thursday?"

He glanced at her and then away. "Leave it alone, Pru," he said, taking his mug to the sink.

"No, I won't leave it alone."

"You shouldn't be a part of this," he said, looking out the window.

"After I heard you argue with Ned that day, did you—" But she'd left it too long. Fergal walked in, and gave her a sharp look.

"We've got to be off."

"We'll see you tomorrow, Pru," Liam said.

"I don't think we'll be able to," Fergal said.

"Stop it, wouldya?" Liam pushed past his brother and Fergal followed without a word.

CHAPTER 18

Pru went down and around the side of the yew walk — still unsheared, it was too overgrown to walk down the middle — and back to her cottage along the lower path, thinking about Fergal's mother-hen act. As she rounded the corner, she saw the *Courier*'s reporter standing in front of her cottage.

"Hugo," she said, startled to find him on her doorstep. She hadn't heard from him since his visit on the previous Wednesday to check on the yew — the day that nothing happened. Surely he wasn't hoping to restart the blog. Look where that had got them.

There had been an article in the *Courier* about Ned's murder, but not written by Hugo. The article mentioned the garden, the Red Book, and Pru, but the focus was Ned and Primrose House, and all quotes were from Davina, except one from Bryan, who said, "Ned was a damn fine human being."

"I'm sorry I didn't ring you after what happened," Hugo said, "but we thought it better to lay off the blog for a while. You understand, I'm sure?"

"Yes, that's fine with me," she said. "But didn't they want you to write the article about Ned? You're more familiar with Primrose House than anyone else at the paper, aren't you?"

Hugo squinted at the horizon, got his phone out of his pocket, glanced at it, and put it away again. "It's probably better that I didn't. Conflict of interest, you know."

"What conflict?" she asked.

His eyes shifted left and right; he took an audible breath. "Ned was my father's cousin. Well, of course, that made him my cousin, too." Hugo paused for so long that Pru thought she might have to remind him of the topic, but before she could, he began again, in a hard voice. "Ned Bobbins made my dad's life a living hell, and I don't mind saying I'm not sorry he's dead."

Pru squirmed. "I'd no idea you were related."

"He as much as killed him." Hugo said, red-faced. "All my dad wanted to do was make a name for himself here, but old Ned would have none of it. No success was allowed without his approval. He ruined my dad. It may have taken years, but it wore him down until he died of heartbreak."

"Was it recent? Your dad?"

Hugo blinked. "November. He died in November. Just a few weeks before Christmas," he said in a voice that sounded like a small, sad boy.

"I'm very sorry," Pru said.

Hugo drew his chin up, took a sharp breath, and pulled out his phone again. "That's not why I stopped. I need to tell you about something that's happened." Hugo frowned and drew his scarf closer around his neck. "Someone posted a comment on the article about the murder, and the editor felt that the tone was threatening."

"Who did it threaten? The Templetons?"

"No, not the Templetons." He shrugged. "Listen, it was vague, nothing specific. It seemed to imply that things needed to be put right in the garden. But we can't take chances about something like this, and we rang the police straight away. The comment's been removed."

"Well, then," Pru said, as her mind begin to spin, "the comment's been removed. No harm done." Except for Ned's murder and now a threat against the garden and — as an extension — her. "Thanks for letting me know, Hugo."

As he got in his car and put it into gear, he said, "Perhaps we can start the blog up again after they find the murderer? If they find the murderer."

Her phone was ringing as he drove off. She slapped her pocket, and realized the ringing came from indoors. She'd left it on her kitchen counter that morning.

"Pru, it's David Hobbes."

She dispensed with hello. "Hugo Jenkins just stopped by to tell me about the comment online," she said as she switched on a light in the kitchen.

"Right, well, that's why I rang. I don't want you to be concerned about this. We're looking into it."

"Can you find out who posted it?" she asked.

"I doubt it. It's too easy for someone to register at the paper's website in order to leave a comment," he said, and then added, "You'll tell Inspector Pearse about this, won't you?"

"Yes, I'll tell him at the weekend." She would have to word it carefully — she didn't need Christopher shifting into superhero protector mode over some vague comment online. But just how vague was it? "What did it say?" she asked Hobbes.

"I don't want you to worry."

"I'll worry more if I don't know. My imagination will go wild. Tell me."

She heard a few taps on a keyboard. "It said, 'Who made this a deadly garden? You see what happens when history is in the wrong hands.'"

History was in her hands — or rather, Repton's version of it was tucked away in a stack of sweaters in her wardrobe. She swallowed hard and took a deliberately casual tone. "Well, thank you for telling me that. I can see why this could be construed as a threat, but really, I don't think it has anything to do with me."

"You'll tell—"

"Yes, yes, I'll tell him."

* * *

128

The lashing rain pelted her slate roof — she heard it before she opened her eyes the next morning. Not a drizzle, not a shower, not even a showery rain, but a real downpour. Pru looked out the window and saw it falling in sheets, as if it had settled in for the long run. She rang Liam and Fergal to say they wouldn't work outdoors today, but suggested that the two come to her cottage and they would spend part of the day planning. Her ulterior motive of questioning Liam about his involvement with Ned was too obvious, apparently, and Fergal begged off.

"If it's all the same to you, Pru," he said, "we'll work here at our own place today. We'll be back in the garden on Friday." Yes, on Friday, when she would be in Hampshire and could not dog them about their alibis.

So, she kept herself busy with plans for the terraced garden and filled the rest of the day by catching up with friends. Mug of coffee in hand, she rang Jo midmorning and they had a fine talk. Later in the afternoon, she sent Lydia in Dallas a long and chatty email, asking after her daughters and making no mention of murder.

* * *

Thursday was cold and gray, but at least there was no rain. A modest crowd gathered inside the old stone church for Ned's service and out in the churchyard for the burial. Pru knew only Cate, Ivy, the Duffys — and almost didn't recognize them in their funeral suits — and Jamie, who stood apart from the graveside group and didn't speak to anyone. When she walked back to her car down the lane, he stood half-way behind an Irish yew waiting for her. He had shaved and changed his clothes and so looked at least marginally better.

"I'm not allowed at the house," he said instead of hello. "Cate asked me to stay away. I don't want to make trouble, Pru, but could you at least talk with her? Tell her she needs to think about Nanda and what's best for her." He appeared earnest, clean-cut, in control.

Pru glanced back at the church. The small crowd had dispersed, and people had left for the reception at Ned's cottage. "I can't tell Cate that, Jamie. It isn't my place."

He jerked his head and jutted out his chin. "You've got what you want, is that it? The head gardener doesn't have time for any lowly Council worker? Lording it over me, are you? Perhaps you weren't the best choice for head gardener after all."

The switch from plea to accusation was so abrupt that Pru was left speechless. And in the blink of an eye, his demeanor changed again, as if she'd switched channels on television. His face crumpled, his shoulders slumped, and he drew his hands out of his pockets and began tugging on his sleeves. "No, I'm sorry, I didn't mean that. Look, I don't want your job, I only want Cate. She needs to understand. I know what I did was terrible, but I'll be better. Can you tell her that?"

"I'm a gardener, not a therapist. You need to talk with your doctor. Sort yourself out."

"I miss my little girl," he said, suddenly breaking out in sobs and barely able to speak. "I miss my wife. Ned wanted to help me, and now I have nothing." The sobs ceased. "This is all Duffy's fault."

She dug for the car key in her bag, got in, saying, "Jamie, I have to go now. Why don't you just leave it for a while? Give yourself some time to . . ." Having no idea how to finish that sentence, she drove off, her hands shaking.

It didn't speak well of Jamie's mental state if his manner was so wildly changeable. He was quite possibly a menace to Cate and probably to Liam, judging from that last threat. She wasn't sure she wanted to interpret his comments to her as a threat, but even so, she knew what she must do. After parking as near to Ned's cottage as she could manage, she rang DS Hobbes and told him what happened.

"I asked Mrs. Templeton about him after you and Inspector Pearse told me what happened with Ms. Bobbins," Hobbes said. "She told me that he'd applied for your post and that Ned had great hopes for him getting it. Did you feel threatened at all by him?"

Pru knew there was little the police could do with no evidence. Jamie couldn't be arrested just because he gave her the creeps. She assured the DS that she felt no threat, but that she would watch out for herself, making certain to lock up at night, and be in the garden only in the presence of others. And she promised him she would tell Christopher. At the weekend.

* * *

Ned's sister, a sturdily built, rosy-cheeked woman with suspiciously black hair for her age, acted as hostess at his cottage for the reception after the burial. Sandwiches and cake accompanied tiny glasses of cream sherry, copious amounts of tea, and — for a few of the men who looked about Ned's age — bottles of beer.

"Pru," Cate said, Ned's sister at her elbow, "this is my aunt Esme. Auntie, Pru is the head gardener at Primrose House . . ."

"Oh you poor, poor dearie." Aunt Esme said, grasping Pru in a tight hug, pinning her arms at her side, and pulling her slightly off balance. "How dreadful for you."

"I'm so sorry about your brother," Pru said, gently pulling free and attempting to keep her balance.

"How will you ever get that garden finished in time without our Edward?" Aunt Esme asked the universe. "It seems an impossible task." She shook her head.

"Ned was a great help," Pru said, wondering what he had told his sister. "He knew so much about the place." She smiled. "We'll just have to soldier on."

CHAPTER 19

The drive to Birdie's house near Romsey passed in a blur, full of hopes and dreams. Pru tried to keep herself grounded by repeating Simon's family situation. Birdie was his mother's sister, and therefore he was not really a Parke relation. But it was no use. She began to imagine Birdie suddenly realizing that her own grandmother had been a Parke, too, and so Pru was actually some second or third cousin of both Birdie's and Simon's as well as a vague relation to Uncle George Parke. Pru spent a good deal of the drive envisioning a family tree on the windscreen and trying to put all the branches in the right place.

When she arrived, she sat in her car a few minutes, breathing in and out slowly. Birdie's cottage was one of six or seven small, older, but well-kept houses on the street. Pru made her way up the boxwood-lined walk to the door and rang the bell. A tall, thin woman with white hair in a pixie cut answered. Her blue eyes, watery with age, were surrounded by smile lines.

"Well, Prunella, here you are," she said. "Come in."

Oh no, Pru thought, *don't start crying now.* No one had ever called her Prunella except her mother — even her dad had seemed faintly embarrassed by her full name.

"It's so good of you to let me visit," Pru said as she followed Birdie into the sitting room, her eyes falling on dozens of photos that populated the walls and tables. She looked closer at a snapshot of a young man with one foot up on the tire of some kind of vintage sports car caught her eye. "That's Simon?"

Birdie leaned her head to one side. "Hmmm, but it wasn't his Aston Martin." She smiled. "That was his 007 period."

Pru glanced at the other photos and thought they must all be of Simon at various ages. In one, she saw a boy holding a cricket bat almost as tall as he was and another, a group photo from a wedding. Several snapshots showed Simon and a woman who must be his wife along with two girls from toddler to teens.

Pru sat on the cushy sofa and glanced around the room, crowded with the memories of a long life. Birdie took a photo album from the coffee table and sat down in an armchair. "You know, you've changed very little since the last time I saw you, even though you're all grown up now."

Pru broke out in goosebumps. "Did I meet you when I came over with my parents? I was only eight, and I don't remember much about the trip. Did we visit you here?" She looked around at the walls, the furniture, the Staffordshire pottery spaniels over the fireplace, longing for something to look familiar.

Pru could see Birdie's hand, with its paper-thin skin, grasp the album tighter, and the knuckles whiten. "What did Jenny tell you?" the older woman asked.

"Tell me about you? I can't really remember anything. I didn't think my mother had any relatives left here, but" — she gave a little shrug — "I still hoped I might find someone. When I heard Simon's surname, I thought that might lead me to a distant cousin."

"Oh, child." Birdie shook her head slightly. "I didn't mean for it to last this long." She opened the album, turned a few pages, and handed it to Pru. "But you know, the older you get, the faster time passes without you realizing it. I didn't even know Jenny had died until Vernona told me. We'd lost touch over the years."

Pru looked down at the photo, taken outside the very cottage she sat in now. In the photo, her parents stood next to another couple. The woman Pru recognized from her pencillike physique as a much younger Birdie. An eight-year-old version of Pru stood with them — her brown hair barely contained in a ponytail — and next to her was a young man, perhaps in his early twenties, his own brown frizzy hair forming a halo around his face. The room was quiet, but a buzzing sound like a swarm of bees filled Pru's head. No thoughts, no words, just sound. Birdie spoke again, and the buzzing stopped.

"Simon is your brother."

The words made no sense to Pru, and yet she couldn't take her eyes off the photo.

Birdie took a deep breath. "At the end of the war," she said, "your father left for America, promising to come back for Jenny when she was of age. We all liked Robert, but many American soldiers said the same thing to many English girls, and very few of them returned.

"Jenny's mother told her not to hope that Robert would come back, but Jenny couldn't help but hope, because she was going to have his baby. She didn't tell Robert before he left, because she said that would be blackmail." Birdie looked out the window, as if looking back through the years. "It was a difficult time after the war — not the big boom you had in the States. That was no time for a girl of fifteen to have a baby of her own. George and I — Jenny was our niece, although we weren't very much older than her, did you know that?"

Out of the depths where Pru now found herself came a tiny reply. "No."

"George and I were married, and we had no children, so we took Simon when he was born." She looked down into her lap, one hand clenched in the other. "The next year, Robert wrote, and eventually he came back for Jenny, but Simon was ours by then, and Jenny understood it wouldn't be right to take him away from us."

"But he was theirs, not your. Their son." How could Birdie suggest that her parents would give up a child of their own?

"He belonged to *us*," Birdie said. "Jenny could see that he was happy, and she came to understand that to surprise Robert with a child he didn't know he had would be a shock." As if speaking to herself, she said, "She could see that it was better for Simon to stay here." Birdie's eyes rested on Pru, and she shook her head. "You both look so much like him — not like a Parke at all."

Pru gasped, as if coming up for air, and realized her face was wet with tears. "My grandmother, why didn't my grandmother take him?"

"Esther died just after Simon was born," Birdie said.

Pru recalled hearing the story of her grandmother's death. But it was the only piece of family history to which she was able to cling. "Simon said his parents died in a car crash after the war," she said, using her sleeve to wipe her face. "Why didn't he tell me?"

Birdie's face lost its color, except for her cheeks, where two red spots formed. "Simon didn't know, not until now. When you rang, I knew it was time." She leaned over to place her warm, dry hand over Pru's. "He barely remembers your visit — he had come down only for the day before going back to work in Surrey. I believe he's always suspected he didn't know the whole story of his birth, but he never asked any questions." Her voice came sharp now, and Pru saw tears in her eyes. "But he knew we loved him. We've always loved him."

The questions in Pru's head were screaming to get out, but they were all questions for her mother, not for Birdie. She tried to see back all those years, hoping to understand the decisions that tore what little family she had apart. "She never said anything. Why didn't she tell me?" A thought hit her with cold dread. "Did my dad even know he had a son?"

"I don't know when she told him, but he knew," Birdie said. "When you came over, we thought they would tell Simon. I believe they wanted to take him away from us." She lifted her chin. "But he was ours. We had adopted him when Jenny gave him to us. They saw he was happy and settled, and we asked them to let it be for a while longer. We thought it would be easier when you were both older."

They sat in silence except for the clock on the mantel and Pru's ragged breathing. She searched in her bag for a tissue to mop up her face, as Birdie got up and walked out. Pru heard her filling a kettle.

This was not a subject for which Pru had prepared, and she could barely think of a question to ask this woman who had reared her brother. Her mind seemed to be frozen. She tried to picture her mother sitting where she sat now — her mother pregnant with Simon, her mother giving birth and handing over her son — and that's when she became aware of the anger heating up inside.

Pru was unmindful of Birdie serving the tea and didn't realize she'd picked up a cup. She put it back down again. "I need to see Simon," she said.

"Give him some time, Prunella, don't try to talk now," Birdie said. "He'll be all right after a while."

"And let how much more time pass?" Pru shot back. She could not let this lie. "Is he working today? Do you know if he's at the Wilsons'?"

"Oh yes, you'll find him in the garden," Birdie said with a little smile. "That's where I could always find him when he had a problem to sort through. When he first met Polly, she was going with another fellow. Simon was so taken with her that he stewed about it for a month — and planted that boxwood along the front walk — before he got up his nerve and asked her out." Birdie looked out the window at the neatly trimmed box. "That was thirty years ago."

As Pru got ready to leave, she took a deep breath and asked the worst question. "Didn't my mother want Simon?"

Birdie drew back as if Pru had slapped her. "Of course she wanted him. But she understood what was best."

* * *

Pru parked in the gravel yard at Greenoak and walked back to the walled garden, passing the spot where Simon had dug up snowdrops for her to take back to Primrose House. The air was cold, the sun bright. It was as it had been on Boxing Day — Pru with the sun in her eyes and Simon bent over one of the beds. Now she knew the reason for that queer feeling when she'd first caught sight of him. Seeing Simon's silhouette, it was as if she were looking at her father kneeling over a row of bush beans he'd planted out their back door in Dallas. Pru's heart was in her throat.

Simon saw her and rose slowly but didn't move. He wore his sheepskin coat. She stopped about ten paces from him. Her hands were shaking, and so she crossed her arms to hold them still. "Simon," she said. He didn't reply. "I just talked to Birdie."

"Did you know?" he asked.

"No, I didn't know," she said. "I didn't know anything until today." Pru saw the ten steps between them as wide as the ocean that had separated them their whole lives.

"Well, no," he said. "Why would they need to tell you? They had their family. You were all they needed, what did they want with an extra one?"

"You weren't extra — you were their son."

"I wasn't very convenient, though, was I? Good thing they had someone to pass me off on, or I'd've ended up in Australia with the rest of the abandoned children." His voice remained quiet, but it was as if a pot had started to simmer. He pulled a shovel out of the soil where it stood and then plunged it back in again.

"They wouldn't have done that. Mother . . ." Pru was unable to offer a defense for something she thought indefensible herself. "She thought she was doing what was best for you. And Birdie loves you."

"What do you want?"

"I want . . ." *A brother,* she thought to herself, but the word wouldn't come out. "I thought you might want to know about our parents."

He boiled over. "*I know enough about them*," he shouted as he took several steps toward her. "Why should I want to know about them when they never wanted to know about me? You think I'm going to beg you for stories about people who treated me like excess baggage? No, you keep your happy little American family to yourself. I've no use for any of you."

"But we're family, you and I," Pru said, trying not to beg.

"We're nothing but strangers with the same last name. We're not family. I've got a family; I don't need you." He yanked the shovel out and walked away, leaving Pru rooted to the ground.

* * *

She was twenty miles away from Romsey before she even noticed her surroundings. Pulling into a layby, she parked just past the tea caravan, pried her right hand off the steering wheel, and massaged it before getting out of the car.

"What'll it be, luv?" asked a young black man behind the counter.

"Tea, please."

As he dropped a tea bag into a polystyrene cup and filled it with scalding water, he said, "Good day for a drive, now. Are you off for the weekend? Up to London?"

She looked east and saw a clear sky with thin strips of indigo clouds on the horizon. She contemplated driving up to London, past London, and continuing north until she could be as far away from Hampshire as possible. "No, off home, near Tunbridge Wells," she said.

"Right," he said, as he took her money, "safe journey."

CHAPTER 20

Her journey was safe, as far as she could remember, but by the time she pulled into the drive in late afternoon, all she could think about was the solitary sanctuary of her cottage.

Ivy Fox stood at her front door, coat buttoned up to her chin and hands stuck in her pockets.

When Pru got out of her Mini, she asked, "Ivy, is Robbie all right?"

"Oh yes, thanks for asking. He's spending the weekend at my sister's in Bristol. A little holiday for him, you know." Ivy's eyes followed a car down the road before saying, "Pru, I hope you don't mind, I didn't know who else to talk to. I need some advice."

"Come in and warm up," Pru said. She tried to shift her attention from the war going on inside her head to Ivy. "Would you like some tea?"

"I could just do with a drink," Ivy said.

Pru knew how she felt. "Sure, what would you like? Wine, brandy, whisky?"

"A whisky would be lovely — just a small one."

Pru got down the bottle of single malt Bryan and Davina had given her as a housewarming gift and poured them each barely enough to cover the bottoms of their glasses. They sat at the kitchen table.

"Cheers," they both said.

"Now Ivy, what's wrong?" Pru asked.

Brow knitted, Ivy said, "I've been trying to think what to do about this all week. You know I'm so grateful to the Templetons. Robbie and I would have a difficult time if I didn't have this work. I would never want to get them in trouble." She looked down into her glass.

"They haven't fired you, have they?"

"Oh no, not at all. It's just that . . ." Ivy downed the last few drops of whisky, and Pru poured them both another. "We're very sad about Ned."

"Yes," Pru said, unsure of where Ivy was going with this, "we are."

"You know that the Templetons left for London on Thursday morning — the day it happened," Ivy began. Pru nodded. "And then they left for Brussels the next day." Ivy twisted her hands together in her lap. "Oh dear," she said. "It's just that, I drove up the lane that Thursday afternoon. I'd been working at the Brickdales', and I was on my way to collect Robbie at Chaffinch's." She paused again, using the sleeve of her coat to wipe up an imaginary spot from the table and not looking at Pru. "I saw Mrs. Templeton getting out of her car at Primrose House," she whispered.

"But they said that they didn't come back," Pru said.

"Yes, I know. I heard her say that to the inspector on the phone." Ivy shook her head. "That isn't what I saw. But I can't tell the police, because what would that look like?" Ivy's eyes were large and focused on Pru.

"It would look like you're telling the truth," Pru said, a queasy feeling settling in her stomach. She took another sip of her whisky and let it burn its way down her throat. "Perhaps Davina just forgot that she'd come back here that afternoon." That sounded as ludicrous aloud as it did in her head. "Really, Ivy, you need to tell the police."

"Oh, I know that's true." Ivy slumped down in her chair. "But do you think it would be all right if I told Sergeant Hobbes, and not that inspector?"

Pru laughed. "I know what you mean. Yes, ring the DS and tell him."

"It's probably nothing," Ivy said, shaking her head. "It just slipped her mind." It was unlikely that Ivy could fathom Davina being a suspect, as she had come up with her own theory about the murder. Ivy thought it had been committed by a passing stranger looking for money — a random, violent act — and ignored the fact that Ned never looked as if he had two tuppence to rub together. Still, Pru couldn't help liking the idea, mostly because it allowed her to imagine the black cloud of suspicion that hung over Liam blowing away.

"Ned was such a help, wasn't he?" Ivy said as she unbuttoned her coat and slipped it off. "Even before you started here at Primrose House, he was always popping by just to see if there was anything the Templetons needed doing or to tell them something about the history of the place."

It occurred to Pru that Ivy might possess information that Pru could use as she looked into Ned's murder. Ivy might know why Davina implied that Ned was blackmailing her. Pru recalled Davina's comment about hiring him. "It isn't as if we had the choice." Talking with Ivy involved no risk on Pru's part. *I'm being careful,* she told Christopher in her head, remembering with a rush of pleasure that he was due to arrive that evening.

"Ivy, let's get a fire going, shall we? Can't you stay awhile?"

"Well," Ivy said as she took the whisky bottle and poured them both another, "I do seem to have a free evening, now don't I?"

It wasn't one of Christopher's creations, and they smoked up the cottage a bit, but it was a fire and it was warm. The two women settled down with the whisky and a small plate of cheese and crackers and put their feet up on the sofa. They chatted about gardening, housekeeping, Robbie's love of Robin Hood, and the village hall, which was in sad need of repair. Pru took comfort in both the company and the drink, and the chance to ignore her own troubles for a while.

"Is Robbie's dad around?" Pru asked, wondering if this was a topic for discussion.

Ivy shook her head. "No, Bertie left when Robbie was about five. It was very hard for him, you know, the way Robbie is. He just didn't have the strength for it."

Pru pressed her lips together to keep from saying what she thought about Bertie and his strength. Instead, she said, "You've done such a fine job with Robbie."

Ivy got tears in her eyes. "Oh, he's my heart, that boy."

In her mind, Pru saw Birdie's sitting room filled to the brim with photos of Simon, and realized that he was Birdie's heart. But that thought brought her too close to despair, and so she turned away from it.

"What kinds of things did Ned tell the Templetons?" Pru asked.

"Just this and that." Ivy held her glass up to the fire and the whisky glowed golden brown. "He knew so much about the village, and all the ancient goings-on. Do you know about the Domesday Book?"

"William the Conqueror, it's a recording of all the towns and villages at the time?" Pru offered.

"And who owned what land. Well, I once heard Ned talking to the Templetons about the Domesday Book and land rights. I remember he said, 'Well, who do you think owns it?' Isn't that funny, that he would know so much about things so long ago? He was just like the rest of us, didn't even own his cottage. It belongs to the estate, to Lord Hamilton."

Pru poured another round as she smiled. "You don't think Ned wanted to be the earl, do you?"

Ivy snorted into her glass. "I'd say he would've taken it if it was offered."

"Do you know his daughter, Cate?" Pru asked.

Ivy nibbled on a bit of cheese. "Poor sausage. To be left with no parents and her so young. I hope she'll be all right. I hope she'll be" — Ivy cut her eyes at Pru — "safe."

"You know about Jamie, then?" Pru took the poker and gave the fire a stab, causing a shower of sparks to rise and a cloud of smoke to billow out into the room. Her eyes burned, and she coughed.

"News gets around," Ivy said, giving a cough herself and reaching for the bottle. "I asked Ned about her one day — just enquiring, you know, after her welfare — and he said very little, just that he would take care of her."

"But he wanted her to stay with Jamie, didn't he?"

"Ned had a traditional view of the world," Ivy said. "Thought there should be a mother and a father in every home. He even thought I should track down Robbie's dad and make him come back to us." Ivy shook her head. "Ned didn't realize that families don't all have to be the same to be happy."

No more talk of family, Pru thought, she couldn't take it. "Did Ned think that Jamie would get the head gardener job? This job?"

"He may have," Ivy said, giving her a sympathetic look. "But you know that Mrs. Templeton cannot be talked into anything. I did hear a sharp word or two between them one day, something to do with the garden. But that was ages ago, before you started here. The Templetons love everything you're doing." Ivy reached out and gave Pru's arm a squeeze.

Talk of the garden reminded Pru of the task still ahead of her — a finished landscape. "I don't know how we're going to get it all done," she said, shaking her head.

Their talk wandered off into other subjects, and they laughed over stories of dealing with employers. Pru was surprised to find that the whisky was well more than half gone. She wasn't sure she could stand up. "Ivy," she said, "perhaps you should stay here tonight."

"Oh, Pru, no," Ivy said, leaning over to reach for her handbag on the floor and almost falling off the sofa. "Aren't you expecting your Mr. Pearse? I'm not sure he'd like to find me asleep on the sofa when he arrives." She pulled out her phone, punched in a number, and said, "Tommy? It's

Ivy. Could you come collect me at the gardener's cottage at Primrose House?"

She rang off and said to Pru, "He's lovely, your Mr. Pearse is. Now then, how did the two of you meet?"

Pru told their story, going light on details of the London murder, and ended with, "And he said if I had gone back to Texas, he would've come to get me. Isn't that lovely?" She drained her glass and reached for the bottle.

"It's just like in the films," Ivy said. "You're so lucky to have found such a wonderful man." Ivy gave her a shrewd glance. "To have a boyfriend."

Pru burst out laughing. "No, Ivy, don't say that word. How embarrassing." She covered her face.

Ivy picked up on it immediately. "Oh go on," she said, laughing and elbowing Pru, "you say it."

"I can't," Pru said, turning scarlet. "I can't. I'm too old to say it."

"Well, you aren't too old to do it," Ivy said, and they both erupted in peals of laughter as Christopher suddenly walked in the cottage door, causing another puff of smoke to escape from the fireplace into the room.

His eyes moved from Pru to Ivy to the almost-empty whisky bottle. "Ladies," he said, a smile slowly spreading across his face.

Pru could see him clearly, although it seemed as if she were looking through the bottom of her glass.

Ivy stood up, holding onto the sofa and her handbag. "Mr. Pearse, how lovely to see you again. I'll be on my way now." But she didn't move, eyeing the distance to her coat at the table.

"Hi." Pru smiled up at him. *God I love him*, she thought.

Christopher reached for Ivy and her coat at the same time. "You aren't thinking of driving home, are you?"

"Not at all," Ivy said. "My car is up at the big house, and I rang for Tommy, our local taxi." As if on cue, tires crunched on the gravel and a horn honked. "There we are. Bye now, Pru."

"Goodbye, Ivy, thanks for stopping." Pru momentarily forgot the reason for Ivy's visit, and thought they'd just had a friendly chat.

"Let me walk you out," Christopher said, holding firmly to Ivy's elbow to escort her to the waiting taxi. When he returned, Pru hadn't moved, although she'd tried to reclip her hair with little success. He sat on the edge of the sofa and said, "How are you?"

"I've had a bit to drink," she said.

"Have you now," he said, smoothing her hair down and kissing her forehead. "Would you like some tea?"

"Yes, please." She kissed him on the mouth and wondered why he tasted like whisky. Then she remembered she was the one that tasted like whisky. "Can you fix the fire?"

"Is it broken?" he asked, and she giggled. He put the kettle on and worked his Boy Scout magic with the logs. Pru stayed where she was. She drank the strong tea, and on the second cup her head began to clear just a bit. That brought the events of the day back into focus.

"Did you visit Birdie today?" he asked.

Yes, there it was. The pain that had receded briefly was back and as sharp as her moment of discovery. She took a few breaths and stared into the fire.

"Simon is my brother." She could think of no way to introduce the topic, and blurted out the one sentence that rested at the top of the pile of memories and longings.

Christopher was quiet, searching her face. "Did Birdie tell you that?" he asked.

Pru cocked her head. "You don't seem surprised."

"You look very much alike," he said.

"We look like our dad," Pru said in a hoarse voice.

"Did your mother never say anything?"

Pru shook her head. It felt as if an earthquake was passing through her body. She swallowed hard, trying to stay in control.

"What happened?" he asked.

"She gave him away," Pru said, putting her mug on the floor and trying for a matter-of-fact tone. "She passed him off to Birdie and George. He wasn't convenient."

"Is that what Birdie told you?" Christopher took her hands.

Pru grabbed them away. "She *abandoned* him." Now shaking with rage, she got up and stood by the fireplace, holding onto the mantel to steady herself. "She was pregnant when my dad left at the end of the war. Birdie said they didn't know if he'd come back for her or not. She had the baby and gave him to Birdie. He was discarded like an old pair of shoes."

"She was a *girl*," Christopher said, standing and putting a hand over hers on the mantel. "She was an unmarried girl, and she allowed her son to be brought up by others. Think of the sacrifice that must've been for her. Come here, sit down." She sat, now holding tight to his hands as if they were her anchor at sea. "It's too easy for us to look back and judge," he said. "We don't know what it was like — it was a different time." He put his hand under her chin and lifted it up. "Did he have a good life here? Does Birdie love him?"

Reluctantly she nodded. "Yes, Birdie loves him."

"Does he know about his parents?"

"He does now," she whispered.

"And did you see him — talk with him?"

Pru's eyes grew unfocused. "He was so angry."

Christopher's hand tightened on hers. "What did he do?"

She shook her head. "He didn't do anything except make it abundantly clear that he has no interest in getting to know me. He already has a family." Her voice cracked, and she cleared her throat. "They abandoned him, so why should he want a sister who would be a reminder of that every day?" Tears came into her eyes, but didn't fall. "All my life I've wanted a sibling, and now that I have a brother, he wants nothing to do with me."

She took comfort in his arms. They didn't speak for a while, until at last Christopher asked, "Have you eaten? Or was it just whisky for dinner?"

She laughed a little. "It was mostly whisky," she admitted. She dragged herself away from the brink of the abyss and on to news of the evening. "Ivy was waiting for me when I got back." She told him that Ivy had seen the Templeton's car at the house that day. "The two of them are up and down from London so often, Davina probably forgot she'd stopped back by," Pru said.

"There's no reason for her to lie about it?" he asked. "Do you believe they got along with Ned?"

Pru shrugged. "She's made a couple of odd statements before about him. She made it sound as if they'd been forced into hiring him. But she's never explained what that was about. And she seems really sad that he's dead."

Christopher grinned and kissed her hand. "Will Ivy tell Tatt?"

"She asked if it was all right to ring DS Hobbes instead. I gave her my permission."

They returned to staring at the fire. Although she tried, Pru couldn't keep the voices out of her head — snatches of her conversation with Birdie, and Simon shouting at her. Finally, she lifted her head. "I'm very poor company tonight. I'm sorry."

"You, my darling, are always the best company. Although, I'm not sure what tomorrow morning will bring." He pulled her up. "Let's go to bed."

CHAPTER 21

Pru heard small sounds in the kitchen the next morning. Christopher was up. She reached for his pillow and put it over her ears, hoping to stop the throbbing pain in her head.

"Coffee?" he asked in a quiet voice.

"Coffee," she said, her head still under the pillow, "would be lovely." She peered out, squinting her eyes against the flood lamp aimed straight at her. It turned out to be only pale sunshine through the window. She sat up and took the mug, relishing its heat and the fragrance of the coffee. She took a test sip. "God. What time is it?"

"It's after ten." He was dressed, proving that the day had already started for some people.

"I'll fix us breakfast?" she said, hoping he would decline the offer.

"I've had breakfast already." Christopher gave her a kiss. "I have something I must do today," he said. "I'll be back this evening."

"I should've been up earlier — I didn't know you'd have to leave." Their time was limited and precious, and here she had squandered some of it.

"If that bottle started out full yesterday, I'd say it's just as well you slept in." He took her hand. "It's just for today."

"If you can't make it back, that's all right, I'll understand," she said, putting on a brave, but transparent, front.

"I'll see you," he said, "this evening."

* * *

Although she kept busy for most of the day, Pru ended the afternoon sitting in the kitchen, the only light in the cottage from the sofa lamp. She thought about her childhood — her happy childhood with two parents who loved her and whom she loved. She marveled at how alone she felt now that evidence of their deceit had been revealed. She belonged nowhere and to no one.

When she was about five, she had made up a sibling — a sister named Barbie who had a smooth, blond ponytail just like her Barbie doll. Barbie had become her constant companion. Pru had requested two of everything — cookies, bowls of cereal — so that Barbie would have her own. She couldn't remember how long that lasted. Had she come to her senses one day or had Barbie disappeared from her life gradually? When her mother poured Barbie a glass of Kool-Aid, did she think to herself that she could've been pouring it for Simon?

She thought of the black humor in that situation — she pretended she had a sibling while her mother pretended she didn't. The betrayal cut deep and uncovering the years of her mother's lies opened a chasm between her and the loving woman she thought she knew, a mother who could give up her baby.

Her mind hovered in a shadowy place, and she was surprised when Christopher walked in. She hadn't even heard his car.

He stood just inside the door. "What are you doing in the dark?"

"What time is it?" she asked.

"It's gone five. Are you all right?"

She got up and kissed him. He winced. "What's wrong?" she asked.

149

His face didn't look right. She switched on the kitchen light for a better look.

"Oh my God, Christopher." His right eye was black and blue and swollen almost completely shut.

"I'm all right," he reassured her, but she could see otherwise.

"What happened?"

He put his arms around her waist and looked into her eyes. Well, one eye looked, one eye squinted. "I will tell you what happened. I promise that I will tell you," he said, and she could tell by his tone that he wouldn't. "I promise I will tell you," he repeated. "Just not right now." He continued to look and she continued to be silent. "I promise," he said again. "All right?"

"All right," she said in a small voice. The huge pool of misery inside her, brimming with family secrets and lies, shifted slightly to allow room now for this — worry. An open case, she thought. It was too easy to forget he had a dangerous job. A policeman could be injured in the line of duty at any time and here's proof. And he couldn't talk about it.

"I'm sorry I had to leave you today," he said.

"I was fine," she said. She kissed him, her lips barely touching his. "You're the one who's hurt."

He gave her half a smile and began to massage that spot low on her back. "It's just my eye. The rest of me still works."

She cupped his uninjured cheek in her hand. "Does it?" She drew close and kissed him again, with more intent. "We'd better find out, don't you think? Just to be sure," she said, taking his hand and leading him to the bedroom.

She took care pulling off his sweater, making sure it didn't rub against his bruised face. She kissed him at the base of his throat and worked her way up to his mouth, standing on tiptoes to do so. He took care, too. He traced the shape of the fan pendant against her skin and followed the path of the chain with his lips. And when he reached for her, he took care to remind her that she did belong. That they belonged to each other.

* * *

Pru nestled her head into Christopher's shoulder, his arm around her. "How is your face?" she asked. "Do you want something for the pain?"

"I've just had something for the pain," he said, "and I feel much better. Shall we go into town for a meal?"

She stuck her chin out. "I cooked," she said.

"No," he replied with proper amazement. "What brought this on?"

"I wanted to stay busy," she said, getting up to dress. "I rang Ivy after you left — she was worse off than me — and she talked me through it, from going to the shops to chopping the shallots." She acquired a lofty attitude. "I made boeuf bourguignon. Although in Texas we'd just call it beef stew."

* * *

She waited until after he'd had seconds — the first meal she'd cooked in her cottage, and a rousing success — to tell him about the online comment, thought by the *Courier* and the police to be menacing. Christopher didn't take it well.

"I'll ring Hobbes," he said, pulling out his phone.

"No, there's nothing to it. They took the comment down, and nothing's happened." She put her hand over his. "I couldn't keep it from you, but I don't want you to worry." She kept her eyes on him while she bit her lower lip.

"And?" he asked, realizing there was more.

"I saw Jamie at Ned's funeral. He's miserable and wants Cate back," she said, holding onto Christopher's hand. "He's upset about Ned's murder — he thought Ned would sort everything out for him. He blames it all on Liam. And he did make some reference to me being selected as head gardener." She tried to throw that in as an offhand remark, but it was no good.

She could see the muscles in his jaw tightening as he stared a hole through her. She could only wait it out, until he reasoned with himself and, she hoped, came to the conclusion that she was in no danger.

He looked around the cottage. "You shouldn't stay here alone."

"I'll be fine. Sergeant Hobbes said the police will be patrolling the area."

"Why don't you move back to your little room up at the house?" he asked.

"Davina and Bryan are gone more than they're here these days," she said. "I'd be no safer up there than here in my own cottage. And I will be safe *here*. I'll lock the door. I'll let no one in."

"I don't like it," he said.

"You could ring every hour to check on me." He said nothing. "I could get a guard badger," she said.

She saw the corner of his mouth twitch. "Keep your phone handy."

CHAPTER 22

The winter sun did its best to blaze through the kitchen window on Sunday afternoon, reminding her of the young plants in the glasshouse. "I'd better go and open the vents a few inches," she told him. "With the sun so bright, it'll heat up inside, and the primroses aren't ready for that yet."

He stood up from arranging firewood. "I'll come with you," he said.

"I'll be right back. You keep going with your building project."

She walked through the front gate of the walled garden and into the glasshouse, pushing open the roof vents a few inches. Movement beyond the back gate caught her eye. She froze, staring at the opening, waiting. For a second, she considered going back to get Christopher, but then decided that would be excessive. This was her garden, and she was in charge of who was allowed. She crept as quietly as possible to the lower gate and peered out. The tape had been removed from the murder scene, and it was a clear view to the potting shed.

"Liam?"

He started as he emerged from the shed. "Pru, I didn't want to disturb you. I brought the paraffin heater back." He nodded toward the interior of the shed. She didn't reply. "Do you remember, you asked me to collect it after it was repaired?"

"Yes, sure, of course I remember. Thanks." Liam didn't move. "You and Fergal are working tomorrow?"

"We'll be here," he said, looking up at the sky. "Hope the fine weather holds."

"Liam," she said, after taking a deep breath. "I want to ask you something."

Fergal came round the far corner of the walled garden. "Right, I'm ready now. Oh hi, Pru." He looked none too happy to see her. "We didn't mean to disturb you. I only wanted to leave the tools we borrowed — the pruning saw and those long loppers. We'll be on our way now."

"Do you have a few minutes? You could come up to the cottage. Christopher is here. I only want to chat." They were as skittish as rabbits when she got them alone.

"Is everything all right?" Christopher appeared down the path from her cottage. She saw the brothers take note of his black eye, but make no comment.

She smiled at him. "Everything's fine, I was just asking Liam and Fergal back for a cup of tea."

"Sorry, we can't stay," Fergal said. "Come on, Liam." He nodded the way.

Pru's gaze followed Fergal's gesture, and she saw their car parked on the access track. "Do you drive down this way often?" she asked.

"Sometimes," Liam said. "I came down this way last week, didn't I? I brought that stack of seed trays in."

She didn't remember, but was happy to take his word for it.

Fergal was acting like a herding dog, trying to get his brother to move, but Liam didn't budge. "Christopher," he said, "when someone tells the police something that may not be exactly true—"

He got no further, as Tatt came stomping through the lower gate of the garden.

The inspector surveyed the group and said in a quiet and self-satisfied voice, "Well, well, well — what do we have here? A meeting of the minds? Getting your stories straight? And what are you doing, Pearse, coaching them?" He caught sight of Christopher's face. "Run into a disagreement, did you?"

Pru put her hands on her hips. "Inspector Tatt, what do you want?"

"I want to know what the Duffys are doing here on a Sunday afternoon, Ms. Parke, that's what I want. You've yet to account for your whereabouts," he said, pointing to Liam. "Although others seem eager to do so."

"Who?" Pru asked.

"I also wanted to let you know of an interesting discovery we made." Tatt paused, took two steps back, his eyes sweeping the small group. "We've found the victim's mobile phone, and guess where it was. Of all places," he said with a chuckle, "at the Duffy cottage."

"That's not true," Liam shouted, making a move toward Tatt. Fergal grabbed him.

"It is true, and I'd say we'll have a few questions for you about it before long." Tatt patted his stomach as if he'd just eaten a large and satisfactory meal.

"Where was it?" Christopher asked.

"Behind a loose stone," Tatt said, sounding eager to brag. "No one had noticed until—" He caught himself. "That isn't really any of your business now, is it Pearse?" He turned back to the Duffys. "And what are the two of you doing here?"

"Leaving," Fergal said.

"We'll see you tomorrow, Pru," Liam said.

"Sergeant Hobbes will be stopping for a visit," Tatt called after them.

Pru could barely hold still in her fury and fear, and she latched onto the one topic she could control. "Inspector, there's nothing sinister in my gardeners coming over on a Sunday afternoon. We've worked plenty of weekends." She would not let her own suspicions about Liam creep out for

Tatt to see. "We're starting on a new phase of the garden, and we needed to go over a few details. And you've no right to suggest that Christopher is here for any other reason than to see me. That feels a bit like police harassment," she said.

"Spare me your American television dramatics, Ms. Parke," Tatt said, one hand in his pocket jangling his keys. "I was passing your cottage and decided to stop and ask about Mrs. Templeton. Did you know that she returned to Primrose House on the afternoon of the murder?"

It seemed that Ivy wasted no time. "No, I didn't know that. As I told you, I was in Tunbridge Wells. Did you check all the places I told you I'd been?"

"Yes, yes, you are not a suspect," Tatt replied. "Has either Mr. or Mrs. Templeton ever voiced any dissatisfaction with Bobbins or his work? Mrs. Templeton made him sound too good to be true."

"I don't know of any difficulties," she replied, feeling Christopher's eyes on her.

"Very well. Until next time, Ms. Parke. Pearse." Tatt walked away, and Christopher stepped over to Pru's side.

"There's something wrong about that," she said. "Police just now finding Ned's mobile at Liam's. Did it sound suspicious to you?"

"It sounded convenient," Christopher said as they walked back to her cottage.

* * *

"The fire is ready for you to light later. You'll stay in this evening?"

"I'll be here," she said in a small voice as she stared at the cold fireplace and contemplated the quiet evening that stretched out before her — an evening full of misery, as far as she could tell. The past was waiting in the wings, eager to lay claim to her mind. Time to dwell on the stories her mother never told her.

Pru watched Christopher take the poker and move one of the logs a millimeter as she planned to fill her week with work. "I have a few questions for Davina. And, I'll talk with Liam and Fergal, too." Christopher stood up and she realized she'd spoken those words aloud. "Talk to them about the garden," she added to no avail.

"Pru, leave it to the police."

"I can talk to Cate," she said. "Just a friendly chat. I believe she was lying about Liam not being at her flat."

Both his grip on the poker and his voice tightened. "You've been threatened, and we don't know where it's come from. If you push the wrong person, you could end up in danger."

"I haven't been threatened — it was only a vague statement," she said, unconsciously crossing her arms in defiance. "I can talk to people. I can ask questions."

"*No.*" He thrust the poker back onto its stand causing the whole set to rattle. "Not after this."

"*I have to stay busy,*" she shouted at him.

Silence. After a moment, he walked over to her and they held each other. She knew that her stubborn streak was rearing its ugly head, but she had no inclination to back down. He looked at her with a lopsided smile. "Come up to London next weekend. You can get away, can't you? We'll take Jo, Cordelia, and Lucy to dinner."

He was throwing her a life preserver, and she willingly took hold. "To Gasparetti's?"

"Of course."

Her eyes widened as her mind filled with possibilities. "The Garden Museum has a new exhibit on Lawrence Johnston and Hidcote that I was hoping to see. And we could go to the Sunday recital at Westminster." A tiny spark of excitement ignited inside her. A weekend in the city, away from the garden, the murder, and the family history she never knew she had. She kissed him soundly.

Primrose House

Monday, 1 February

Dear Pru,

We've thought further about the statue of Ned in the oval, and decided that perhaps that's not the best way to honor his memory. I've had a vision of something so much better! I see that all the little apple trees have been delivered for the walled garden. As you had already planned to espalier these in various patterns along the wall, why don't we spell out Ned's name in branches? Wouldn't that be so sweet? We'll chat more this week.

Best,
Davina

CHAPTER 23

The upcoming weekend in London shone like a beacon, guiding Pru through the morass of the week as she tried to untangle the three balls of knotted intrigue in her life — Ned's murder, Jamie's obsession with his wife and his barely-disguised desire to be head gardener at Primrose House, and her own newly revised family situation. She glanced down at Davina's note, which had been stuck in her front door that morning as usual. Under no circumstances would she let this latest wild hair divert her. Pru shuddered to think what visitors would say if they saw "BOBBINS" spelled out in branches in the walled garden.

She did, however, have something to talk with Davina about, and so while the workers, including Liam and Fergal, began preliminary excavations for leveling the terraces, she popped into the kitchen of Primrose House midmorning on Monday. Ivy had gone to the shops.

"Coffee, Pru?" Davina was poised to pour.

"Thanks." Pru sat at the table, and took a deep breath. She hoped to do this without implicating Ivy. "Davina, Inspector Tatt mentioned that you had stopped back by here on that Thursday" — *that Thursday* had emerged as the most popular euphemism for the day Ned was murdered. "You'd probably forgotten that," she added in a rush.

Davina didn't answer at first, instead taking an inordinate amount of time to arrange the many flowing layers of thin material around her before she sat down. She looked down into her coffee. "It didn't seem relevant at the time," she said. "I wonder that the inspector thought to mention it to you. Is it because Christopher is involved in the investigation?"

"No, certainly not, he has nothing to do with this." A fear that Christopher could be reprimanded for meddling lodged in her mind. Could Tatt complain? "It's only me. I didn't want to pry, it's just that I can't help but hear things from Tatt, of course." Trying to appear casual, Pru took the milk and poured an extra dash into her mug, resulting in more milk than coffee, and cooling the liquid to a tepid state.

Davina waved her hand at Pru and smiled. "No, don't mind me. How can you help but be involved in all this? You may as well know" — Davina's eyes bounced around the kitchen from table to sink to dish drainer, never hitting Pru — "I did come back to see Ned." Davina's statement put a stop to all movement in the kitchen. Pru sensed that even the clock held its breath before its next tick.

"Oh," she said.

"I rang and asked him to come up to the house and see me that afternoon. I needed to talk with him." She glanced out the window as they heard a small earthmover roar past below the balustrade. "Bryan and I have put a lot into Primrose House — not just a great deal of money, but our time, too. We will not give up now."

"You've done an amazing job on the restoration," Pru said, an uneasy feeling in the pit of her stomach. "Did Ned want you to give up?"

Davina turned an even gaze on Pru. "I hope you aren't letting all this business draw you away from what needs to be done in the garden, Pru," she said, putting an effective end to any more talk about Ned, and causing Pru's face to turn quite hot.

"I haven't let it interfere with my work," Pru said, putting her mug down. "We're doing fine." What a lie that was

— they were far behind schedule. "I know what needs to be done and I hope you know that I'm committed to having the garden ready and that I will work as many hours a day as it takes." Pru wondered how her resume would look if her first — and possibly only — head-gardener post lasted only three months.

Davina melted into her usual convivial self. "Of course we're very pleased with the progress," she said.

Pru thought Davina was also quite pleased at successfully changing the subject away from Ned. "Well," she said, "I'll just get back to it then."

She was at the kitchen door when Davina said, "He never showed up. I waited here past our time, and I even drove down that little road you have at the bottom of the garden, but I didn't get out of my car and I didn't see him." Her eyebrows drew together. "I didn't see anything amiss, and I had to get back to London for a dinner that evening."

Pru turned. "Did you tell the police that was why you came back?"

"God, no," Davina said, her face flushed. "How would that look? I didn't see him, and so it doesn't really matter, now does it?" She watched Pru's face, as if daring her to say it did indeed matter.

"Well, I suppose that the police like to know everything, don't they?" She couldn't keep herself from one more reckless question. *Go ahead,* she thought, *fire me.* "What did you want to talk with him about?"

"Ned knew a great deal about this area, its history, its laws. I only wanted to" — Davina looked off into space for a moment — "chat with him about that."

That hardly seemed a good reason for the hour's drive from London when she'd just gone up that morning. "What would he know that—"

"You should leave this alone, Pru," Davina cut in.

I will not leave it alone, Pru thought, but she was prevented from asking another question when Ivy walked in carrying three shopping bags in each hand. Davina launched into a detailed conversation with her about an upcoming dinner party.

Pru left, checking in briefly with Gordon about the terracing and the next load of dairy manure — this one not quite as fresh as the first — that he would deliver and dump at the base of the balustrade terrace the following week. After that, she skirted the construction work and walked down to the meadow and beech wood. The meadow would be dug out in April. They'd found the stream source that Repton used to fill it and a new channel would be constructed.

It had occurred to her that a bench near the water would create a lovely scene from the balustrade, and that the bench could be a focal point if they lined it up with the central staircase through the terraced beds. It would mean a large hole cut in the yew walk, but she had lost interest in the yew and planned to cut it down drastically, creating a low hedge lining the path instead of a hallway with green walls. This wasn't Sissinghurst, after all. She mulled over what kind of bench would get Repton's approval, telling herself she should know his tastes by now. Then she remembered Liam's advice to include something of herself in the garden. Perhaps she would.

She stroked the smooth gray bark of a huge beech and leaned against it, craning her head to see up through its branches. In front of her was the yew walk, and beyond that and perpendicular to it the boxwood allée ran straight down the hill. It was far enough to the side that the new terraced beds would not interfere, although she thought the boxwood had outlived its usefulness with all the new additions to the landscape. Off and up to the right she could see the terracing work and the balustrade. The ground-floor windows of the house were hidden.

She scuffed around in the thick leaf duff, and her foot caught on something. It was an archer's bow. At first, Pru thought it must be the one Fergal made for Robbie the day he was Will Scarlet, but on closer inspection, she saw that although it wasn't the finest quality, it was a real bow — polished wood with a leaf motif carved into it and a taut string. She picked it up and looked round for arrows or signs of target practice, but saw nothing. The land belonged to the Templetons, but a copse could attract anyone looking for a piece of woodland to enjoy. Thinking if no one claimed the bow she could give it to Robbie — sans arrows, of course, and with Ivy's permission — she took it back with her and propped it up outside the shed.

* * *

She had arranged a video call with Lydia in Dallas for that evening. She and Lydia had known each other for many years, and Pru had practically become a member of the family, welcomed in by Lydia, her husband, Ray Morales, their daughters, and Lydia's brother, Marcus Rojas. Pru had worked with Ray and Marcus at the Dallas Arboretum, and she and Marcus had been in an on-again, off-again relationship for a few years until it was completely off.

She and Lydia chatted a while before Pru got to her point. "Lyd, you have all my boxes, remember?"

"All? You own next to nothing. The boxes are in the closet in the spare bedroom," Lydia said.

"I need one of them — the one with Mom's things in it. It's marked, you'll know which one." Pru took a deep breath and a sip of wine and explained why.

To Pru, the box had always been special. She had thought of it as keepsakes from her mother's girlhood in England, but was more than that. Pru had opened the box after her mother died, but found her grief still too fresh to examine the letters and photos without the heartache of loss. She hadn't looked at it since, but hoped that it might hold a clue to the family's recently uncovered past.

"Pru, *mija*, I'm so sorry for you," Lydia said after she'd heard the story. "I never thought your mom would be one for such secrets. I'll send it tomorrow."

* * *

163

The highlight of her week, Pru decided, was her visit to Cate. She arrived in time to wave hello to Mrs. Sock and Trevor, who were either on their way out or just returning from a walk. When Cate came to the door, Nanda stood just behind her, peering around her mother's leg at Pru.

Nanda saw Trevor across the road and yipped. Trevor yipped back and wagged his tail.

Nanda got over her shyness soon after Pru arrived, and that allowed Cate to get a few things done around the flat without her daughter at her heels. Cate said housekeeping was the least she could do for Francine, who had opened her home to them on such short notice. Not only did Nanda talk to Pru, but, by the little girl's bedtime, she wouldn't stop talking. She squealed in delight as Pru turned her hair clip into a monster that tried to eat Nanda up, and Pru had four tea parties with Nanda's collection of stuffed animals, which included Paddington Bear, Madeline — with her big round hat and blue French school uniform — a giraffe, and a pig.

Christopher rang during one of the tea parties. They had time for only a short chat, because Nanda kept calling to her, "Pwu, dwink your tea" in a three-year-old's version of a motherly tone, but at least he knew she was safe and sound.

"Nanda, would you like to say hello to Christopher?"

Pru held the phone out and Nanda leaned in, shouting, "Pwu is busy now!" Then she took the phone and began a long one-sided conversation that sounded as if it had something to do with Paddington Bear getting into trouble.

When Pru reached over to rescue Christopher, Nanda wandered away, phone to her ear, into her mother's bedroom. Pru followed and watched Nanda walk over to the open closet door and drop the phone into a tall, black, high-heeled boot at the very back. "Bye-bye." She waved down the boot.

"Nanda?" Cate called from the kitchen. Off Nanda trotted, and Pru stuck her hand down the boot.

"Pru?" she could hear Christopher's voice coming from her phone.

Pru laughed. "Did you get all that? What's the scoop on Paddington Bear?"

* * *

Pru was stretched out on the sofa when Cate came out from putting Nanda to bed. "I could never be a granny," Pru said. "I don't have the stamina."

"You're not old enough to be a granny, Pru," Cate said. "You're more like an auntie."

Grateful for the compliment and feeling immediately younger, Pru sat up and reclipped her hair. "I didn't realize that Hugo Jenkins was a cousin of yours," Pru said.

"Hugo — I saw that he was writing the blog. Did he tell you his tale of woe?" she asked, sitting on the sofa. "I've hardly seen him in years after that hoo-ha about the pub. He's still blaming Dad, isn't he?"

"He did mention that your dad and his had a disagreement."

Cate gave a disapproving click of her tongue. "Hugo's dad was a con man, always looking for the easiest way to make a quick million," she said. "This was years ago. Fred — Hugo's dad — was going to reopen an old pub up near High Brooms. It was the 'oldest pub in Kent and Surrey', he said" — Cate's fingers wiggled air quotes — "and 'Henry VIII stopped here.' Honestly." She rolled her eyes. "Fred thought it would draw in coachloads of tourists. He'd bought adverts and got it written up in pub guides. Began fixing the old place up."

"That must've cost him," Pru said, picking up Nanda's pig from the floor.

"He'd borrowed loads. Except it wasn't the oldest pub in Kent and Surrey — that's the Red Lion in Rusthall. Dad said it opened in 1415. That's all he did, just point out that Fred's pub just wasn't the oldest." Cate set Paddington Bear and Madeline back up on their little chairs. "The whole scheme fell apart, Fred lost buckets of other people's money, and he and Hugo blamed Dad. It was the talk of the village for a while, but then most people forgot it."

"Hugo still seems upset."

"I'm sorry about Fred dying. But now Hugo thinks he has to clear his dad's name. I can't believe anyone could hold a grudge that long," Cate said, after which her face clouded up. "Apart from Jamie, that is."

"Is he leaving you alone?" Pru asked.

"Mostly. I didn't tell him I'm starting back to work nursing a couple of evenings a week. I don't want to get into that again."

"You were brave to break away," Pru said.

"I should've done it sooner," Cate said. She pushed her sleek hair behind her ear, picked up the giraffe, and began to fiddle with its legs.

Pru took a deep breath. "Cate, I want to ask you about Liam."

Cate's eyes looked like huge dark pools. She hugged the giraffe to her breast. "Oh God," she whispered. Pru could see her trembling. "I've made such a terrible mistake."

"A mistake?" A wave of cold washed over Pru as she reached out a hand to calm Cate.

"It's just that—"

Nanda cried from her room. "Mummy! Mummy!"

Cate dropped the stuffed toy, threw off her look of fear, and stood up. "Sorry, Pru. She's having some trouble getting to sleep these days." She turned as she got to the door of Nanda's room. "Usually if I read her a story, she'll drop off. I don't know how long it will take, but you're welcome to stay."

Somehow that welcome did not come across in her voice. "No, I'll be off now, and I'll see you again soon," Pru said, standing to gather her coat and bag.

Cate walked her to the door and reached for the latch to open it.

Pru took a quick breath and plunged in. "Cate, you heard that they found your dad's phone?"

"That's a lie, Pru, it can't be true. Liam would never have Dad's mobile."

"Mummy!"

"I'll see you soon," Cate said, opening the door and putting an end to questions.

Pru walked out to her car, kicking herself for not getting to the point earlier, but she'd had no desire to talk about Jamie or Liam in front of Nanda. Cate's alarm at the mention of Liam alarmed Pru. Was Cate scared of him, too?

Pru took the car keys from her bag, and they slipped out of her hands, falling to the pavement at the same moment she heard rustling in the laurel hedge alongside the drive. She stopped and listened, but heard nothing else except Cate putting the chain on the door behind her. She bent down slowly to pick up her keys and as she did so, cut her eyes over to the base of the hedge, which was bare of branches. She saw, among the thick brown stems emerging from the ground, a pair of work boots.

She stood up abruptly, not making eye contact with the hedge as she continued to her car. Perhaps Jamie isn't bothering Cate, but he is spying on her, Pru thought, and decided to ring DS Hobbes first thing in the morning to make sure that the police were keeping an eye out.

CHAPTER 24

If Pru had only the garden to attend to, there still wouldn't have been enough hours in the week, but even so, she filled every unclaimed second and each evening with sorting through questions about Ned's murder and seeking out those who might have a clue even if they didn't realize it. On Tuesday afternoon, she had the opportunity to chat with Robbie.

They sat on the stairs at the end of the balustrade terrace that led down to where the workers continued to level the slope and prepare for the stonework. Robbie was trying to retie the string on his makeshift bow, and Pru sat down to help.

"My mate said he would teach me to shoot an arrow straight," Robbie said.

Pru was beginning to think Robbie's mate was much like her sister, Barbie — imaginary. "Who is this mate of yours, Robbie? Do I know him? Is he from Chaffinch's? Is it someone who comes round here?"

"It's a secret, Pru," he replied, thrusting out his chest. "I can keep a secret."

Before she could try to get further, one of Gordon's crew called her over to see about the soil mix for the new terraced beds, and by the time she was free again, Ivy was giving her a wave as she and Robbie left for the day.

* * *

Since talking with Cate, Pru's mind had been stuck on Hugo and how he blamed Ned for his own dad's death. She rang Hugo with the pretense of chatting about resuming the blog, but she'd had to leave a message, and he hadn't phoned her back. So at lunch on Wednesday, she made the short trip up to the *Courier's* offices to talk with him in person.

She asked for him at the front desk, but instead of the receptionist answering, a woman passing behind her, hair in a topknot and glasses perched on the end of her nose said, "He'd better not be around. I told him to get over to Stone Cross. A couple of pensioners were cheesed off at the Council for canceling the village fête this spring, and started a protest." She took her glasses off and let them dangle on their beaded lanyard. "May I help you?"

"Thanks," Pru said, "it's nothing important."

The woman's eyes narrowed. "Are you the American?"

Pru thought it was quite obvious that she was, at the very least, some American, but knew what the woman meant. "I'm Pru Parke. I work at Primrose House."

"I'm Anna Clegg-Hill, editor here at the *Courier*. Why don't you come through and we'll chat. Coffee?"

Pru had no desire to talk with Ms. Clegg-Hill, but the woman began herding her toward a hallway, and she had no reason to be rude, either. "Sure, thanks."

"Carmen?" the editor said over her shoulder to the woman behind the reception desk.

"Yes, coffee," Carmen replied.

Pru imagined that the newspaper's editor would love to get a few words from the head gardener of a local murder site — that is, garden — but perhaps Pru could get a bit of information out of Clegg-Hill, too. The editor settled in behind a desk that was oddly void of paper, and Pru took the chair opposite. Carmen was on their heels with the coffee tray.

"Ms. Parke, how are things going at Primrose House?" the editor asked, hands folded in front of her and her face full of concern as she leaned over her desk. "What's the atmosphere like? Tense? Is it difficult to walk every day past the place you found Ned Bobbins' body without it catching at your heart? How is the investigation going? Are you privy to any new discoveries you might share with our readers? They do so love to read about you and the garden."

"I'm surprised you didn't ask Hugo to cover Ned's murder, Ms. Clegg-Hill. Wouldn't that have made the most sense? After all, he's been writing the blog about us. Was he not available that day?" *I see your bid and raise you,* thought Pru.

The editor blinked. "Hugo was—" she began, and then leaned back in her chair. "Hugo was nowhere to be found the day of the murder. Or the next."

Nowhere to be found? "You mean, he was supposed to be at work, and wasn't?"

"I mean that Hugo is a young reporter with a great many ideas bouncing around in his head," Clegg-Hill said. "When I asked him later where he was, he said he was in London doing research. I didn't pursue it. I know I'll see the end result sometime." If she suspected Hugo of anything else, she didn't let on.

Pru wanted to ask if the editor thought Hugo's disappearance had anything to do with his connection to Ned, but thought that might result in being drilled again about what she herself knew. And lunch was almost over. "Thanks for your time," she said to the editor. "I need to get back."

As she opened the door, Clegg-Hill asked, "Shall I tell Hugo you stopped by?"

Pru looked back and smiled, knowing the question was really *Do you want Hugo to know you're checking up on him?* The editor was fishing, but Pru wouldn't bite. "Yes, of course, please tell him."

* * *

Christopher rang if not every hour, then certainly more often than usual. She saw DS Hobbes twice during the week, and for no reason. Once, he was parked in front of her cottage as she walked back at the end of the day.

"Don't you have a home to go to?" she asked.

He grinned. "Just dropped by on my way. Everything all right? You're usually back by now, aren't you?"

"I'm putting in a few extra hours these days," she replied. "Will you phone the all clear into Christopher or shall I?"

Hobbes blushed. "I don't mind stopping, and Inspector Pearse is right to be concerned." He started the engine, and then nodded in the direction of their access road, saying, "We found clay from down there on the tires of two cars — Liam Duffy's and the Templetons'." He looked behind him, as if afraid that Tatt sat in the back seat listening as he passed along evidence on the case. "I suppose Duffy could have a reason to be there, but Mrs. Templeton? Does she ever come down this way?"

The thought of Davina pulling down the road, finding the hatchet in the shed and confronting Ned made Pru queasy, but when she swept the image from her mind, it was replaced with one of Liam doing the same thing. "Have you asked her?"

"As soon as she's back in town, I will," he said, putting his car in gear.

"Sergeant Hobbes," Pru said, laying a hand on his arm, "can you tell me about finding Ned's mobile? How was it missed the first time police went to see the Duffys?"

Hobbes shook his head. "It's a bit of a mess, and the inspector isn't best pleased. He got an anonymous tip, which seems too easy, if you ask me. The phone couldn't've been in a more obvious place — the stone was sticking halfway out of the wall with the phone behind it. It wasn't there on our first visit, I'm sure of it. Instead of the best place to hide, if that's what Liam was about, it was the worse place."

"Were there fingerprints?"

"Not Liam's. Ned's blood was smeared on the phone" — Pru took a deep breath — "and there may be a partial print, but it isn't clear. But it's just one more piece, Pru. We're not finished."

* * *

Pru drove back to Cate's flat after work on Thursday, hoping to resume their conversation and pin her down about Liam's whereabouts. Was he trying to hide an alibi or was it that he didn't have one?

But only Francine was home. "Just tell her I stopped," Pru said.

"Can I ask you something?" Francine said, standing at the door as Pru turned to leave. "Robbie helps you in the garden, doesn't he?"

"You know Robbie?" Pru asked.

"I'm the nurse at Chaffinch's, the day care center he attends," Francine reminded her.

"Yes, sure, I forgot that."

Francine dug her thumbnail into the wood of the door-jamb, idly working off a piece of peeling paint. "On the day that Cate's dad was killed, that afternoon, there was an hour or so when we couldn't find him. Robbie, I mean."

"He left Chaffinch' on his own? Is that allowed?"

"It doesn't happen very often," Francine said, "but occasionally someone might wander off. We're right in town, though." Francine took her long auburn hair and twisted it until it twisted upon itself and made a bun. She tucked in the end. "No one's ever gone for long. And Robbie's never done that before. We just thought he was out in the garden, digging. And really, before we could sound any alarm, here he came again, as if he'd just been around the block. Very chuffed he was, too, as if he'd done something he was proud of."

"Does his mum know that happened?"

"We told her as soon as she came to collect him, later that afternoon. It's the law. But he was safe."

"Do you know if the police were told?"

172

"I was there when the sergeant visited the next afternoon after, well, after you found Cate's dad," Francine said. "It didn't come up. I don't think the director wanted to call attention to it, and Ivy, Robbie's mum, asked if we could keep it quiet." Francine wrinkled her nose. "I don't know where he could have got to, anyway. It was such a short time."

"What did he say when you found him?" Pru asked, holding onto her car key so tightly that it dug into the palm of her hand.

Francine shook her head. "Some nonsense about Robin Hood. Nothing we could really figure out. But I thought I'd mention it to you," she said, looking at the ground.

As she drove home, Pru added Ivy to her to-do list.

* * *

She'd just got out of the cold and into her cottage when she heard a car pull in. DS Hobbes again, she thought, and opened the door to find Tatt, who wore a tartan coat and a deerstalker.

"Inspector, what can I do for you?" *Oh fine,* she thought, as a few snowflakes danced above his head like albino fireflies. "Come in, why don't you," she said. "It's freezing out there."

Tatt stepped just inside, and she closed the door as a blast of cold air tried to follow him.

"Ms. Parke," he said, clearing his throat, "have you had any further contact with Cate Bobbins?"

"Yes, of course I have. We're friends."

He jangled the keys in his pocket. "Right, well, we expect you to report any information you may come across that is pertinent to this case." He glanced around the room. "I noticed yellow tape around an area down below the house. I don't believe that's a crime scene, is it?"

"No, it isn't police tape. It's streamers from some gala the Templetons sponsored. It's circling a new planting — an area I didn't want anyone trampling." *This is a waste of police time,* Pru thought.

"Yes," he said, and got a small notebook out of his jacket pocket. "Your fingerprints, Ms. Parke. Have you stopped by the station to have them taken?"

"You already have my . . ." she started, then the realization hit her. "You were told to stop by and check up on me," she accused him.

He sputtered like a too-full kettle come to boil. "I do not take direction, I'll have you know."

She laughed. "No," she said, "I don't suppose you do." If Christopher had pulled a few strings that resulted in Tatt's being advised to keep an eye on the American gardener — she could imagine that didn't go over well.

He stuck the notebook back in his pocket. "It's just that I'd prefer not to have an international incident on my watch, if you please."

"Inspector, really, I'm fine."

His phone rang. He looked at the screen, and said to Pru, "I'm sorry, do you mind if I take this?"

Pru gave her permission with a nod. Tatt turned away and took a couple of steps. "Hello," he said quietly. "Yes . . . I have the chops already . . . Well, there are still a few sprouts left . . . Yes, I'll be home soon."

Pru was mortified to overhear this personal conversation and busied herself by brushing nonexistent crumbs off the counter and into the sink. When Tatt finished, he said, "Ms. Parke, you'll let me know if Mrs. Templeton says anything else about her journey back to Primrose House that afternoon."

"Yes, of course I will. But you don't really suspect her, do you?" she asked, hoping to keep Tatt in this unusually friendly mood.

He shrugged off the suggestion. "She's on CCTV at the London hotel, leaving just when she said she did, and returning not three hours later. She would have to have made a quick job of it, if she did it, but still, it's possible."

Pru couldn't get used to speaking about murder in such an offhanded manner, but thought that police must have to harden themselves to it.

Tatt pulled a set of keys out of his pocket and said, not looking at her, "You'll mention that I looked in on you?"

"I'll be sure to say so."

Alone at last, she poured herself wine and swirled the red liquid around in its glass as bits and pieces of people's stories swirled around in her mind. Perhaps the results of her enquiries would mean nothing to the investigation, but just in case, she jotted down what she knew on the first piece of paper at hand, which turned out to be the back of a stray plant list. But when it came time to pack her bag for London, she didn't have the heart to pack her list of clues as well.

CHAPTER 25

On Friday morning, Pru was almost to Primrose House when she realized she hadn't put her phone in her pocket. Fearing Christopher would try to check in and get no response, which would not be the best way to start the weekend, she trooped back to her cottage. As she neared, she heard her phone ringing and raced to get there before it stopped.

"Hi," she said, catching her breath.

"You aren't directing the excavation, are you?" Christopher asked.

"No," she said, laughing. "They're pretty much on their own doing the terracing. I forgot my phone and just came to the cottage to get it." She glanced at her weekend bag, sitting in the middle of the room all ready to go. "Ivy and Robbie are taking me to the station. I'll be in at seven."

"You'll ring when you arrive at Charing Cross?"

"Of course I will."

* * *

But he rang first, just as the train pulled in.

"I've been held up, and I didn't want you to wait," he said.

"I'll get the Tube," Pru said. "I can meet you at your flat."

"Too many changes. Take a taxi."

"But couldn't I just take the Northern line to Embankment and then—"

"Please take a taxi. I'm sorry I can't be there to collect you, and I don't want to imagine you traipsing about on the Underground." He wasn't all that fond of public transport, she knew, and his voice held a note of frustration. She thought it better to accommodate him.

"Yes, a taxi. To your flat?"

"There's a pub just on the corner from my building — the Green Man — I'll meet you there. I'll be there as soon as I can."

"Don't worry," she said. "I'm quite good at entertaining myself."

At the pub — a posh place with polished brass fixtures and wood waxed to within an inch of its old life — she settled into a booth with a pint of London Pride in hand, lucky enough to arrive between crowds: The after-work drinkers had left and the Friday-night partyers had yet to arrive. She kept her coat on for a while, but finally shed it and tried to nurse her beer along. About nine-thirty, the pub began to fill again, the noise level rose, and she noticed people eyeing her as she sat in a booth on her own. She got another pint. She was halfway through it when Christopher walked up, slid into the booth, and put his arm around her.

"God, I'm sorry to be so late," he said. "I wanted to finish up a few things to have the weekend free, and it took longer than I expected."

The lines on his face looked deeper than usual — a trick of the light or a reflection of how hard he'd been working. She reached up and tried to smooth out the furrow between his brows with her thumb.

"I've been fine, just sitting here thinking. Pleasant thoughts," she assured him.

His lips brushed her temple. She raised her chin and gave him a brief kiss, but thought better of it and kissed him again, lingering this time. The pub chatter receded until a burly fellow bumped the table as he passed and brought them back to reality.

She gave a small, embarrassed smile. "I can quite forget myself around you."

He grinned and nodded toward her pint. "Same again?"

"No, that's my second. Would you like it?"

"I wouldn't mind. Cheers," he said, and took a long drink.

She admired the right side of his face, which had progressed from the swollen, black-and-blue condition of the previous weekend to a mottled yellow-and-green. "Nice," she said. "It looks like an impressionist painting of daffodils."

"I suffer for my art," Christopher said, and she laughed. "Are you ready?" he asked.

"Christopher, we won't talk about it this weekend, will we?"

She hadn't needed to say what it was, he understood. "Not a word. We have two days to ourselves."

"Good," she said, hand resting lightly on his knee, "Then I am ready."

He helped her with her coat as four women squeezed by to take possession of the table. "I'm glad you're here," he whispered in her ear.

"I'm glad, too," she said.

A bitter wind whipped down the street as they walked to his flat. Snow had been predicted even in London. "I got the primroses planted this week," she said, pulling her coat collar higher. "I can only hope that if it snows in Sussex, it covers them completely so they don't freeze."

"Will someone check on them?" Christopher asked.

"No, they must brave the elements on their own now."

When they reached his flat, she stood just inside the door, taking it all in. "I wasn't able to get a good look at the place the first time I was here," she said, referring to the dinner that his son, Graham, had cooked for them before she started at Primrose House.

Christopher took her coat. "Well," he said, "here's your chance."

The furnishings — leather sofa and chairs, dark wood tables, and scant ornament — were decidedly masculine. Pru stopped at a table with the only decoration in the room — three framed photos. She looked closer and saw an old photo of a couple with a young boy and even younger girl, one of Graham as a teenager, and a photo of her and Christopher taken at the hotel in Kent where they'd spent the weekend. In the photo, she was wearing the dress that Jo gave her — the one she'd brought along this weekend for dinner at Gasparetti's. *He's going to think it's the only dress I own,* she thought. The fact that it was true wasn't the point.

Bookshelves covered half a wall, and she began perusing the titles. At least two shelves were taken up with natural histories of various parts of Britain. There was half a shelf of police-related titles — Pru wondered just how captivating *The Gathering and Analysis of Evidence* could be — another shelf of international thrillers, and, on the bottom shelf, Harry Potter books, *The Hobbit*, *Lord of the Rings*, and a row of old, cloth-bound books with frayed edges and faded titles. She bent over to take a closer look.

"That's Graham's shelf," Christopher said from behind her, "for when he visited. By the time I finished reading him *The Hobbit*, he was well able to read it back to me."

Pru pulled out one of the old books, sat back on the sofa, and opened it. "*The Happy Return,*" she read.

Christopher smiled. "Horatio Hornblower. Those were mine," he said, "and I'll give them to Graham when he's settled. Have you read them?"

"No seafaring sagas for me. I read Pollyanna."

"I don't know it," he said, shaking his head.

"No, you wouldn't." Pru said. "They aren't really boys books. My sixth-grade teacher brought her own copies into our classroom. I read them all and carried on so much about them, for Christmas that year I got the whole set from my folks." Her smile faded.

He sat down next to her. "For a while, I wanted to go to sea."

"You may have given that up," Pru said, "but I've always played Pollyanna's Glad Game — looking on the bright side of things. So much so that I've been compared to her most of my life. It can become a bit tiresome."

Christopher leaned back and pulled her after him and they sat quietly. She liked being in his flat. A host of problems awaited her back at Primrose House, but she felt an incredible lightness in London, there with Christopher's arms around her and with his bed to look forward to.

"I need to freshen up a bit," she said, sitting up. "We're working far too many hours a day, and I came straight from the garden."

"More manure?" he asked.

"Not today," she said, laughing. "At least I don't have to worry about that."

"All right," he said. "I'll meet you in bed."

* * *

She walked into the bedroom. He'd left a lamp on, and he had one arm stretched across the empty pillow. She heard his breathing, deep and regular. She clicked off the lamp and he stirred.

"Pru?"

"Yes?"

"I'm not asleep," he mumbled.

"Of course you aren't," she said. She heard him snore lightly. She crawled in bed, displacing his arm just long enough to get under it so that she could snuggle her backside against him. He sighed, put his face against her neck. She was awake only a few minutes herself, just long enough to listen to the sounds of life in the city — traffic, a distant siren, the rumble of the Underground now actually above ground this far out of the city center.

She awoke to a pearly gray light in the flat and Christopher's hand on her thigh. She turned onto her back and found him watching her, head propped up on his hand.

"I've dreamed of waking up and finding you in my bed," he said.

* * *

It was an escape — she would be the first to admit it. A weekend away with no thought to what she'd left behind and only friends and entertainment to be had. Christopher did his best to be interested when they visited the Garden Museum, listening and asking questions as she explained the Arts and Crafts movement, how it related to garden design, and the importance of Hidcote Manor as a lasting example of the style.

She took him upstairs to the permanent exhibit of gardening through the ages. He enjoyed the collection of old tools. She was examining a row of grafting and budding knives — one with a carved mahogany handle, another with Bakelite — when she noticed Christopher patting his pockets in the never-ending search for his reading glasses. She went over to see he stood at a case with several long, straight glass tubes, each about two inches wide.

He turned slightly pink when she went up to him, and she laughed. "It says they're cucumber straighteners," she said. "Just what do you think we get up to in the garden?"

* * *

They walked over Lambeth Bridge and along the Victoria Embankment. The pavement was clear, but a fine sifting of snow like powdered sugar remained on the bare tree branches and the tops of evergreens. That afternoon, Christopher left her at Jo's, as he needed to check on a few things at the station.

The five of them met at Gasparetti's that evening, Riccardo greeted Pru with open arms and a kiss on each cheek. They were a happy gathering, despite the obvious discomfort of Cordelia, Jo's daughter, who was quite pregnant and due in a week's time. Cordelia and her partner, Lucy, had announced the pregnancy not long before Pru left London and in the few months she'd been away, Cordelia's tall, thin outline had morphed into something quite different. "I look like a whale," she said, "and I can't sleep at all."

Pru thought Lucy looked as if she might be missing some sleep, too, but they kept up their sides of the lively dinner conversation, regardless. Cordelia told the story of how her father, Alan, who lived in Edinburgh, had shopped for an antique pram for his impending grandchild and had it completely refitted to be twenty-first-century safe. Jo, a property manager with no knowledge of gardening but a great love of flowers, revealed she had a wealthy new client with a large town garden. Jo said she wished Pru still lived in London so she could design it. "And besides," Jo said, reaching across the table to take Pru's hand, "I miss you."

* * *

"Subtle," Pru said, checking Christopher's small fridge the next morning when he returned from getting the newspaper. Inside, she'd found a half pint of buttermilk. "Hoping I'd fix you some biscuits?"

A small smile. "Perhaps I got it just to hear you talk Texan."

"You might oughta think twice about that," she said, pulling him close and slipping into her best Texas accent, "'cause when I start, I can talk a 'coon right out of a tree."

* * *

Jo sent a text on Sunday afternoon to say Cordelia had gone into labor — speculating it had something to do with the lasagna the night before — and said they were headed to hospital. And so, as Pru and Christopher left the Westminster Abbey after an organ recital, Pru switched her phone back on in case there was news. It rang immediately.

"The baby!" she exclaimed, gripping Christopher's arm for a second before walking a few steps away to answer. She returned not a minute later, her face white as a sheet.

"That was Cate. Liam's been arrested."

CHAPTER 26

"Has he been charged?" Christopher asked. "Or have they taken him in for questioning?"

"He's . . . they're . . . I don't know." Pru shook her head. "I could barely understand Cate, she was crying so hard. They've taken him in because" — Her voice caught in her throat — "remember last week they found Ned's phone at Liam and Fergal's cottage?" He nodded. "It was planted there. That was obvious, wasn't it? That's why they didn't take him in at the time." She searched his face, willing Christopher to say that this was true.

Christopher cocked his head, a noncommittal reply. "And so why take him in now?"

Pru frowned. "Call records, something about Ned's phone service being canceled and so it took a while to find the . . . It's Tatt," she spat out his name. "He's just grand-standing. Make a big show of hauling Liam in on a Sunday."

Christopher put his arm around her and directed her toward Parliament Square and a taxi.

"Come on, I'll drive you back," he said.

"No." She stopped in her tracks to make the point. "No, you will not. There's no reason for you to take me home, and it would put you back far too late. I'll take the train and go to the police station. You won't be able to do anything — Tatt won't let you. Put me on the train."

She looked away so that he wouldn't see the longing in her eyes. She would, of course, prefer that he be there, but he couldn't fix this, and she wouldn't ask him to try.

"And leave you to march in and fight Liam's battle for him?" he asked. "I won't let you do that."

It was a standoff. She felt him watching as she looked from park bench to tree to Big Ben across the road.

"I won't go to the police station tonight," she said. "You're right, I can't help tonight." He continued to watch. "I'll ring you when I get home, and I'll ring in the morning. But I want to be available for Cate."

"What if Liam—" he asked.

"I don't *want* him to be guilty," she said. "How could he have done that? How?"

"You don't know what a moment of rage can do," he said, "although you've certainly seen the results." He sighed, put his arm back around her, and began propelling her once more toward a taxi. "Do you want to stop and get your things or can you leave them here?"

A compromise. "Oh, I can leave them here for some future weekend."

"Weekends," he said. She detected a bitter tone, and stopped before they got to the curb to look at him. "Our weekends," he said, "are—"

"Amazing?" she offered.

He smiled. "Not enough." He stuck his hand out to a passing cab, which pulled over. "We need time."

She nodded, crawled into the taxi, and settled into the roomy bench seat, tucking her arm through his and resting her head on his shoulder. There was nothing to discuss. What could they do? They both had responsibilities that left no space to even think about spending more time together.

As they rode to the station, he reached into his pocket and pulled out a key. "So you don't have to wait in the pub next time. I'm sorry I didn't have it for you last weekend."

Her hand clasped his as she took it. "Thanks." She dropped the key in her bag.

At the rail station, they stood just outside the gate to the platform. He took her hands. "Tomorrow, I'll see if I can talk with Hobbes, although I don't know if he'll be able to tell me much."

She nodded as she began her own mental checklist, all the while remembering that she was not a police officer.

"If Liam was with Cate, why didn't she say so?" Christopher asked. "You've tried to find that out, haven't you?"

"Yes," Pru said, confessing her foray into the investigation. "Neither of them will say." But she would try again, she thought.

"It's almost certain that Ned was killed in the afternoon," Christopher said.

"How do you know that?"

"The body was . . ." He raised his eyebrows.

"Yes?"

"It was well past the rigor mortis stage. After twelve hours or so the stiffness begins to leave . . ."

She took a deep breath and swallowed, trying to clear from her mind the picture of Ned lying on top of the yew with a pool of blood on his chest.

"If Liam was with Cate, was it all night, or did he go home," Christopher said. "The body had been moved after death — pushed to the side." He searched her face. "Are you all right?"

Christopher was using her as a sounding board, talking aloud through what he knew about the case. She wouldn't spoil the moment by becoming nauseous. "Yes," she said. Barely. "But when was it moved?"

"Probably sometime during the night. Do you remember the pocketknife? It could be the murderer's. He could've missed it and come back to look."

Pocketknife, she repeated to herself. *Why is the pocketknife a clue?* "A light!" she shouted, startling not just the other people

185

near the gate, but herself as well. "I saw a light during the night," she finished in a frantic whisper. "I just remembered."

"What time?"

The memory had only just popped into her mind. "About three, I think. I wasn't sleeping well, and I got up to get a glass of water. When I went back to bed, I looked out the window — it faces toward the bottom of the walled garden and the wood — and I saw a light." She frowned as she tried to remember the moment. "There's a lot of growth between my cottage and down where Ned was, but it's mostly just bare branches now. The light seemed to be jumping around. I was groggy and thought that it must've been headlights from the lane reflecting on the tree trunks. I got back in bed and went to sleep. It was sort of like a dream." She looked up at him. "I was at home when the murderer came back."

That was the wrong thing to point out to him. His face grew taut, and he grabbed her and held her close. But it didn't scare her — the discovery gave her a thrill of excitement.

"Was it headlights, do you think?" she asked. "The track is uneven, and so headlights would bounce." Her eyes lit up. "Or it could've been a torch! If someone was looking for the pocketknife, he would need a light. That's why the light was jumping." She raised her eyebrows, waiting for his response.

"You'll tell Hobbes about it immediately?"

"Yes, first thing tomorrow."

"And let the police manage the rest. Please don't—"

"Go off half-cocked?" she offered.

He laughed. "It's 'go off at half-cock' here."

She kissed him. "Is it? I'll remember that."

* * *

Only two other passengers were in her train carriage, both wearing ear buds, which allowed her the pretense of privacy when she rang Cate, who had little more to offer.

"They won't tell me anything," Cate said, sounding weepy but strong. "Fergal rang. There's a call on Dad's mobile from Liam. That's all I know."

186

"Cate, Liam needs to say where he was that afternoon and evening." Cate offered no reply, and so after a moment, Pru asked, "Do you know if they will keep him at the police station overnight? Is Fergal with him?"

Cate thought he was, but she didn't know if or when they would let Liam go. "I wanted to be there," she said, "but I don't want to make it worse for him."

Or for you. "You're right to stay away," she said. "You have to think of Nanda."

When the train approached the Frant station, she rang Tommy, and just as Tommy pulled his taxi into her drive, she rang Christopher.

"Did you leave a light on?" he asked.

"Yes," she said as she got out, "and everything looks fine."

"Ask Tommy to wait until you're inside."

To ease his mind — and hers, too — she walked through the cottage, looked under the bed, in the shower, and she opened the wardrobe. It took all of thirty seconds.

"Right, I'm alone," she reported as she waved Tommy on his way.

"I should be there," Christopher said.

CHAPTER 27

"Sergeant Hobbes? It's Pru. Can you talk?"

She heard background noise from the station, then scuffling, a click, and quiet. "Yes, just for a moment. You heard, I suppose?"

"Cate rang last night. I was in London, but I'm home now. Can you tell me what happened?"

"We've got Ned's mobile records, and they show two unanswered calls from Liam — one the evening before Ned died and the other, the next evening."

"After Ned had been killed? If Liam had done it, why would he try to ring Ned?"

"This is Tatt's show, Pru, and he's trying to make the most of it."

"Is Liam still there?"

"We're letting him go this afternoon."

"So, Liam isn't a suspect?" she asked.

"He isn't clear," Hobbes said. "He won't tell us where he was that afternoon or evening — just 'out,' he says. It's as if he wants to make himself look suspicious."

"Christopher said that Ned's body had been moved," she said, keeping her voice even and the image off the screen in her mind. "That perhaps the murderer came back looking for something — maybe the pocketknife?"

"Inspector Pearse told you that?"

"I saw a light during that night," and told him what she'd told Christopher.

"A torch. It's possible," he said. "Do you keep torches in the shed there?"

"No," she replied. "I have one in my cottage — you can come take a look. And one in my car. I don't know what they might have at Primrose House."

"Any more thoughts about the pocketknife?" he asked.

Why was the pocketknife coming back to haunt her? "No, not at the moment."

Primrose House

9 February

Pru,

    I do hate to bring this up, but I want to make sure that we are focused on our goals for the garden, and not all of this extraneous activity. I realize you are great friends with Liam and Fergal, but really you cannot let what's happened take you away from readying the gardens for summer. How wonderful for the Duffys to have such a supporter in you, but the police must do their work, and we must do ours.

    We may not be able to keep the Duffys on, of course, depending on how things turn out. I'm sure we'll fill in with other workers eventually, but in the meantime, I hope you don't mind picking up the slack.

    Best,
    Davina

The amount of daylight increased ever so slightly — sunrise was stretching itself toward seven in the morning, and sunset wasn't upon them until five. It afforded them more time to work, and Pru, in an effort to show Davina that she took her job seriously, took advantage of every second of it. Pru consulted with Gordon's workers, who still seemed to be discussing, not building, the terraced beds and stairway. She planted half of the six dozen roses that were waiting to go in the walled garden, including English, species, and landscape. She hoped Liam and Fergal would return to work Tuesday, regardless of Davina's threat, as she needed them to work on the path between the house and the walled garden, stopping just short of the approach to the brush pile. Police tape or no, it wasn't a place anyone headed on purpose.

* * *

She had put the garden and murder out of her mind during the weekend in London until the end, when word came in about Liam, but now she had plenty of time to mull over the details, including Robbie's brief disappearance from Chaffinch's, and Hugo's activities on that Thursday. She picked up the plant list she'd used to write down clues, adding and amending what she had. She underlined Hugo's name as his whereabouts gained prominence in her mind. Perhaps the police didn't even know Hugo and Ned were related.

Hugo had seemed a nice enough fellow, but he seemed to carry a long-term family grudge against Ned. Hadn't she read somewhere that most victims were murdered by a family member?

But first, as soon as she could on Monday, she rang Ivy, who had never mentioned to Pru or the police why she had driven past Primrose House and happened to see Davina's car that Thursday afternoon. Now, Pru knew that Ivy had been heading for Chaffinch's, because Robbie had gone missing. Did Ivy suspect her son had something to do with Ned's murder?

"I thought I'd stop by at the end of the day," Pru said on the phone, "just to say hello." She added, "For a cup of tea."

Ivy laughed. "Yes, we'd better stick to tea for a while, now hadn't we?"

* * *

Ivy and Robbie lived at the edge of town in Victorian terraced housing, brick first floors and pebbledash above. Pru picked out their house at first glance. The tidy front garden and the shiny green door set against the tatty appearance of the rest of the row were a dead giveaway. The inside of the two-up-two-down house was neat as a pin, too.

Robbie was thrilled to see Pru at his own house and took great pains to show her every special thing that he owned, from Robin Hood action figures to photos of his visit to his aunt Viola in Bristol. When his mother called him to the kitchen for his tea — their early-evening meal — Pru settled into a chair in the sitting room.

Ivy came out with two cups. "There now, he'll be quite busy. I let him watch *Blue Peter* on the telly while he eats." She sighed. "Tell me now, Pru, how are you doing? It seems as if you're running a race every day in the garden."

Pru brushed off Ivy's concern. "Oh, we've a great deal to do, but I believe it will get done." She thought for a moment. "I hope it will get done." She put her cup down on the coffee table. "Ivy, did you know that Cate, Ned's daughter, is staying with Francine Rosse at the moment?"

"Francine mentioned it," Ivy said. "Isn't she lovely to help Cate out like that?"

"She is, yes" Pru replied, looking down in her lap. "Francine told me that there was a small problem with Robbie on that Thursday. They couldn't find him for just an hour or so." She glanced up at Ivy.

Ghostly white and with eyes like saucers, Ivy whispered, "Oh no, Pru, he didn't do anything. You don't think that of Robbie, do you?"

"Certainly not," Pru said. "But Ivy, could someone have wanted to use him as a scapegoat? Set it up and let Robbie take the blame for what happened? After all, his jacket was wrapped around the hatchet."

"No," Ivy said as she shook her head. "No one could be that beastly, could they? Robbie must've left it somewhere and that evil person picked it up and used it."

"Did Robbie tell you where he went?" Pru asked.

Ivy smiled and shrugged. "You know how he loves his stories," she said. "It isn't always easy to sort out where the Merry Men leave off and the real world begins." She picked up the hem of her apron and ran her fingers down the edge. "You won't say anything to Sergeant Hobbes, will you? Or that inspector?"

"But Ivy," Pru said, "I don't think they would actually accuse Robbie of being involved in Ned's murder."

"Oh, it isn't that," Ivy said, shaking her head, her face pinched with anxiety. "It's Chaffinch's. I wouldn't want to get them in trouble. It's a good place, and it's just a tiny mistake. But if Chaffinch's gets into trouble over this, they might have to close and" — she swallowed hard and Pru could see tears in her eyes — "then what would Robbie do? Where would he go? I could never have him with me every day while I work, and there are no other places nearby. At least none I'd send him to."

Let others cover up murder. Ivy's only concern was a comfortable and happy place for her son to stay while she cooked and cleaned in other people's houses. It didn't answer the question of where Robbie had got to for that hour, but Pru couldn't see herself pursuing the matter.

"I can't imagine one little mistake would lead to their closure, but don't worry. I will not tell the sergeant or Inspector Tatt," Pru said. "I hope it's all right that I tell Christopher."

"Oh, of course you tell your Mr. Pearse." Ivy smiled, her good humor restored.

"Do you know all of Robbie's mates at Chaffinch's?" Pru asked. "It's just that he told me something about keeping

193

a secret for someone. You don't think that had anything to do with the time he was missing?"

Ivy dismissed Pru's question with a wave. "Oh, his secret. Yes, Robbie told me about it. He and little Andrew at Chaffinch's both love to play Robin Hood. When they're outdoors, they'll go hide in the wood there on the grounds and call it Sherwood Forest even though there's only about three trees. It seems to occupy them and there's no harm in it. But Robbie likes to think no one knows, so he calls it a secret."

Robbie's television show had finished, and he appeared in the doorway, ready to read them a story about an adventure Robin Hood had one day when he was out hunting for acorns.

Pru stayed and had her own tea with Ivy — chicken-and-leek pie. Ivy insisted that Pru take the remainder of the pie home. They wouldn't need it, she said, because, the next day, Robbie would have his pint at the Two Bells, and Ivy always gave him egg and chips for his tea on those evenings. After a feeble protest, Pru accepted.

Before she left, she remembered the archer's bow she had found in the wood and described it to Ivy. "It isn't his, is it?"

"No, Robbie wouldn't have anything so fine," Ivy said.

"If no one claims it, could he have it?" Pru asked. "Maybe he could play with it only when someone else is around? No arrows, of course."

* * *

Pru's life seemed to revolve around three activities — gardening, which took every daylight hour, asking questions about Ned's murder, which carried on seemingly nonstop, and talking with Christopher. She wished that last activity could take most of her time, but in reality it took the least. On Tuesday, as soon as she could get away from the garden, she dashed to the flat to talk with Cate.

When Pru pressed the bell, she noticed the dirt under her fingernails, and wondered if there was a point to showering at all these days, as she seemed to be in the dirt more than out of it. She stuck her hands in her pockets and waited. Pru's surprise visits weren't going well. This was the second try and the second time Cate wasn't home. She reached out to press the bell one more time, when she heard a voice across the road.

"She's gone out with the little miss, about an hour ago."

It was, of course, Arabella Sock, whose country accent was as broad as her smile. She had Trevor in tow. Pru walked to the end of the drive. "Thanks," she said, wondering if Mrs. Sock was taking messages for the house now. "I'll come back later."

"You're welcome to wait here for them. I can put the kettle on."

Mrs. Sock and Trevor looked dressed for a walk. "I don't want to hold you up if you were about to leave," Pru said.

"Oh, Trevor and I are in no hurry, are we now, boy?" The beagle sat down.

Well, why not? "Thanks so much," Pru said as she walked across the road and up Mrs. Sock's front path past twiggy spires, thorny roses, and a tangled mass of clematis, all waiting for spring. "I'm Pru Parke, a friend of Cate's."

"I'm Arabella Sock, and this is Trevor." Trevor stood and Pru knelt, putting a hand out for the dog to sniff.

"Hello, Trevor," she said, petting him as his back half wagged. "That's a very nice name you have."

Pru followed her hosts down a narrow hall, careful not to jostle a wall shelf teeming with photos. On the way, Mrs. Sock pointed to a jolly-looking man standing next to a brown-and-white cow in one of the frames. "There's my Trevor," she said as they walked into the kitchen.

"Trevor?" Pru asked. The beagle gave a minor yip.

"My dear husband Trevor died three years ago," Mrs. Sock said as she put the kettle on and reached for the tea tin. "So, I sold our dairy farm and moved here to be near our two boys.

They thought I needed a companion, seeing as how I didn't have my own Trevor any longer, and a friend of theirs knew about this re-homing for beagles. Well, when they told me they had a beagle named Trevor that were looking for a family, I knew we were meant for each other. Isn't that right?" Mrs. Sock looked down at Trevor, who sat at her feet and whined.

"Do you need a bickie?" she asked him. Trevor stood, his tail a metronome set on allegro. Mrs. Sock reached in the pocket of her coat and pulled out a treat.

"I think Nanda would love to meet Trevor," Pru said, taking her own treat from the plate that Mrs. Sock put out. She remembered how Nanda and Trevor barked at each other across the road.

"She's a cute one, that little miss," Mrs. Sock said, pouring the tea. "And her mum is lovely. I notice she has a friend who looks in on her. I'd say he's a mite more helpful than that other one lurking in the laurel." She raised an eyebrow.

Whoa, Pru thought. *Mrs. Sock really does keep an eye on things.*

It was just one cup of tea and a generous slice of Bakewell tart, but it was a restorative visit. They talked about gardens and cows — the Socks had raised Ayrshires. In the course of the conversation, Mrs. Sock asked Pru if she had any family.

Pru opened her mouth and after a moment stumbled over a few words. "I have . . . We don't . . ."

"Trevor does so love the little ones," Mrs. Sock said, deftly changing the subject.

When the woman noticed Cate arrive home — there was an excellent view of Francine's drive and front step from the window in Mrs. Sock's front room — Pru stood to leave.

At the door, Mrs. Sock said, "You know, Pru, there were a good few years when my sister and I didn't speak to each other. I don't even remember what it was about now. But I was too proud and she was too stubborn — or maybe it were the other way round — to do anything about it." Mrs. Sock smiled. "Then, one day, she rang me — or I rang her — and it was as if nothing had ever happened." She shrugged. "Families. You just be patient." She patted Pru's arm.

Tears sprang to Pru's eyes before she could stop them. She had the sudden urge to tell Arabella Sock the entire story of her family in hopes that she would ring Simon and sort it all out.

"Thanks for the tea, Mrs. Sock."

CHAPTER 28

"Pru, come in. Cup of tea?" Cate asked.

"I'd love one, thanks," Pru said. Even if she ended up floating back to her cottage, she knew that tea made a fine conversation lubricant. "Where's Nanda?"

"I dropped her at Chaffinch's. Francine was finished for the day, and they've gone to the shops," Cate said. "It's a great entertainment, and Nanda gets an ice lolly at the end of it all." She hesitated, and then said, "Jamie often rings about this time, and it's easier if Nanda isn't around to hear. If I don't answer, he stops by."

With tea in hand, Pru asked more about Jamie.

"We were a bad match from the beginning," Cate said, "but I was dazzled by him. He was older, good-looking, a charmer, and I was itching to leave home. It was only after we'd married I found out what a control freak he is. He would always say, 'I'll take care of it' to whatever I wanted to do myself. It was easier to just go along with it. Then I found his red book."

Pru started. "Red book?"

"He has a little red diary," Cate said, frowning, "and inside was what looked like an accounting. He kept track of people that he thought had wronged him." She looked up at Pru, her eyes wide in amazement. "Can you imagine? Every little thing he thought someone had done to him, in a tidy list."

So different from Repton's Red Book that only promised a beautiful landscape. "Did you recognize any of the names?"

Cate stared into her tea and nodded almost imperceptibly. "The first one I saw was a fellow he worked with last year, who gave Nanda that little pig there. He was just being nice, but Jamie didn't like it." She looked up at Pru, her face hard. "That fellow's name was crossed off, and I remembered not long after the pig, this same fellow got blamed for mixing up sprayers at work. Instead of spraying fertilizer on flats of annuals to go out as summer bedding, it was a herbicide — killed them all off."

"You think Jamie did that — mixed up the sprayers on purpose?"

"I don't know," Cate said, as if arguing with herself. "The fellow admitted to the mistake, so maybe not, but it was awfully convenient and Jamie seemed pleased. There were other grievances in his red book — petty things, little jealousies."

"And other people were punished?" Pru asked.

"No, not that I knew of," Cate said. "Yet. I know it sounds as if I'm imagining it, but it worries me, because I saw Liam's name in it."

"What had Liam done?"

"Talked to me in the Two Bells, that's all. I'd gone to meet Francine — quite rare, Jamie actually letting me out on my own. I couldn't have said more than two words to Liam, but someone must've seen and told Jamie."

"Is that when he hit you?" Pru asked.

Cate wrapped her arms around herself. "He hit me when he saw me with his red book. He hit me and then he fell on the sofa and cried and cried. Such drama," she said in a bitter tone. "I took Nanda and left. I rang Francine, and we came here. The next day, when I was sure he was at work, I went back and packed a couple of bags."

"Is he bothering you?"

"So far he's mostly ringing. He's very upset about Dad."

"Did your dad really want you to stay with him?" Pru asked, unwilling to paint Ned as an enabler.

Cate shrugged, and poured them both more tea. "Dad always thought about his own growing up — just his mum and him, no dad — and how hard it was. Then, when Mum died, only him and me. 'Two parents, Catie,' he'd say, 'you need the two.' I was going to tell him what happened after we were settled here, but I never got the chance." Tears filled her eyes. "It's just as well."

Pru thought back to the timing of that event. Perhaps Ned supported Jamie because he didn't know how his daughter was being treated. But Liam knew. And right after the holidays, Liam suddenly couldn't stand to be in Ned's presence. He argued with Ned, and shouted at him that something needed to be done. An incredible sadness filled Pru's heart. Did Liam blame Ned for what Jamie had done?

Francine and Nanda tumbled in the door, and after many greetings and several goodbyes, Pru left for home, having missed another opportunity to ask about Liam's whereabouts. She thought about Jamie's red book, the list of petty grievances and little jealousies — things other people had done to him. Did he think she had taken a job meant for him? Was her name in his red book?

* * *

That night, she tucked herself up in bed and waited for Christopher to ring. Without him as a living hot-water bottle beside her, she had gone through her usual routine of laying wool socks on the warm Aga until they were toasty, at which point she pulled them on, dived under the covers, and peered out to admire her surroundings. She loved her cottage in lamplight, the way the two-foot-thick brick walls gave off a warm glow and the huge oak beams cast shadows on the ceiling. No well-planed wood here, but rustic, massive pieces that suited the cottage's former cowshed persona. When her phone rang, she snuggled down and began with the news of the day.

"It's a boy," she said. "Cordelia was in labor for eight hours, and finally, out he came. No problems. Jo says he looks just like Alan — seems a bit of a stretch for a newborn to already look like his grandfather."

"That's good news. What's he called?"

"They've named him Oliver. Oliver Alan. I'm not sure what surname they're using," she mused.

"And who is Oliver?" Christopher asked.

"Don't know," Pru said. "Maybe it's another family name. The weekend went awfully quickly, didn't it?"

"It's always a rush," he said.

"There isn't much we can do about it at the moment," Pru said. "Perhaps when this is all finished . . . the garden, you know." He had said it before — they needed more time together.

"Perhaps I'll take you away somewhere."

"I will let you," she whispered. "Now, time to catch you up."

She launched into telling him what she hadn't said over the weekend about Hugo and the chat with the *Courier*'s editor. "I thought I'd try again to talk with him," she said. "It's getting difficult to take any time away from the garden, though. I can't let Davina think I'm a slacker."

That elicited a small laugh. 'How could anyone think that?"

"And there's something else." Briefly, she told him the story of Robbie's one-hour vanishing act, and went into greater length to explain why Ivy didn't want attention called to it. "What should I do?" she asked.

"Would it do any good to talk with Robbie?" Christopher asked. "Or find out from Francine if he's close to any adult — either someone who works there or who visits Chaffinch's. It isn't ideal, keeping it from the police. At the very least, Hobbes should know. But I understand her concern."

She wasn't quite ready to alarm him with the story of Jamie and his red book — perhaps she would save that for the weekend — and so she veered off into a long and involved account of her tea with Arabella Sock and Trevor. "Wouldn't it be lovely if Cate got to know her. Nanda would have a granny figure around."

"What did you learn from Cate about Liam?"

"Foiled again — Francine and Nanda arrived before I could get to it. I'll ask more as soon as I can get Liam or Cate on their own."

This collaboration eased her mind. Christopher had allowed her equal say in the evidence, and it gave her a sense of power. "Thank you for talking me through this." A bit of gloominess crept in. "I miss you," she said.

He was silent a moment. "I'll see you on Friday."

CHAPTER 29

Midweek, the box arrived. The delivery truck pulled off the lane just as Pru got to her front door at the end of the day. Lydia had taken great care in packing — inside the shipping box was another box, and inside that was the box from Titche's department store in Dallas, from the days when department-store boxes were worth keeping. A whole life in a shirt box, Pru thought, as she took it out and set it on the sofa. When she lifted the lid, she caught a whiff of old paper and perhaps a memory of her mother's favorite cologne, Youth Dew.

The contents had shifted slightly, but everything looked intact. Under the packet of letters that were tied with a faded blue ribbon, Pru saw her school awards and an article about her dad, who had worked for the highway department, and his involvement in building the Dallas-Fort Worth turnpike in the '50s. Below that were old photos, and it was to those that Pru first went, sorting through the people she recognized, looking deeper to find — and there it was.

A copy of the same photo that Birdie had shown Pru had been within Pru's reach nearly her entire life. Her parents, Birdie and George, Pru and Simon — the whole family, such as it was.

Pru stared at it for a few minutes and then went back to the packet of letters. She had tried to look at them just after her mother died and had discovered they were letters her mother had written but never sent. Both the letters and the unaddressed envelopes were yellow with age, and brittle. She took one out gingerly, and, heart beating too fast for comfort, she began to read.

> *My sweet baby boy,*
> *I will never see you grow up. I will never clap as you stand for the first time, and I will not make you custard for your tea. I will never hear you call me "mama." I wish you could know how much I love you.*

Pru trembled as she put the letter down gently. Tears started flowing with the realization of what she held. She'd read the letter before, but had assumed that her mother had had a miscarriage, and she was writing through her grief for a lost child. This had been too much for Pru to bear, and she had put the letters away, not wanting to intrude on her mother's grief. Now, Pru knew the truth. Her mother was indeed grieving for a lost child, but not one who had died — one she had given up. It was a letter to Simon.

She took another out and read a few lines.

> *My dear boy,*
> *You should be playing cricket by now. Is the bat too much for you? And what about football? Your father wishes he could teach you American football — he wishes he could just see you, hold you. You're probably too old for that these days, aren't you?*

Although they weren't dated, Pru realized that the letters followed the passage of the years. She opened another and read:

> *Dear boy,*
> *You have a sister. I hope someday you will know that. She looks like you. Are you surprised?*

Pru's crying became sobs. "Why?" she asked the air. "Why didn't you tell us?" She carefully put the letters back in their envelopes. These letters were not hers to read. They belonged to Simon, and she must give them to him.

* * *

Pru was so very happy to see Friday come, and thought she might just be able to take the entire weekend off. Perhaps she and Christopher could go for a drive somewhere — they might have dinner at the hotel where they had spent their first weekend. The memory of that time, sitting by the fire and walking to the wood, distracted her at the end of the workday.

She lingered near Primrose House after everyone had left the site. The stonework should begin soon, and after that they could plant. She would need to overplant in order to fill the space and make it a good show for the open garden day in July. She made her way down the slope, enjoying the silence and the emptiness of the winter landscape. There was still no sign of green from the trees, but she had noticed new growth pushing up out of the earth, displacing the damp, matted cover of decaying leaves. Wood anemones, columbine, perhaps a clump of snake's head fritillary in the damp spots of the meadow. It would be Pru's first spring to see native wildflowers in their habitat. And with any luck, a few primroses.

The light was growing dim as she walked just inside the beech wood, and then turned to look out toward the site of the pond. She heard the arrow sing past her ear and heard it "thunk" into the tree trunk before she realized what had happened. It hit the tree almost directly in front of her face, and still quivered from its swift journey from bow to trunk. She swung round and looked out, realizing it must've passed inches from her head. Her chest tightened, her knees went wobbly, and she stumbled as she spun left and right trying to see deeper into the copse, but it was too dark to make anything out, and she heard no sound.

"Hello?" she called, bracing herself against the beech trunk. "Is someone there?" Was that a shadow darting between trees? "Who is it? I see you in there — you'd better come out now." A bogus threat, and one that went unheeded. Had someone really just tried to skewer her? She made a fine target in her yellow waterproof jacket.

She backed out of the wood, staring into the darkness before she turned and ran, her heart beating furiously and her only thought to get far away. She dashed out of the wood and alongside the yew walk. Primrose House was dark, so she kept running, taking the lower and quicker path toward the walled garden and up to her cottage. Even as she fled, she realized if someone wanted to hit her, she was an easy target the whole way.

She slammed the door and threw the lock before sinking down to the floor. Breathing hard, she pressed her hand against the stitch in her side. She must ring Tatt or Hobbes — the police needed to know, and she would tell them everything. As her breathing slowed, her mind began to calm. She would wait and tell Christopher first. He could help her sort through what happened, and present it in a reasonable order. Perhaps she hadn't really been part of someone's target practice — maybe it had just been a local hunter. What would anyone be hunting so near a house?

Unsure of what time Christopher would arrive and unable to keep still, Pru bounced from sofa to sink to fireplace as if she were the shiny silver ball in a pinball machine. Who would wish her harm? The murderer, of course. She'd been asking too many questions.

She heard Christopher's car, but he didn't come in straightaway. She peeked out the window and saw that he was on the phone. Work, she thought, there was no escape from it. In a few minutes he finished, got out, and walked in the door, but when he looked at her, he seemed to be seeing something else.

"What's happened?" she asked.

He dropped his keys on the little table and put his arms around her, rubbing her back, and then held onto her arms and looked at her.

"Graham is missing," he said.

CHAPTER 30

"Missing? In Dubai?"

"No one can reach him." Christopher went over to the fireplace and began to set the wood, then stopped and sat down. "Phyl tried to ring him yesterday and thought that he'd just turned his phone off. He hasn't replied to emails. I told Phyl that we had talked with him last weekend, and he was fine." He got up, went to the kitchen, and began filling the kettle.

"Did she try ringing him at work today?" Pru asked, following him in. "Maybe something's wrong with his phone." Dread crept over her.

Christopher put the kettle on and turned to her, his face ashen. "He hadn't been in today, they said. They thought he might have gone out to the site of a new building on the outskirts of the city, but they hadn't heard."

Pru took his hands. "And you tried? You rang him?"

He nodded. "Straight to his voice mail. His phone is off or—"

She jumped into the breach. "His battery's dead. He forgot to charge his phone. I'm always forgetting to charge mine." She dragged him over to the sofa. "His company, the people he works with, they're looking for him, aren't they? What about where he lives? Does he have a flatmate?"

"No, they're just bed-sits really. The company owns the building and puts interns up there."

Dubai was far away, but much of the distance was south, and so there was only a four-hour time difference. Still, she thought, that made it almost midnight there. "When did you find this out?" she asked.

"Phyl rang just before I left my flat."

"You didn't need to come down here for me," she said, feeling immediately guilty that he would try to take care of her as well as his own crisis.

He held both her hands up to his lips. "I was being selfish — I needed to come for me. I couldn't sit in my flat alone with this."

She pressed her cheek against his. "That isn't selfish."

He had put his own call into Graham's supervisor and one to a former London police colleague, Matthew Blount, who now worked in security for the same Dubai firm. The hospitals had been checked, the authorities alerted. Nothing yet, but Matthew promised to ring as soon as he had news.

"I talked to Phyl again just as I got here. I gave her your number in case she couldn't reach me — I hope that was all right." His eyes were empty and scared, and she wanted to hold him close.

"Of course it's all right. Are you going to fly down there?"

"I can't leave yet," he said, shaking his head. "I can't sit on a plane for eight hours not knowing . . ." his voice trailed off and he took her hand and squeezed it.

"We'll wait here for good news," she said, squeezing back. "You make a fire. I'll sort out the tea."

That took up a few minutes, after which they sat and stared at the flames. "Tell me what you've been doing," he said. "Tell me how things are."

Thoughts of red books, an arrow aimed at her head, and her own questions about both Liam's and Davina's innocence flitted through her mind, but she held back. He was always willing to add more to his load of responsibilities, even leaving work the day she found Ned's body, but she could not heap more weight onto the burden he carried now.

"Fine, things are fine. The stone pots arrived this week, the ones for the terrace." she proceeded to go into great detail about the progress they'd made in the garden. She knew he wasn't listening — she barely listened to herself — but it filled the air with sound, and that was what they needed.

The minutes dragged on into an hour, then another. A fresh pot of tea. They sat at the kitchen table and Christopher stared at his phone, left out in front of them. Pru had never seen him look helpless.

She began asking him about Graham as a boy, and he warmed to the subject, telling tales of camping and school trips and holidays — the parts of their father-son lives that overlapped after Christopher and Phyl divorced. When a story ended, they lapsed into silence, but the silence frightened her, and so she would ask for another. Was he a Boy Scout like his father? Who was his best friend when he was ten? Between stories, Christopher would grab her hands across the table. They would go over what they knew again and again. Matthew was looking. The authorities had been alerted. Graham would be found; Matthew would ring as soon as he knew anything.

It was past three o'clock in the morning when she stood up. "I'm going to look for a flight for you."

She had just started searching online when Christopher's phone rang. The occurrence of the one sound they'd been waiting hours to hear frightened her even more than the silence. He leapt up and answered, his back to her.

"Matthew?" A few seconds of silence, and when he turned round, Pru saw the color had come back into his face. "You've seen him? Is he all right?" His voice was thick.

Her eyes filled with tears of relief. As she was about to go to him, her phone rang. She answered, and it was Phyl, who didn't bother with hello. "They found him — did you hear? Does he know?"

"Yes, he's talking with Matthew now. What happened?"

"Graham's hurt, but he's going to be all right. I just spoke with him. I'll let Christopher explain it. Pru," Phyl said in a shaky voice, "it's good he's been there with you."

That was an unnecessary kindness, but one which Pru, who had met Phyl only once and briefly, deeply appreciated. "Thanks."

When he rang off, Christopher took her in his arms and for a moment neither spoke. It was a good silence; she could feel the tension drain out of his body. She looked up at him. "Tell me what happened."

He didn't let her go but began to fill in the details. Graham was in hospital with injuries from a car crash, but he would recover. Just as the firm had suspected, he had been driving out to the site of the new building, but he'd been run off the road — they are not the most disciplined drivers there, Matthew had said. His car ended up hidden from view, and he was pinned in. They found him Friday evening, and only after Matthew urged the police to look for the GPS signal from Graham's phone, which had landed out of his reach. He was conscious, and he'd had bottled water at hand. Broken leg and arm, and a mild concussion, but he was alive.

"There's a flight at seven from Gatwick," Pru said. "You could make that."

His phone rang as she spoke, and when he looked down, his face lit up. "Graham? Sorry, who? Millie?"

Millie? Pru sat back down at the computer to get flight details while Christopher talked with this Millie, and then Graham must've come on the line.

"Son, how do you feel? Is the doctor there? Listen, I'm flying out first thing in the morning, but I won't see you until almost evening." Christopher sat down on the sofa, then stood up by the mantel. They spoke for a few more minutes; he rang off and beamed at Pru. "He sounds good. At least, as well as can be expected. He'll be all right."

"Let me finish your ticket now — I need your passport number," she said. Christopher went over to his jacket. "And who is Millie?" she asked.

"The daughter of one of his co-workers from Newcastle. She's visited Dubai a couple of times. They've been seeing each other. He's mentioned her several times."

"He had to go all the way to Dubai to meet the girl of his dreams from Newcastle?"

"Nonsense," he said, "he won't meet the girl of his dreams for ages yet. I didn't."

She had her back to him and didn't turn, lest she had misinterpreted his remark. "Well," she said in a light tone, "I hope she was worth the wait."

Christopher's arms encircled Pru, and he kissed her behind her ear. "She most definitely was."

When Phyl first rang him, he'd had the forethought — that keen policeman's mind — to grab some clothes and his passport in anticipation of a journey. Now, he could leave for the airport from her cottage. And with Graham safe and Christopher on his way to sort things out, suddenly they were both starving. Pru scrambled eggs and sliced bread for toast.

* * *

They stood at the door, the sky still dark, not quite ready for him to leave. He took her face in his hands and kissed her mouth, her cheeks, her eyelids. "You saved me tonight," he said.

"You've saved me plenty of times," she reminded him.

"I don't like leaving you with all this."

"There is nothing going on," she said. She hoped he would forgive her that small lie. It was for his own good. "I don't want you to worry. I'll be fine here, and you can ring any time you want."

He looked over to the table where the Titche's box awaited its next journey. She saw the direction of his gaze and brushed off the impending concern. "I'm not going to talk with Simon," she said. "I'm going to drive down, give him the box, and come home. I'll do it on Sunday."

"You could stop and see Harry and Vernona," he suggested.

211

She brightened. "Yes, I'll visit the Wilsons. Maybe I could spend the night with them tomorrow — oh, that's today, isn't it? Then, after I deliver Simon's box to him, I will come home." At least part of her journey would be pleasant.

"When I return," he said, "we'll make plans. See if we can find time away from all this."

She looked into his intense gaze and nodded. She wondered where that time would come from. Would elves make their way into Primrose House gardens every night and get all the work done that she couldn't? And where would Christopher find more time? Tell crime victims that he was very sorry, but he was going off with his girlfriend — Pru almost laughed as she thought of him saying that ridiculous word aloud. They needed time, but they had no time to give.

After he left, Pru made another cup of tea to keep herself awake until he rang, which he did once he was settled at the gate, waiting to board. "I talked with Graham again, and I spoke with a doctor," Christopher said. "I'll find out more when I get there. I'll ring you tomorrow after you're home."

She fell into bed about six and willed every single thought to leave her mind. With nothing left in there, she slept.

CHAPTER 31

Pru woke at noon. Groggy, at first she couldn't understand
why the sun poured in her window. She stumbled out of
bed and stretched until she recalled not just the night before,
but also the task ahead. She sat at the kitchen table drinking
coffee and eyeing the Titche's department-store box, as if it
might suddenly come to life and talk to her about the past.
When it didn't, she rang the Wilsons. Pru didn't need to say
much. Mrs. Wilson seemed already aware of the situation
— most likely she'd heard it straight from Birdie — and said
they would have a room ready when she arrived.

On the drive to Romsey, her mind filled to the brim with
questions that came from too many directions — gardens,
murder, family, Graham. When she reached the Wilsons'
home, Greenoak, she realized that the arrow incident had
spilled out in the overflow, unnoticed and unremembered
until that moment. She would ring DS Hobbes when she got
back tomorrow. In the light of day, she realized the sensible
explanation was that a local, using the wood for target practice, had not seen her. She filed it away as the Wilsons' terrier,
Toffee Woof-Woof, greeted her in the vanguard.

The Wilsons were as dear as ever, and they never brought
up the subject of Simon. Mr. Wilson talked about his latest

213

archaeological dig — Roman artifacts being his speciality — and Mrs. Wilson chatted about the Women's Institute, broadly hinting that Pru should join the Tunbridge Wells chapter. Pru listened without comment, fatigued from the drive. She'd had only a few hours' sleep, and thought it might be days before she recovered from the odd hours she'd been keeping.

She left the Wilsons' midmorning on Sunday, after a leisurely breakfast during which she grew nervous with anticipation. After promising another, longer visit soon — and when would that be, she thought? — she followed Mr. Wilson's directions for the short drive to Simon's house. Pru's heart pounded as if it would prefer to run away and hide rather than stay in her chest at that moment. She parked two houses away to compose herself and to admire Simon and Polly's front garden. The last of the snowdrops still carpeted the ground, and the earliest dwarf *Narcissus* were just beginning. Walking up to the door, she passed a couple of small shrubs she couldn't identify, and her heart ached at the thought that she couldn't just drag Simon out and ask him.

Polly — who else could it be — answered the door. She had blond hair, on the faded side, cut stylishly at shoulder length, and she wore glasses with red frames. Whether or not she'd seen the recent photo of Pru, it was clear she recognized her. Pru hadn't meant to surprise them — at least, she hadn't meant to surprise Polly. Simon, she had decided, needed to be caught unawares lest he absent himself before her arrival.

Pru clutched the box to her chest in an attempt to calm her heart. "Hello, I'm Pru. Is Simon at home?"

For a moment, Polly said nothing, only looked at Pru. A radio played somewhere in the house. "Hello, Pru. I'm Polly. Will you come in?" She opened the door wider.

"No, thank you. I only want to give him something. Is he here?"

"Yes, let me get him." Polly left the door open. Pru heard murmured voices followed by footsteps. She tried to steady her breathing.

He said nothing at first, and she opened her mouth to begin, but then he spoke. "Do you want to come in?"

"No, thank you." *Yes, please,* she thought. "I haven't come to talk, I only wanted to give you this." She held out the box and he looked down at it, as if unsure what sort of gift it was. "Take it," she urged, in a tight voice. She took a breath. "Please, take it. It's yours." Simon took it, and she felt a great heaviness lifted from her, out of all proportion to the weight of the box. She hurried on before he banished her from the premise. "It's letters and photos" — it hit her that she was giving up the photo of the family from all those years ago, the one taken at Birdie's, and she felt a stab of pain — "that Mother saved. She saved them for you, and I didn't understand that until now." He remained silent and her eyes dropped to the ground. "That's all I wanted to do — give you the box." She turned to go.

"Pru—" he said as she walked away. She didn't stop.

* * *

Straight home, to her safe, lonely little cottage. But a couple of hours of daylight remained, and a pang of guilt prevented her from retiring indoors. She should get some work done. She stood looking at the walled garden, hearing Humphry Repton's voice in her head in that friendly, insistent, designer-ish tone she had invented for him, telling her that the "bank planted with shrubs would hide the kitchen garden wall."

The broad walk from the house would sweep down and around the walled garden to arrive at the front gate, drawing the bare outer wall into prominence. She must cover the walls, and that meant more rambling roses to peg all along the length of it — the side that faced the house. It took every ounce of effort she could muster just to sigh deeply.

The work inside the walls overwhelmed her, too. Smooth off the hacked yew trunks. Surely the police would let her do that now. The apple trees were ready to plant, and

215

she had heeled them in, digging a trench in one of the beds and burying the bare roots until actual planting took place. She'd chosen a range of old varieties from the list Ned had made, everything from Ballyfatten to Pig's Nose Pippin and Bloody Ploughman. That last one seemed inappropriate in light of recent events, but there was little she could do about it now. Training the apples meant more masonry nails and wires. Perhaps she could set up work lights and start putting in a few hours overnight.

She walked to the glasshouse and put her hand out to open the door, and as she did so, she thought back to the first incident when the primroses and cowslips had been destroyed.

Her hand hovered over the handle. She would leave solving Ned's murder to the police, but the upturned flats, the fire in the shed, and the yew cut down — small events in comparison — she could solve that mystery. She knew no one on her work crew had been involved — why would they destroy their own work? No, those deeds had been aimed at her, head gardener at Primrose House, a job that Jamie Tanner had counted on.

Had police even looked for fingerprints on the glass-house? She couldn't remember. She drew her hand back. Did the police not have Jamie's fingerprints on file? No, she answered her own question, they did not. Cate never reported his abuse, and as far as she knew, he had no police record. She would talk with DS Hobbes.

She walked down to the shed to retrieve the bow she'd come across in the wood by the house so that she'd remember to give it to Robbie. But it was no longer propped up outside where she had left it or inside with the tools. How long had it been gone? In an instant, Pru remembered hearing the arrow zing by her ear in the wood on Friday. The bow had been taken and not for a petulant act of jealousy. Her eyes darted around, as if Ned's murderer waited under the brush pile, behind the shed, or on the far side of the cedar of Lebanon, hoping to get a better shot at her. She backed away, pulled her phone out, and hurried off to her cottage.

Her call went straight to Hobbes' voicemail. Perhaps he didn't work on Sunday afternoons, as other police officers she could name did. "I can't prove anything, but I believe that Jamie Tanner was behind the vandalism in the garden. Do you have his fingerprints on file? Maybe you could give me a ring tomorrow. And," she added, slightly out of breath as she reached her door, "I have something else to tell you about."

* * *

Christopher rang Sunday evening. In Dubai, it was past midnight, and so she didn't get to speak to Graham, but she at least found out that all was as well as could be expected.

"You'll bring him home, won't you?" she asked, stifling a yawn.

"I most certainly will," he said. "And soon — possibly midweek. Phyl's got his old room ready for him." They lapsed into one of those intimate silences for a few moments before he asked, "How did it go with Simon?"

"It went quickly," she said. "We didn't talk. I gave him the box and left." She scratched at a spot on the knee of her trousers in hopes of distracting her emotions. "I met Polly. They have a nice garden." She shouldn't have tried for the last part, because she barely made it to the end of the sentence, and she knew he could tell. "Mrs. Sock knows about family disagreements. She seems to think it'll all work itself out." She tried not to sniff.

"And what does Trevor think?" Christopher asked.

Pru laughed, spilling a tear out onto her cheek. "He didn't offer an opinion."

Usually, a bedtime phone conversation with Christopher relaxed her and almost always ensured pleasant dreams. That night, sleep eluded her. She spent most of the night staring at the ceiling and working out the planting design for the terrace beds. She told herself to go to sleep, but it didn't work this time, and it was only near dawn when her eyes finally closed, immediately after which her alarm went off.

CHAPTER 32

DS Hobbes rang early. Pru had left to walk to Primrose House, but ducked into the walled garden for a moment to take the call.

"We don't have Tanner's fingerprints," Hobbes reported, "and we can't ask for them for no reason. Each time something happened in the garden, he had an alibi. He was at work early, with a witness. We couldn't get any further."

"Yes," she admitted. "I suppose I only suspect him — I've certainly no proof. But now there's something else." She told him about the arrow.

"I'm coming round now. I'll take a look. What about that bow you found the week before?"

"It's gone," Pru said. "I had propped it up just outside the shed, and I checked when I got back yesterday. Should I wait for you here?"

"No, you go on to work. I'll let you know if I find anything."

* * *

If she remained in constant motion, she decided, fatigue could not overtake her. She began her day hounding the stonemasons with innocent questions about just how long it took to set one row of stones, after which she had Liam and Fergal help her adjust the placement of the heavy pots along the balustrade terrace. When she caught a glimpse of Hobbes at the edge of the wood, she went down and found him scuffling along in the damp duff.

With the branches still bare, the morning sunlight shone through to the leaf litter on the ground. It looked a brighter place than it had during the late-afternoon gloom when the arrow was shot.

"It's unlikely whoever used it would leave the bow here," he said, his eyes scanning the ground. "Where were you standing?"

Pru took her position and turned to look out of the copse, just as she had Friday afternoon. No arrow remained stuck in the beech trunk, but when she walked up to examine the bark, she could see fresh splinters bursting from the wood where it had landed and been pulled out.

"That's where it was," she said. "I stood with my back to the wood, and the arrow landed there." Just a few inches and it would've been in the back of her head. She shivered. Should she be grateful his aim was good or bad?

Hobbes photographed the hole in the trunk and before he left asked, "You won't be out here alone again, will you?" She assured him it was the last place she would go without a companion.

The well-aged manure had arrived — left as directed by Pru — and now a large pile sat just below the balustrade terrace at the kitchen end, barely out of the way of the terrace work. They'd have to shift it all soon or Davina and Bryan would get a whiff of it every time they passed a window — although not fresh, there was still no mistaking that aroma. As she darted from task to task, Pru dodged the many holes Robbie had dug. They'd have to be filled in eventually, but the activity kept him occupied and happy.

She kept an eye on the Duffys so that they could not escape her again, and at the end of the day, when she saw

219

them turn their backs to leave, she called out. "Liam, I want to talk with you. Come down to my cottage."

"We can't stay today, Pru," Fergal said. "Sorry."

"Fergal, stay or go as you like, but Liam is staying."

Liam's eyes flashed from his brother to Pru. "Well, I don't know."

Pru pointed to the path and raised her voice. "Liam, you will march right down there this minute and talk to me, do you understand?"

Liam took a step back. Whether she sounded like his mother or his boss, it didn't matter to Pru, because he went along with her, although he kept quiet on the walk. She heard Fergal heave a sigh as he trailed after them.

Once inside, the three of them stood in the chilly darkness, Pru thinking about how to begin.

"Would you like a fire, Pru?" Fergal asked.

"Thanks, yes, that would be great." She really must learn to build a better fire, she thought, as she put the kettle on.

"Liam, why won't you tell the police where you were on that Thursday? Even after they took you in for questioning."

He set his jaw and looked away from her, but she wouldn't let up. "You know what this looks like," she said, trying not to plead. "If you tell the police nothing, who knows what may happen?"

Liam jumped up out of the kitchen chair and walked to the window without speaking.

"Were you at the flat with Cate — in the afternoon or the evening?" She sensed Fergal pause in his work.

Liam's face, contorted into a massive frown, grew bright red. He thrust his chin out. "Didn't Cate already tell the police that I wasn't there?"

"But you were, weren't you?" She turned her back to them while she poured up the tea and put out remnants of a Dundee cake from Ivy.

"I wasn't," he snapped. Pru looked over her shoulder at him, and he took a breath. "At least, I wasn't there the whole time," he said. As he gave up telling the lie, his face relaxed. "I was there that evening."

"Was it because of Jamie? Is that why she wouldn't say?"

"Her only thought was to protect me from Tanner — she didn't think she needed to protect me from the police." He sat down again, resting his arms on the table, his hands clenched together. "But she shouldn't be protecting me," he said in a raised voice. "I should be protecting *her*."

"She thought that if Jamie found out you were helping her, he'd go after you?"

"He's done it before, hasn't he?" Liam asked in a sullen tone. "And she'd seen my name in that diary of his. But if the police found out that I was there and she had already said I wasn't, wouldn't she be in trouble for lying?" Liam pointed a finger at his brother. "And *you* never even asked where I was."

"I didn't think I ought to know anything. For when they questioned me," Fergal said as he put the tea things on the table.

She looked from brother to brother. "Liam, you didn't tell Fergal where you were? Fergal, you have no idea where Liam was on that Thursday? What did you think?"

"*I wasn't here. I didn't kill him!*" Liam dropped his voice and sounded tired. "Do you think I'd do that? Have you been suspecting me all along?"

Pru's "Certainly not" and Fergal's "God, no" piled on top of each other.

Liam slumped back into his chair at the kitchen table and let out a heavy sigh. "I found a little place over near Crawley for Cate and Nanda to move to, a place of their own. I went to look at it for her. It isn't ready to let until next month."

"That was in the afternoon?" Pru asked as she poured the tea and the brothers started to work on the cake. "And then you went over to the flat? For the whole evening?"

"Cate cooked a meal for us — for Nanda and me." He smiled at mention of the little girl's name, and Pru had a sudden vision of Liam sitting down to a tea party with Nanda and her stuffed friends.

"Were you there all night?"

Liam jumped up from the table. "I was not."

Pru raised her hands. "All right, all right. I only want to know where you were, not what you were doing."

"He was home when I arrived home myself," Fergal said. "But it was close to midnight."

"Did you talk to Ned again after I heard you argue earlier that week?"

Liam shook his head. "No, but I tried to ring him. Imagine me ringing his phone and him already dead."

"You have a perfectly good alibi," Pru said. "You have to tell the police where you were."

"I don't want to get Cate in trouble."

Pru ignored his chivalry for the moment. "Did anyone see you?"

Liam stared off into the sitting room, as if a witness might be hiding under the sofa. "I met the man at the Crawley place. He's got Cate's name down on the papers, but he would remember me. That was early afternoon, just after you let us go."

"And that's it? What about the rest of the afternoon? You went nowhere else?"

Liam scratched the side of his face, deep in contemplation. "I stopped at the DIY in Crawley to check out the cost of compressors in case Fergal and I could afford one." He shook his head. "But I didn't buy anything, so I've no proof."

He stood up and stuck his hand in his jeans pocket as if to verify that fact, and pulled out a few coins, a folded-up beer mat with something scribbled on it, and a crumpled piece of paper. He stared at the assortment, picked up the paper, and smoothed it out.

"*Chips!*" he shouted. "I stopped at a chippy in Crawley. Here's the receipt." Pru peered at the paper. She could still read the date and time stamp. She didn't want to ask how a receipt from more than two weeks earlier could still be in his jeans pocket and still be legible. He was a single young man and thought that was a good enough answer.

"There will be CCTV at the store," Pru said. "And if the chip shop doesn't have it, at least you've got the timed receipt." She looked down at the paper — five o'clock. "How long does it take to drive back from Crawley?"

"A good three-quarters of an hour," Fergal said.

"And you went straight to Cate's. She's your witness there."

"I don't want her involved." Liam said, straightening his shoulders.

"And would they consider her a good witness?" Fergal asked. "After she already said he wasn't there."

Liam gave his brother a dark look.

"What did you tell the police?" she asked Fergal.

"The truth. I was out with Angela," Fergal said. "I picked her up from work in the afternoon and we went to a film in town, then to the pub near there and then back to her flat. Liam was home when I arrived. I was away, you see," he said, looking at his brother, "so, I couldn't've said if you had been home or not."

"Didn't you talk when you both got home? Say where you'd been?" she asked.

Fergal snorted. "Do you think we natter on about each other's day? And discuss what we'll wear tomorrow?"

"Yes, yes, all right," Pru said. She turned to Liam. "What time did Francine get home?"

"About eleven," Liam said, sinking back into the chair.

"First thing tomorrow," Pru said, wagging a finger at him, "you will ring the police and tell them all of this. How can they find the real murderer if they keep chasing you around?" She drummed her fingers on the table. "Ask for Sergeant Hobbes."

CHAPTER 33

After they left, Pru remained in front of the fire, piecing together Liam's activities on that Thursday, and hoping that Cate wouldn't be in trouble for first denying he had been with her. Cate's excuse would be her fear of what Jamie might have done, but that meant she would need to report his abuse to the police, which would lead to . . . what?

DS Hobbes had indicated that Ned's mobile, stuck behind a stone in the wall of the Duffy cottage, had been dismissed as evidence against Liam. But how did it get there? And did the police know about the trouble between Ned and Hugo? She pictured Hugo skulking about at the cottage, removing a loose stone and shoving the phone in the hole it left. What could Hugo have against Liam? Or was Liam just an easy target?

Jamie certainly had a grudge against Liam, who had dared to speak to Cate at the Two Bells. But Jamie needed Ned, and she could see no further motive to involve him in Ned's murder. Pru thought back to one of the last times she talked with Ned. The quiet Monday he had wanted to discuss something with her, but he wouldn't stay that day, he said, because he had something to do. That Thursday, he was dead.

She would not wait until morning, but neither would she take Hobbes away from his family. She rang Tatt — let the inspector take care of it.

"Ms. Parke?" Tatt sounded surprised to hear her voice. She heard dishes clattering in the background, and she had a sudden image of Tatt in an apron, washing up. She stifled a giggle, and heard him sigh heavily. "I suppose you're ringing concerning the anonymous tip we received about the Fox boy being at the scene of the crime?"

"What?" Pru shouted. "Robbie was nowhere near Primrose House that afternoon. How can you say that? Why do you even listen to these ridiculous anonymous tips? Aren't you the least bit suspicious that—"

"All right, all right." For once, it was Tatt who was trying to be quiet, and he replied in a furious whisper. "I do not need you to tell me how to run my investigation."

Pru grasped at straws. "Have you questioned Jamie Tanner about Ned? He's a relative, after all, and surely you need—"

"We talked with Tanner as a matter of course," Tatt replied. "He seemed upset about his father-in-law, but nothing out of the ordinary."

Yes, Pru was sure that Jamie looked the picture of sanity when questioned by the police — she'd seem him flash from one emotional state to another at the flip of a switch. "Do you know where he was that afternoon?"

"He was at work," Tatt replied in a short, loud burst, and then grew quiet again. "He was at work, checked in at the proper time, stayed all day with his co-worker as a witness, checked out late in the day after which he was at the Two Bells, confirmed by the barman. And now, Ms. Parke, are you finished with your interrogation?"

Pru missed the days when you could slam a phone receiver down.

* * *

She slept poorly again Monday night, images of the heap of manure waiting at the base of the balustrade stairs haunting her. It did not make for a promising day, but at least she had coffee in hand by the time Christopher rang.

"We're flying back tomorrow," he said, and as tired as she was, a broad smile stretched across her face.

"Will it be a problem for Graham? Will there be enough room for him on the plane?" She pictured his leg — the break was midthigh — in an enormous cast.

"We'll be in first class," Christopher said. "I told him not to expect anything for Christmas this year."

"And you'll see him settled in Oxford?" She infused the question with as much cheer and good will as possible in order to let him know she did not expect to see him immediately.

"We'll see. What about Liam?"

She filled him in on Liam's story. "I ordered those Duffy boys to ring DS Hobbes today," she said. "I had no idea I could be so bossy." A noticeable silence followed that statement. "They'll present Liam's complete alibi, and that should be that."

* * *

Hugo rang as she walked out her door — sounding far too chipper for her state of mind — to say he was in the walled garden.

The heavy wooden gate stood ajar, and she stuck her head in. Hugo had walked up to the center bed and was nudging some of the remaining bits of yew branches with the toe of his shoe. He looked up when she approached.

"Anna said you stopped to talk with me. Sorry I was out."

"Yes, you were busy with the pensioners," Pru said as she reached down to pull up a few bittercress plants, remembering that Repton, big-picture man that he was, had nothing to say about weeds in the garden. "Your editor, Anna, said that you were not at work the day Ned was murdered. Or the next."

"No," Hugo said, "I wasn't." He seemed neither perturbed that Pru had asked nor willing to offer more.

"I suppose you've spoken to the police," she said. "It seems as if they'd want to talk with everyone related to Ned. Did you tell them you were related?"

"Yes, they know," he said, looking chagrined. "They know about the whole thing — Dad's plans, the pub, and the argument I had with Ned two days before he was murdered." He noticed her raised eyebrows. "Hadn't you heard about it? It wasn't exactly private. We were standing in the car park outside Sainsbury's. As it turns out, so was Detective Sergeant Hobbes, looking into a case about stolen trolleys." Hugo shrugged. "I should've told you about my connection when we started the blog."

"I don't think it wouldn't have made a difference. Where were you on that Thursday?"

"I was at the National Archives and the Land Registry," he said. "It's easy enough to check both places — the police already have."

Pru colored slightly. "I wasn't accusing you of anything, Hugo."

"It's all right. I know how I sounded last time." He gave a short laugh. "Turns out Ned was right, of course. Dad's pub wouldn't have been the oldest. But, I made another discovery in the stacks of ancient records about our own village of Bells Yew Green. One that has to do with Primrose House and the Templetons." He paused a moment. "They don't really own it."

"Don't own Primrose House?" Pru asked. "That can't be right. They bought it from Lord Hamilton. Surely as earl he has the right to sell off the manor houses on his estate."

Hugo grinned. "We're an ancient country, Pru, with many layers of antiquated laws. Ned knew what a massive tangle they are — it was what he loved, sorting through stories, decrees, and laws hundreds of years old. He gave me the idea to look. That day we argued in the car park, Ned made a comment about Primrose House and how no one really knew its story. I thought it would make a great series in the paper."

"But Davina and Bryan have put so much into the restoration," Pru said. "They wouldn't have done that if they didn't own the place."

"You're from a young country where the laws are clear," Hugo said. "It's likely the earl didn't know that a freehold sale wasn't possible, that he held only an equitable estate. It has something to do with the Court of Chancery and when the land was registered." He shook his head slightly. "At least I think it does."

"The Court of Chancery? Like in *Bleak House*?"

"Yeah," Hugo laughed. "We're all living in a Dickens novel. We may not even understand it, but Ned did. Do you suppose he told the Templetons that he knew they didn't own the place?"

It took a moment for that to sink in. What would Davina and Bryan do if they discovered the vast amount of money they'd spent had been for nothing? What would they do to cover up the fact that they weren't the true owners?

Davina's comments about Ned fell into place. Ned knew that the Templetons didn't own the house, but he would keep quiet for a price. And that price involved securing a good job for his son-in-law to make sure his daughter was provided for. Maybe Ned had asked for money, too. Had Davina finally had enough of his blackmail and put a stop to it in a fit of pique? The police had found mud from the rough track on her tires. She had no reason to take that rough track unless it was to get to the spot where Ned was murdered. Pru swallowed hard. "And you told the police?"

He nodded. "Just this morning. I was looking for the last pieces, and I wanted to try to get them to agree to let me write it up. They wouldn't, of course. Open case, they said — the usual run around."

"Do you think Ned was blackmailing the Templetons?" Pru asked, hoping Hugo would convince her otherwise.

"He didn't say so. At least, not in so many words," Hugo said. "When we argued, he said something about taking care of Cate. I suppose he could've asked for money, but it had been mentioned that Cate's husband might get the head gardener job. Before you came along, of course."

"I believe it was Jamie who set the fire in the shed and did the rest. To make me look bad. He thought that I would get the boot and it would pave his way to take over. But I'm not sure how to prove it, because he seems to have covered his tracks well."

Hugo surveyed the still-bare inner walls of the garden. "I'm sorry now that I didn't write the piece about the antique apples, but maybe I can do it if we start the blog up again. Tell me, how do you grow actual trees from Victorian times?"

"Fruit-tree varieties are propagated by grafting — inserting a stem of one tree into a cut stem of another. You can take cuttings of trees and put them on new rootstock or you could graft a stem onto another stem. It's an ancient practice, but still used today."

Hugo made a couple of notes before saying he must be on his way. Pru stayed where she was. Something flitted about in her mind, and if she stood still, it might land and she could catch it. It had to do with grafting.

She had tried her hand at grafting in a propagation class at Texas A&M. The knife had slipped once or twice and cut her — unconsciously, she rubbed the pad of her thumb at the memory. An occupational hazard of those in the trade, she knew. If she had kept it up, she would have ended up with scars on her thumb, as so many grafters do. She had seen a variety of antique grafting knives at the Garden Museum in London, but such things didn't need to be specially made. "Anything can be a garden tool," she had told DS Hobbes.

She phoned him and reached his voicemail. "Pru again. The pocketknife you found under Ned's body. It could've been used for grafting or perhaps it was Ned's and he intended to use it to propagate the apples we were going to plant. Or perhaps he wanted to graft roses. I don't suppose this is very helpful, but I thought I'd let you know." She rang off.

CHAPTER 34

At lunch, she chanced a quick trip to Francine's flat to find out from Cate if the police had Liam's alibi. Davina and Bryan were preparing to leave for Liverpool on a three-day meeting with the investor group — Davina had informed her that their next meeting would be at Primrose House in July, so that the investors could all attend the open garden day. A shrill laugh escaped Pru's lips before she could stop it.

She waved at Arabella Sock as she got out of her Mini and walked up to the door of the flat.

"Come into the kitchen," Cate said, "we're just having our lunch."

"I'm sorry to bother you now," Pru said, eyeing Nanda's plate of fish fingers and wishing she had remembered to make herself a sandwich.

"Not at all. Have you eaten? We've plenty, and we know how to share, don't we Nanda-Panda?" Nanda's mouth was full, but she offered Pru the rest of a half-eaten fish finger. "Let's give her a fresh one, shall we?" Cate asked.

As Pru joined them, Cate said, "Sergeant Hobbes rang to say he'd talked with Liam about where he was that Thursday."

"Mummy, Liam likes Paddington Bear," Nanda said, perking up at his name.

Cate smiled at her daughter. "Liam told you a story about Paddington Bear, didn't he?"

Nanda nodded and handed Pru one of her apple slices. "Apple is good for you," she said.

"I hope there won't be a problem about what I said to begin with," Cate said. "What if they don't believe me?" She sat down to her own lunch, shaking her head. "Too bad we don't have CCTV here."

Pru could hear, through the closed kitchen window, a voice call, "Trevor!" She turned her head toward the sound.

"But you do," she said, standing up. "You do have CCTV — or as good as." She saw that Nanda's plate was clean, and she held out her hand to the little girl. "Nanda, would you like to go meet the dog across the street? Would you like to say hello to Trevor?"

* * *

Nanda kept up a steady stream of excited talk all the way out the door and across the road, until they set foot on the path, the door opened, and Trevor emerged, followed by his mistress.

"Hello, Mrs. Sock," Pru said. "Nanda has been wanting to meet Trevor, haven't you, Nanda?" Nanda had turned herself into a barnacle and was stuck to the back of Pru's leg, peering at Trevor with one eye.

"Well," Mrs. Sock said, "we're very happy to meet you, now aren't we, Trevor?" Trevor's tail set an andante pace and he whined slightly, peering back at Nanda. "Why don't you and the little miss come in?"

They followed Mrs. Sock down the hall to the kitchen, where a plate of custard cream biscuits appeared as if by magic. Mrs. Sock offered the plate to Nanda, who took one biscuit, said a tiny "Thank you," and sat down on the floor next to Trevor. Soon the beagle was giving the little girl's face a thorough washing, causing a fountain of giggles to bubble forth.

As she nibbled on her own custard cream, Pru laid her cards on the table, explaining in vague terms for Nanda's benefit the day in question. "And so, I wonder if you remember seeing Liam that evening."

"I do indeed," Arabella Sock replied. "You see, that was the day that Trevor and I had been to visit our doctor, and we returned just about five o'clock, didn't we, Trevor?" Pru looked down at the dog just as Nanda offered him her second custard cream. He gave it a lick, after which she resumed eating it herself.

"Oh, um, Nanda . . ." Pru began. She wondered if she could be fired as an aunt before she ever got started.

"Don't you worry about those two," Mrs. Sock said. "My boys grew up sharing their bickies with our dogs, and tweren't never any trouble." She patted the palms of her hands on her expansive lap in contemplation, and then said, "Now, let me see, we did see the young man arrive. He parks his car round the corner and up a ways. I noticed it there that evening, on our walk, isn't that right?" Again, she looked down to Trevor for confirmation, but the dog was unable to reply as Nanda had him round the neck in a gentle hug. Trevor must have been taught how to behave in the company of little children in his former life, Pru thought.

"It might be necessary for you to tell that to the *police*." Pru whispered the last word. "You see . . ."

Mrs. Sock put her hand up. "No, no, now, you don't need to tell me any more. I'm happy to help."

* * *

Pru drove back to work with a lighter load now she could cross Liam off the suspect list and hoped that the police would do the same. The next name that floated to the surface was Robbie. Tatt's latest anonymous tip echoed in her mind. Ivy had dismissed Robbie's brief disappearance from Chaffinch's on that Thursday afternoon, and Pru would like nothing better than to do the same, but the fact remained that for

232

an hour, no one knew where he was. A "mate" could have easily persuaded him to hand over his red fleece jacket, but could he be persuaded to participate in murder? Pru shook her head. Robbie hadn't understood the situation when he'd found Ned's body. If he'd been there when the murder had occurred, he would've said so.

The rest of the afternoon while her hands were busy, Pru's mind was on overdrive. Who would this mate be? Robbie led a sheltered life, and his only outlet for socializing, other than Chaffinch's, came at the Two Bells. Who was Robbie's drinking mate on his weekly visits? Ivy said Ted behind the bar kept an eye on him, but Pru had been in the Bells often enough to know that it could get busy. She doubted that Ted could keep track of Robbie's every conversation.

She stood up from digging, stretched out her back, and glanced down to the edge of the pond, where Robbie stood on a wide beech stump — his parapet where he could survey all of Sherwood Forest. He was holding a bow, and it looked like a real archer's bow, not Fergal's makeshift variety.

She ran down the slope, narrowly avoiding one of his holes.

"Robbie," she said, gasping to catch her breath. "Where did you . . . What a fine bow that is. Where did it come from?"

Robbie threw back his shoulders proudly and held the bow out for Pru to admire. Smooth yew with a carved leaf motif. It was the bow she had found in the wood. The one that had disappeared from outside the shed.

Robbie raised the bow, pulling back the string. "My mate gave it to me. It's just like Will Scarlet's." He let loose the string and his eyes followed the path of the pretend arrow.

Pru looked back over her shoulder at the Duffys, putting on their coats. "Fergal gave it to you?"

"No, Pru, not Fergal. My mate that knows Robin Hood."

"Robbie!" Ivy called to her son from the balustrade terrace.

"I'm off to the pub, Pru, to have a pint with my mates," Robbie said, jumping down from the stump.

"May I borrow your bow, Robbie?" Pru asked. "Just to look at it. I'll give it back on Friday when you're here again. Is that all right?"

Robbie looked at the bow before thrusting it at Pru. "I can share. But don't let the sheriff find it. He would get Robin in trouble."

"Not a word to the sheriff," Pru said, taking the bow. "Thanks."

Ivy called again. "Robbie, come along now. We're to stop by the Brickdales'," his mother said.

Robbie climbed the slope. "But Mum, I get to have my pint."

"I'll leave you at the Bells after that. You'll have your pint."

Pru waved goodbye to them and hurried back to her cottage on the lower path, bow in hand. Forming a small plan as she went, she stopped briefly to put the bow inside the shed, and then rang DS Hobbes to leave a message.

"The bow must've been in the wood," she said, "because Robbie had it." She was reluctant to say anything that might implicate the boy. "I've put it in the shed, so stop by if you want to get it. I'll be out this evening, but I'll explain more tomorrow."

She didn't stop in her cottage, but headed straight for the pub.

CHAPTER 35

She pulled her Mini in behind the Bells, a two-story building of stone below and brick above with several chimneys
sprouting from its slate roof and a garden off to the side.
She parked in an out-of-the-way place between a wooden
outbuilding and a couple of stainless-steel tanks Ted had
acquired recently. He hoped to start brewing his own beer
using local ingredients and had been talking with a few farm-
ers about growing hops.

Not quite five o'clock, she saw only four or five regulars
when she cracked one of the doors open. She walked up to
the bar, glancing around on the way, searching for a shadowy
alcove. If Robbie caught sight of her, all covert surveillance
would be finished.

"All right there, Pru?" Ted asked.

"Ted," Pru said, by way of greeting. "I'll have a pint of
the Sussex Mild. You haven't seen Robbie Fox yet?"

"Ah, it's Robbie's day, that's right," he said, pulling her
pint. "No, he'll be in soon."

"Does Ivy stay with him ever?"

"Good woman that she is, she doesn't. She gives the lad
some time to be just a lad."

"Does Robbie have friends here?" Pru continued to look round for a good hiding place as she asked. The fireplace that stuck out in the middle of the room offered no cover. Everything was within full view.

"Well, he does, I suppose." Ted took a cloth that had seen better cleaning days and began to polish the wood bar. "There are a few that talk with him. He doesn't get into any trouble."

Behind Ted, Pru saw a small window, just large enough to get a couple of pints through, at counter level. It had a louvered wooden door that moved up and down, and seemed to be stuck open a couple of inches. Pru could see only darkness beyond.

"Ted, do you have a snug here?"

Ted glanced over his shoulder at the little window. "We do, yes, but it's more a box room these days than a snug, though."

"It's just that, I'd love some peace and quiet for a while," Pru said, scanning the wall behind the bar until she saw the doorway to the snug off to the right. "Would you mind if I took my pint in there?"

Ted looked as if he thought that was a preposterous idea. "There's no real place for you to sit, I don't think."

"Just a bit of dark and quiet. It's been very difficult at Primrose House, as you can imagine." She gave him a significant look.

"Sure, yeah, go ahead." He made a halfhearted move toward the door. "Let me shift a few things for you."

"No, please don't bother." She waved him away. "I'll find a place to sit. Thanks so much. Oh, you won't say I'm back there, will you?"

"Not a word," he said as he turned away to the next customer.

Pru took her pint and pulled open the door to the snug. No longer the hidden room for a quiet drink, it now held boxes of cleaning supplies and glassware, a few broken chairs, and a stack of bench cushions. When she closed the door, the only light came through the two-inch opening from the little window. She blinked a few times. and when her eyes adjusted to the dim light, she took a low stool and positioned it so she could see into the pub and view the whole bar area by leaning left or right. If she stayed back far enough, she would be hidden in the shadows.

She got settled just in time. Robbie entered the pub, a bundle of excitement, and walked up to the bar. She heard him order proudly. "I'll have a pint, Ted," and saw Ted pull a pint of a low-alcohol beer.

The sound of a phone ringing made her jump. She saw Ted reach for the phone behind the bar, but still, it was a good reminder not to call attention. She leaned back, stuck her leg out — kicking a box of glasses and setting them to rattle in the process — and wrestled the phone out of her pocket. She switched it off and set it down quietly on the floor at her feet.

Ted exchanged a few words with Robbie, but soon became occupied with his bartending duties. Pru's stomach growled. The Two Bells did not serve food, and the fish fingers at Cate's seemed ages ago. If only she could reach out of the louvered window and grab one of the packets of sour-cream-and-onion crisps that hung at the back of the bar.

Not long after Robbie arrived, Jamie Tanner strode in and up to the bar, standing next to Robbie.

"Robbie, how are you?" he asked in a jovial manner.

"I'm here for my pint," Robbie said, beaming.

The noise level of the pub had increased, and Pru wasn't able to hear the entire conversation, but it was obvious from Robbie's manner that meeting Jamie at the pub was not an uncommon occurrence. Was this Robbie's secret, that he knew Jamie? It was certainly Jamie's secret — he had professed not to know Robbie. If he hid that fact, what else was he hiding? Jamie and Robbie were mates, but that led Pru nowhere in her effort to absolve Robbie of guilt. According to Tatt, Jamie had an airtight alibi for that Thursday.

Pru could get no more evidence from her undercover work, but neither could she go anywhere, and so she drank her beer and waited for Ivy to collect Robbie and Jamie to leave. After that, she would find out from Francine if Jamie had even been spotted near Chaffinch's and let Hobbes know about the situation. Reluctantly, she admitted to herself it was unlikely to be of much help.

When Ivy collected Robbie, she was quite discreet about it, not making a show of Mummy coming to get her little boy. Pru couldn't see Jamie, but then he returned to the bar and ordered another pint. Here's a problem, Pru thought when she saw Ted reach for the pump handle. It was the same session beer that Robbie drank — low alcohol and designed to keep the drinker at the pub, ordering pint after pint all evening with little worry of getting drunk. She was in for a long evening.

Pru eyed the crisps at the bar again. Tired, hungry, and uncomfortable, she grabbed a few of the cushions and made a nest for herself on the floor. Every few minutes Pru checked on Jamie who stood alone at the bar, but gradually, another more pressing need overtook her stakeout. She needed the loo. That's what she got for downing her entire pint so quickly. The door of the snug, in full view of Jamie at the bar, opened out and might just cover the door to the women's toilet. Could she slip out and back in again without him noticing? The more she thought about it, the more she realized she had no choice.

Cracking open the snug door, she stayed out of the light that streamed in, and waited until a woman pushed in the door to the loo. At that second, Pru pushed out the snug door and slipped in behind the woman. Returning to the snug wouldn't be so easy, because there was no way she could keep an eye on Jamie from the toilet, and dash out when he wasn't looking. At least the snug door stood open and would provide some cover.

She reversed her steps, but another woman, entering the toilet as she left, moved the snug door, and for a split second, Pru thought she might have been seen by anyone at the bar before she made it back into the dark snug. Once inside, she stood breathing heavily and shaking. She eased her way to the edge of the louvered window, peered out, and locked eyes with Jamie. A cold wave of fear rippled down her back. She jumped out of the way so quickly, she knocked into a stack of boxes and the one at the top tumbled to the floor. She closed her eyes tight and waited for the crash of glass, which would surely alert the crowd to her presence even if Jamie hadn't seen her, but the box landed with little noise. She put her hand to her chest and waited for the pounding to subside. *Aren't you just the picture of a suave police officer on a stakeout?*

When she had the nerve to check the bar again, Jamie was reading the sports page over another fellow's shoulder. He remained a solitary drinker until a man with a red ponytail walked up to the bar. Pru recognized him as Jamie's co-worker. She had met him when she went looking for Jamie after the yew had been destroyed.

Pru sighed, and sat down again. Her eyes lit on the fallen box. Its contents had spilled out, and on the floor lay a pile of riches — packets of crisps. *Put it on my tab, Ted.* She grabbed a bag at the top, saw that it was prawn cocktail flavor, tossed it aside, and then rummaged around for something more palatable.

She was on her second packet when the door of the snug opened, and Pru jumped. It was the barmaid. Hayley? Heidi? Pru couldn't remember.

"Hello!" Pru said in a cheery whisper.

"What are you doing in here?" Hayley or Heidi demanded. Then she peered closer and recognized Pru. "Oh, it's you."

"I asked Ted if it was all right. You see, I wanted to come to the pub, but I still needed a little peace and quiet, what with all that's going on at Primrose House these days. He said it would be fine for me to sit in here on my own. You go ahead and ask him, really, but it's just that I didn't feel like anyone knowing I'm here, you know what I mean?" Breathless, Pru held up an empty bag. "How much are the crisps?"

Hayley or Heidi nodded. She must hear all sorts of stories in this job. "Don't worry about it," she said. "Would you like another pint?"

"No thanks," Pru smiled. "I'll be leaving after a bit."

Hayley or Heidi went back to serving behind the bar. Pru checked on Jamie, who was involved in an agitated conversation, jabbing his index finger into the chest of the red ponytail guy, whose face was as red as his hair. Jamie nodded at Ted, who pulled two more pints.

Pru sat down again, tugging at her cushions to rearrange them. She sighed and looked around the dim mustiness of the snug, now box room. A fine place to spend an evening, she thought. Her muscles ached with fatigue, and her skin ached to feel Christopher' arms holding her as they drifted off to sleep. She reached inside her sweater, pulled out her necklace, and held the fan pendant to her lips. Her chin began to quiver.

Some detective you are, she thought. Here she was trapped in a room with the only exit in full view of the one person she didn't want to meet. Did she really think she could make a difference? Solve a mystery? You're a gardener, and even that skill is debatable at the moment. She took a ragged breath before swallowing hard. She must get a grip. As soon as Jamie leaves, she would go home to bed, and tomorrow morning she would get up and by God get to work on that garden. She took another breath and let it out slowly. She leaned her head back into the corner and closed her eyes just for a moment, until she noticed the badger walk in.

"Here now, this is a funny sort of place for a drink," he said as he hopped up onto a box of glasses.

"I just wanted some peace and quiet," she said, hoping he wouldn't take offense.

"You're a long way from peace and quiet. I would think you'd know that," he said.

"I thought I might be able to find out who did it."

"You know who did it," the badger replied.

"I don't," Pru said crossly. "I remember now that's what Ned told me, but I don't know."

The badger peered down his snout at her, and said, "I had a cousin once, who was a Boy Scout down in Dorset—"

She snorted. "Badgers can't be Boy Scouts." He ignored the interruption and carried on with the story. Pru had no idea badgers could be so loquacious. The story, although interesting, was long, and she began to lose track of it. Then, in the distance, she heard Ted slap his hand on the bar and call, "Time! Time, please, ladies and gentlemen."

The badger hopped off the box. "Well, that's me away," he said. He started to leave, but then turned and added, "He'll be looking for you, you know."

"Will he?" she asked. Perhaps that should make her afraid, but it didn't.

He seemed about to say something else, but instead walked out, leaving Pru confused. Should she hide because he would be looking for her or should she go find him first?

* * *

"Look! I told you — here she is!" Pru started with fright, unable to figure out if he had found her or if the badger had come back. But when she opened her eyes, it was to Ted and Hayley or Heidi standing over her.

"Oh, sorry," she said, trying to get her bearings, stand up, and sound coherent. "I must've dropped off. Is it closing time?"

"Closing time?" Ted asked. "It's morning. You must've slept the whole night. We forgot all about you until a bit ago when Hattie said, what about that American woman — didn't you, love?"

Hattie, yes, that was it.

Pru shook her head, trying to dislodge a few of the cobwebs in her brain, but the only thing dislodged was her hair clip. "I'm sorry you had to come back over to get me."

"It was no trouble," Hattie said. "We live upstairs. Would you like a cappuccino?"

A cappuccino sounded like the most wonderful thing in the world. "Yes, thanks, that would be lovely," she said, trying to stretch out the kinks. It had been a long time since she'd slept on a floor.

"Double?" Ted asked, when Pru emerged from the toilet, having attempted to stick her hair back up into its clip.

Pru nodded. "So, I happened to see Robbie talking with Jamie Tanner last evening. You know Jamie?" she asked as she pulled the cup across the bar and scooped a spoonful of the deliciously bitter foam into her mouth.

The two exchanged glances. "Look, I'm sorry I don't have time to keep them apart," Ted said.

"Does Jamie cause problems?"

"He gets into it now and then. Nothing we need to ring the station for, and he cools off quickly. But," Ted caught himself, "he's never that way with Robbie."

"And the fellow with the red ponytail. Do you know him?" Pru asked.

"Those two," Hattie said, shaking her head. "They argue constantly, but they're always stuck to each other at the bar. Last night, did you hear, Ted?" — she turned to her partner — "Tanner was bossing the fellow around again. 'You'll do what I tell you to do.' That sort of thing. He's a bully, if you ask me."

"Yes, certainly sounds like it," Pru said as she replayed Jamie's statement in her mind. She remembered talking with the red ponytail guy who said he and Jamie worked together up at Dunorlan Park, but hadn't they lost track of each other about midday? Tatt had said Jamie had an alibi, but if that was it, it certainly didn't sound airtight.

"Thanks very much for the coffee," Pru said, hand on her bag.

"That's lovely, that is," Hattie said, nodding at the fan pendant. "It looks old. Wherever did you find it?"

Pru touched her necklace, her talisman, resting on the outside of her jacket. "It was a gift." She smiled. "From . . . from my . . ." There she went again.

Hattie seemed to understand. "Your fellow?"

"Yeah," Pru said, and gave a little laugh. That wasn't too bad. "My fellow."

Primrose House

16 February

Pru,

 Just a note as Bryan and I dash off to Liverpool. I want to have a good, long talk when we return. There are several things we need to get straight. I don't want to alarm you, but I know you will understand that it's better to leave things alone rather than to stir up what could possibly end up being a great deal of trouble for you. We'll say nothing else now, but do watch yourself.

 Best,
 Davina

 P.S. I've left something for you in the walled garden.

CHAPTER 36

She had seen Davina's note stuck in the front door as she pulled her Mini up to the cottage. She read and reread it, attempting to decipher its veiled and mildly threatening tone. God, she felt alone. She needed some spark, some push to get her going. She needed Repton. Time and again she got out the Red Book, whether she was in need of inspiration or merely to hear his voice as she read his kind but pointed comments. Perhaps today, if she carried the Red Book along with her, she would absorb some of Repton's wisdom about the landscape and clear her head of everything else.

She retrieved the leather-bound book from its safe placed under a stack of sweaters in her wardrobe, scattering a few sweaters onto the floor in the process. She wasn't in the mood for tidying, and ignored them. She walked, opened the book to a random page and read.

"I suppose every person who visits Primrose House will observe that the house is too near the road, but the house is not in fact too near the road but the road is unluckily too near the house. This is the great defect of the place, and although it cannot be turned in reality, it may so far be removed in appearance that it will be no longer be an objection." Sorry to say, Humphry, the road had gone nowhere.

She pushed open the gate to the walled garden. Now what would Davina leave her here? Had she come up with a new idea for that lasting memorial to Ned? Perhaps she wanted a mural of him painted on the walls — or did she expect Pru to shear a topiary figure of the old man out of the yew? Pru glanced up to the center of the garden where two of the yews remained untouched and two remained a picture of devastation from the day they were hacked to pieces, leaving only uneven stumps. Sunk deep into the broken top of one was an ax.

Her breath came quick and shallow, and she blinked several times to clear the sight away, but it remained. She was alone, she was sure of that — there was nowhere to hide in the walled garden, they'd cleared everything away. She edged forward, making no sound on the bare dirt, and the thought came to her, unbidden, that she would need to order a load of gravel to finish off the paths. She crept up to the ax, as if it could fly out of the trunk of its own accord and attack her.

Pru attempted to make sense of what she saw. Davina had left something for her in the walled garden. Was it this ax? Without touching it, Pru took a close look and could almost swear it was the one that had gone missing from the tool shed — she could still see a sheen on the wood handle from the oiling Liam and Fergal gave it. Surely Davina didn't do this. Hadn't the Templetons been away when the yews were destroyed?

Two tools for cutting had been taken from Pru's garden shed. The hatchet had been used on Ned, but this ax had cut wood. That brought to mind one more tool for cutting wood — the pocketknife found with blood on it under Ned's body. Just yesterday, she had left DS Hobbes a message to say that a pocketknife was a handy tool for grafting.

Her eyes fell on the blank walls and the bare-root apple trees heeled into one of the beds. Yes, yes, she told them silently, I'll get you planted. She pressed fingertips to her eyelids. Two seconds — could she not go two seconds without worrying about what to do in the garden? The sight of the apples had loosened that shred of memory again, and she tried to catch it before it floated out of reach. She repeated what she knew. Old varieties grafted onto dwarfing rootstock. Grafting. She rubbed her hands on her trousers and looked down at her palms. Instead of her own hands, she saw another pair. Scars marred the pad of his left thumb. He held them up to her on that first day they met. "Snap," Jamie had said, "gardeners' hands."

* * *

She had no more registered that memory than she noticed something flutter at her feet — a small red diary lay open, its pages caught by the breeze.

As she reached for it, clutching Repton's book to her chest, she could see pages of neatly printed names, some crossed off, others not. The chill wind that swirled around inside the walls froze the sweat that broke out on her forehead. This was Jamie Tanner's red book. What was it doing in the walled garden?

Picking it up and paging through, she noticed that far into the book, the handwriting deteriorated, with fewer names written in poorer penmanship. By the time she reached the page with Liam's name, the letters were large and badly formed. But still it continued, because when she turned the page, she saw the next name had been written in block letters, each letter traced and retraced with the point of the pen until there was no need for ink to read it. NED. An X tore through both the name and the paper.

A creeping dread came over her and she had to steel her nerve to turn the page. On it, she saw that his handwriting had changed from large and uncontrolled to tiny and precise. PRU PARKE. A shudder swept through her.

Ring the police. She slapped her pocket to locate her phone. Where was her phone? The second she remembered leaving it on the floor in the snug of the Two Bells was a second too late.

He grabbed hold of the back of her collar and jerked hard, throwing her off balance. Something cut into her neck, and for a split second she couldn't breathe. A snap, and she gasped as he let go and shoved her up against the yew stump. Repton's Red Book went flying out of her hands, and the handle of the ax, its blade deep in the yew trunk, hovered over her.

"I've been looking for you."

She had seen Jamie in various states before — tidy, unkempt, cool and collected, an emotional wreck — but she hadn't seen this. His bloodshot eyes burned, the muscles in his neck bulged, and his fists clenched.

"Jamie, you need to calm down," she said, putting her hand up as if to stop him.

"You shouldn't've done that, Pru," he said. "You will help pretty boy Liam, but you won't help me. You chose the wrong side, and you shouldn't've interfered." He leaned down into her face. "She's *my* wife and this should've been *my* job. You can't just come in here and take what's mine."

"It wasn't your job," Pru said, digging her heels into the ground and sitting up bit by bit, hoping to get in a better position to run. "What made you think it was?"

"*He promised!*" Jamie shouted in her face, spraying her with spit. "He promised me the job. He said it was to keep an eye on me, to make sure Cate was all right. I didn't care how he did it, but he failed, didn't he? He couldn't even do that for her. But now with you gone, they'll pick me, like they should've done to begin with." He waved his arm vaguely in the direction of Primrose House.

"Ned tried to get you the job?" Pru scooted a tiny bit farther as Jamie looked away for a moment, still quaking. He was a talker, and although he now seemed a distorted version of his saner self, perhaps she could keep him talking until a better idea occurred to her.

"He told me he'd get me the job, and then he turned around and told me he'd see me in jail first for what I did to her. It was Liam, you see. He's the one who turned Ned against me. Ned said to keep away from her, that he was on his way to the police. I couldn't let him do that — let him keep me from Cate." Jamie looked over the walls and grew quiet.

"Did you steal Robbie's jacket? Did you go to Chaffinch's and take him away?"

Jamie turned his attention back to her and tapped his finger on his temple. "You see, I know how to take care of things," he said in a loud whisper. "It takes brains to organize something this good — who would care what a half-wit does? It isn't as if he'd get in trouble."

Her foot shot out to kick at him before she could stop herself. "He isn't a half-wit."

The kick barely grazed him, but it made an impact. He lunged, shouting as he shook her, "I took care of it. I always take care of it. And they'd have Duffy locked up now if it wasn't for your interfering." He threw her back down again.

"You're checking us off your list, are you?" She glanced past him to the open front gate. They weren't scheduled to work in the walled garden today, and so no one would know where she was. She must get out of here.

He looked left and right in a panic. "Where is it? What did you do with it?"

She knew he wasn't talking about Repton's Red Book — she could see that off to her right where it landed in one of the beds. It was his own red book Jamie wanted. Pru thought she was sitting on it, but flung her hand out, pointing behind him. "It's over there," she said.

He turned and she scrambled, but he recovered, grabbing and hoisting her up, trapping her in a chokehold.

She tried to pry his arm off her and stand up, but her feet could not find purchase. "You *pushed* my Cate and Duffy together," he said. "You *encouraged* it," he said. With every word, he squeezed tighter. "You couldn't take a few friendly hints — the plants, the shed, the yews. You need to be taught a lesson, and an ax is as good as a hatchet for that," Jamie said, reaching for the handle.

But the yew had a better grip on the ax than he did. He couldn't pull it free with one hand and the brief diversion gave Pru the chance to wiggle away, and the added advantage of stomping on his foot as she did so.

It wasn't much of an advantage, but she took it, running to the side gate and out toward Primrose House and people. There was no point in trying to get to her empty cottage — what could she do without her phone?

As she ran, she shouted, hoping that if he thought people were already on site, he wouldn't follow. She wasn't even sure what time it was. Would Liam and Fergal be there? Ivy? No Davina and Bryan, she at least remembered that.

The air seared her lungs as Pru gasped for breath, barely making it to the back of the house where the stone stairs led up to the balustrade terrace. A glance behind her told her that he hadn't followed. Yet. She dragged herself up the steps and got to the kitchen door.

"Ivy!" She banged on the door and peered in the darkened windows. No response. Would she even work today with no Templetons at home? Pru's hands went to her pockets. Another useless gesture — she no longer carried a key to Primrose House with her.

Pru looked toward the walled garden. Perhaps she had scared Jamie away. If he was crazy enough to attack her there, he may be crazy enough to go on about his business now — she'd seen him change in a flash from sanity to insanity and back again. Leaning up against the cold brick of the house, she scanned her surroundings and her eyes fell on Repton's beech wood. Just the place to hide until Ivy or the Duffys appeared.

She flew down the stairs past the towering pile of manure, continued down the terraced slope, and headed for the safety of the wood. Sit quiet, watch, and wait, she thought. Someone will arrive.

Her eyes darted back and forth, behind and in front, in case Jamie should try to surprise her, and she scanned the ground until she found a piece of fallen branch about three feet long with twigs down its length. She stood behind a scrubby holly for camouflage and stood cradling her club and keeping an eye out toward the yew walk, Primrose House, and beyond. The skin around her neck burned, and she shivered in the cold. Her breath created little clouds. *Would spring ever come?* Pru thought. There was still so much to do. Where was everyone?

Car tires on the gravel drive up by the house brought her back to her immediate predicament. She came out from behind the holly. Jamie wouldn't be bold enough to pull into the drive — someone has arrived. Someone to help.

But Jamie had arrived, too. He knew his way around the grounds well, and must have gone out to the lane and circled around the house to the wood. His footsteps behind her had made no noise on the wet, decaying leaves, until just he stepped on a twig a few feet away.

Pru turned as he pounced, and her improvised club caught him right in the stomach. He gasped and seized the branch. She let go and ran toward the stone steps, but when she got to the terracing, she looked over her shoulder, and that moment's distraction caused her to step in one of Robbie's holes. Her right ankle bent awkwardly beneath her and she shouted in pain and collapsed.

Jamie was on her in an instant, shouting what sounded like his mantra, "It's your fault," as he took hold of her hair, clip and all, and yanked her head back. His legs were the only things in reach. She grabbed one and pulled. Unbalanced, he fell on his back and rolled partway down the slope.

But now she had lost her ability to run and had to drag herself back up the stairs to the terrace, each step on the ankle a stab of pain that made her cry out. She got to the top on her knees, but no farther. He had run up after, picked her up, and threw her halfway over the balustrade, so that she was hanging face down.

"You don't like heights, do you, Pru?" He pushed her further over, trying to unbalance her. "You shouldn't admit to a weakness like that — and the first time we met."

She did hate heights, but he had miscalculated her fear. As he forced her farther over the wide stone rail, she saw that the thirty-foot drop had been cut to fifteen, and below was a mountain of soft, fluffy manure mixed with wood shavings. She swung her arms wildly, as if flailing in panic, and reached up, fastening onto enough of Jamie to unbalance them both. They tipped over sideways and dropped.

The mountain of manure, just recently dumped onto the site, still had a great deal of loft to it — not quite as soft as a mattress, but enough to cushion their fall. If she had been a cat, she could've turned herself in midair and landed right on top of him, but as it was, they landed on their sides, still holding onto each other. Jamie recovered quickly and was stronger than she was. He pinned her shoulders down. She reached back, got a handful of manure and smashed it into his face.

"*Bitch!*" he shouted and slapped her hard, causing her world to spin. She pushed against his hold and they both rolled down the manure mountain together and came to a stop at the bottom of the pile. She tried to stand, but the pain in her ankle was a swift reminder that she couldn't go far. Jamie shoved her down again. He put his hands around her throat and his thumbs pressed on her windpipe, squeezing until she made a gurgling sound. Sparkles appeared in front of her eyes, and the world began to fade until a pair of hands clamped onto Jamie's shoulders.

"*Get off her!*" Pru jerked forward for a moment as the hands wrenched Jamie backward and threw him to the side.

She collapsed, drew a torturous breath, and looked up. She squinted, trying to regain her vision, and saw frizzy brown and gray hair on a figure in a sheepskin coat.

"Simon!" she croaked, and broke out in a fit of coughing.

Jamie had rolled down the slope, and Simon paid him no heed. He bent down to Pru. "Are you all right? Did he hurt you?"

She wasn't entirely sure that he wasn't an apparition. She opened her mouth to say something, but only gagged.

251

Over Simon's shoulder, she saw Jamie rush up, screaming something incomprehensible, holding her makeshift club high, about to strike. Simon turned in time to catch the branch, wrench it out of his hands, and use it to give Jamie a ferocious push that threw him back down the slope once again.

"Hold it right there!" DS Hobbes came running down the stone stairs. He pointed, and two policemen, bringing up the rear, were on Jamie before he could get up. Hobbes grabbed hold of Simon.

"No, no — it's Simon," Pru squawked, waving her arms.

Simon didn't try to escape Hobbes' grasp. "I'm her brother," he said.

The DS looked at Pru, who nodded, choked back a sob, and winced at the pain.

He let go of Simon and leaned over Pru. "Are you hurt?"

"My ankle," she mouthed, pointing to her right foot. She began another painful coughing jag.

"More than your ankle," Hobbes said. "I'll get an ambulance."

"I'll stay with her," Simon said, kneeling down beside Pru.

The sergeant ran up the slope, phone to his ear. Jamie was resisting the two policemen, but with little success.

"Who is he?" Simon asked her, nodding at Jamie.

"He's Ned's murderer," she tried to say, without much sound coming out.

"Ah," Simon said, observing Jamie being dragged off. "Harry told me about Ned — the old fellow who was killed." He put his hand on the stone railing to stand up. "Guess I'd better watch who I'm calling an 'old fellow.'"

The police activity faded to the background as, for a moment, Pru and Simon fell into an awkward silence. Finally, she whispered, "Where did you come from?"

"I've been looking for you," he said, glancing up to the several police vehicles parked on the gravel. He didn't look back at her, but continued. "I drove up and down the lane before I decided this was Primrose House. It . . . it wasn't fair of me the way I treated you. I wanted you to stay on Sunday, when you brought me the box, but I didn't know how to ask. Birdie's been saying I should come and talk with you, and last night Polly said it had better be soon or I'd never have another good night's sleep. I left at first light. I didn't want to arrive too early."

"Not too early," Pru rasped. "Just in time."

DS Hobbes returned and said, "Ambulance is on its way. You can wait here, Pru, and they'll bring down a stretcher for you."

"Here now, the two of us can carry you," Simon said. They made a litter out of their arms, and she held onto their shoulders as they carried her up to the stone terrace near the kitchen door.

The ambulance pulled in, and attendants hopped out. One of them took her shoe off and asked if she was in pain. "It's not too bad," she said, which was not true, but in light of such sudden joy, the pain took a momentary back seat.

When they'd got her settled in the ambulance, Simon took hold of the door handle and put his foot up to get in.

"Sorry, sir, you can't ride in the back."

"He's my brother," Pru shouted in squeaks and pops. An electric thrill shot up her spine at the very use of the word, but she realized she was practically unintelligible. She tried again. "He's my brother."

CHAPTER 37

Pru and Simon had no time for familial conversation during the ambulance journey, as the attendant began an assessment of her injuries. Nor did they upon arrival at the hospital where she was admitted into the emergency room, had an X-ray taken of her ankle, and was installed in a curtained-off alcove. At last, activity slowed while she sat up on the paper-covered bed, still in her clothes, which were smeared with manure, and waited for a doctor.

Simon sat in a chair next to her bed. He leaned forward, elbows on his knees, clasping and unclasping his hands. "Does your foot hurt much?" he asked.

Pru, the brave little sister, shrugged. "It's nothing." Her voice was still a whisper.

"What's it like — Texas?" he asked. It broke the ice, if only a crack.

"Hot." She shrugged. Stopping every few words for a cough, and trying to swallow without screwing her face up, she said, "It was a good place to live, but all my life I listened to my . . . to Mother's stories about England, and as far back as I can remember, this is where I wanted to live." Tears welled up and fell as she attempted to blink them away. "I always wanted a brother or sister."

"I always wanted a brother," Simon said. "You know, someone to kick a ball around with." He looked hopeful. "You don't play football, do you?"

Pru wheezed a laugh. "No, but I played softball in high school." Before she could go into the finer points of slow-pitch, the doctor walked in.

"Well, Ms . . ." he glanced down at the chart in his hand, "Ms. Parke, I'm Dr. Laurence." He lifted her chin and examined her face and neck, then looked at her ankle. A nurse had cleaned up the scrapes and wrapped her foot. "How does your throat feel?"

"It hurts," Pru said.

He held an X-ray of her foot up to the ceiling lights. "I'm happy to report you have no broken bones, but a rather nasty sprain, in addition to several abrasions, the bruises at your throat and the accompanying mild laryngeal trauma. Stay still, don't talk, and" — He took stock of her clothes and most likely caught a whiff of her — "You're a gardener, aren't you?"

She nodded, thinking police would've informed him of the situation.

Dr. Laurence wagged a finger at her wrapped ankle. "You stay off that foot," he admonished. He turned to Simon and shook his head. "Gardeners," he said. "They never listen. She'll be out there tomorrow mucking about, saying the peonies need dividing or some such."

"Hang on," Simon protested.

The doctor looked down his nose at him. "You, too?"

"Yes, my sister and I are both gardeners."

Pru broke out in a huge grin. "Can I go home? I'm not going back out in the garden, I promise." Today.

The doctor looked skeptical, but said, "Yes, right, fine. Just give us a few minutes for paperwork."

He left and the siblings sat in silence, until Simon cleared his throat. "I'm sorry for the way I acted," he said.

Pru shook her head. "It was a shock for both of us. I don't understand why they didn't tell you. Or me."

"They knew I'd be fine with Birdie and George, and I was. I've nothing to complain about, really. I've a good life." He looked over at her. "Did you read those letters?"

Pru blushed. "A few lines. When I realized that she had written them to you, I put them away."

He smiled, and Pru could see their dad's smile. Her heart lurched. "There was one toward the end where she wrote 'Someday she will find you.'" He raised his eyebrows. "And you did."

DS Hobbes stepped into the room, carrying a flat parcel wrapped in plastic. Pru introduced Simon properly, and then nodded to the package Hobbes held, and said, "Is that the Red Book? Is it all right?" She would heal, but damage to her beloved Repton epistle might be irreparable.

Hobbes took the Red Book out of the plastic. "It's not too bad, doesn't look as if it's torn. No mud. Good thing it wasn't raining today." He offered it to Pru.

"Simon, you look at it."

Simon took the piece of history with all the reverence it deserved, as she knew he would. The hospital room around them fell away as he opened the book and read the first page, then carefully turned to look at more. "Can you still see Repton's landscape?" he asked. "Is any of it left?"

Pru started to explain the Repton features she'd discovered, but Hobbes interrupted, clearing his throat. "Pru," he began. "I'm sorry to bother you here, but I thought you should know—"

"Will we need to give the Red Book back for now?" she asked. "It's evidence, I suppose." Simon closed the book and stroked its cover before handing it back to the sergeant. What about Jamie?"

"Looks as if there will be plenty of evidence for a murder charge," Hobbes said. "But there's something else." He shifted his weight from one foot to another, and took a deep breath before he began. "I spoke with Inspector Pearse."

Out of the corner of her eye, Pru saw Simon sit up straight, but her mind was all on Christopher. This can't be good, she thought. "Did you tell him what happened?"

"That's the thing," Hobbes said. "I spoke to him just before his flight left. He hadn't been able to get hold of you." She thought of her phone on the floor of the snug at the Two Bells. "I had gone to your cottage, looking for you," he continued, "and then out to the walled garden. He rang just after I found the note from Mrs. Templeton and your necklace on the ground."

Her hand flew to her throat. That was what had cut off her breath when Jamie grabbed hold of her collar. "Oh no — you told Christopher you'd found my necklace, but you didn't know where I was?"

The sergeant's red face told her more than he could say about Christopher's reaction. "I described the necklace to him, and he said that it was yours. I told him what I saw — the ax and the note — before I realized his situation. He told me where he was and I promised to ring him back as soon as I had news, but by the time I'd found you, he was already in flight."

Pru pictured it. Christopher on a plane for eight hours not knowing if she were alive or dead. She covered her face with her hands.

"I left him a long message, explaining that you're all right, as such. I told him what happened." Hobbes shook his head. "But he won't hear that for another four hours."

"I need to ring him," she said, automatically going for her pocket. "I need to leave him a message, too. But my phone is at the Bells."

"Use mine." Simon held his out.

"Thanks," Pru said shyly as she took it. "David, can Simon give his statement soon? He drove all the way from Hampshire this morning, but I'm sure he needs to get home."

"Yes," the DS said, "that's fine. You stop by the station before you go. Pru, I'll get your phone and your necklace and deliver them to you later."

After Hobbes left, Pru said, "Christopher is my . . . well, he and I are . . ." She could feel her face reddening.

"Oh." Simon nodded. "Sure. Does he live round here?"

"No, he lives in London. He's a DCI with the Met."

Simon's eyes grew large. "Cor," he said quietly.

"Yeah, I know," Pru said, acknowledging the unusual pairing of a gardener and a policeman.

"Would you like me to leave while you ring him?" He nodded to the phone.

"No." Pru smiled as she made the call. "You stay."

It was a comfort to hear Christopher's voice, even if it was only his terse recording: "Pearse. Leave a message."

"Christopher, I'm all right." Regrettably, her voice did not back her up on that statement. She filled her brief message with reassurance and ended with, "Ring me when you have a chance. After you get Graham to Phyl's house in Oxford. It's all right, really it is." She sighed deeply and handed the phone back to Simon. "You've come all this way, and we won't really have time to talk."

"It doesn't matter," he replied. "We'll have time after today."

Pru fiddled with the paper covering on the bed. She could feel the tears again. "I've taken a whole day in the garden away from you, and it's such a busy time now."

He nodded. "I've just got in six new roses to plant. Vernona picked them out from an article she read." The corner of his mouth went up. "She's been dying to talk to me about you, but Harry told her not to interfere. She'll be quite happy about this." His eyes flickered to her ankle. "Well, not this, but you know what I mean."

Pru laughed soundlessly. "You go on home."

"I don't want to leave you, not without anyone here," he said, shaking his head. "I'll get you a cup of tea, shall I?" A cup of tea sounded just the trick, and Pru thought that Simon looked as if he needed a useful activity.

While he was gone, an orderly popped his head in to find out if Pru had seen the doctor yet, and after that the nurse came in to say that she would be discharged soon. In the next quiet moment, Ivy rushed in.

"Oh, Pru, I can't believe this," she said, taking Pru's hands in hers. "There were police everywhere at Primrose

House when I arrived — Sergeant Hobbes, too, and he told me what happened." She noticed Simon standing in the doorway with two cups of tea. "I'm very sorry, you already have a visitor."

"Ivy," Pru said, beaming as she took her tea from him, "this is my brother, Simon Parke. He's a gardener, too. He lives near Romsey."

Ivy did a fair job of hiding her surprise at hearing Pru had a brother, and fussed over Pru's voice instead. Pru realized she'd now have to give a revised family history to anyone who knew her. She quite looked forward to that.

Simon offered his tea to Ivy, who said, "No thank you. I only wanted to see you, Pru, for myself and tell you this. I took Robbie in to Chaffinch's myself this morning — that's why I was late to Primrose House. I didn't think it would matter, what with the Templetons off to Liverpool. I'm so sorry I wasn't there to help." Pru tried to picture just what Ivy could've done, and came up with an image of her going after Jamie with a frying pan.

"No, Ivy, it was all right," Pru said. Sure, she was unable to walk, she'd been hit and choked, but after all, she was sitting here with her brother and cautiously drinking a cup of tepid tea. Other than longing for Christopher to be in the room, what more could she ask?

Ivy offered Simon a lift back to Primrose House to collect his car, after which she would return to shuttle Pru to her cottage. While Ivy went off to make a phone call, Pru and Simon were alone to say goodbye. They smiled at each other, and then looked at the floor. Pru tried to figure out just how to handle this newfound intimacy

"I'll want to see the garden," Simon said.

"And I want you to meet Christopher," she said, hoping she wasn't assuming too much.

He looked at her for a moment, and said, "Yes, of course."

"We've so much to do," Pru replied, although at that moment, not even an unfinished garden daunted her. "All that new terracing where . . . where you found me will have to be finished and planted up. Davina wants to have an open garden day in July. It'll be so new, I can't imagine who would want to see it." She caught herself as she began to babble. Her throat hurt. She took a sip of tea.

"Well, we'll be there," Simon said.

They went on to promise visits and phone calls, and finally he leaned over and they embraced. Pru burst into tears.

"No, no," she squeaked, laughing at the look of concern he gave her. He had three women in the house — surely he was accustomed to an occasional cry. "I'm fine. You go."

CHAPTER 38

It was past midday before she left hospital. Mostly she waited for her official discharge, but she did at least give her statement to DS Hobbes, who said Jamie was in a cell at the station where he alternated between threatening retaliation for his treatment and acquiescing to police requests. They at last had his fingerprints and were checking them against the partial found on the hatchet and the pocketknife. For Hobbes, it was all in a day's work — albeit an unusual day — and he ended on a practical note. "Are you hungry?"

Starving, she said, and asked if he could find her some soup. He brought her a cup of creamy vegetable. *Step one on the road to recovery*, she thought as she blew on the surface to cool it off.

She got her phone back, but not her necklace. It had apparently found its way into the hands of Inspector Tatt, who said he would return it. *Oh, joy*. Pru stared at the screen on her phone for a few minutes, trying to figure out if it would help or hurt to leave Christopher another message. She decided against it, but while she considered, Davina rang, having heard from the police.

"Pru, my God, are you all right?"

Pru gave a brief account, but Davina had difficulty following it. "We must have a bad connection," she said.

Happy to blame the phone service rather than to go into detail about why her voice was so spotty, Pru asked Davina only one question of her own. The answer left her laughing in a wheezy fashion.

"Gloves? Was that what your note was about — you left me gloves?"

"They're lovely," Davina said. "Suede. We picked them up in Paris. They're gauntlet-style to protect you when you prune the roses." *It's true,* Pru thought, *those ramblers can be vicious.* "I put them in the glasshouse," Davina continued. "I thought you'd see them right off. Sorry about the mix-up."

Pru stopped short of replying "no harm done."

"Rest up," Davina said, "and we'll have a good chin-wag when I return."

* * *

Pru hobbled out of her bedroom after a sit-down shower taken with Cate's assistance, and found her cottage a hive of activity. Ivy was at the Aga, standing over a pot of something with a spicy fragrance. Fergal and Liam were building a fire. Robbie was helping Cate fluff pillows. When they saw her, they all stopped what they were doing and got quite busy settling her on the sofa. Robbie rearranged the pillows behind her several times. Cate rewrapped Pru's ankle as she worried aloud how she would explain to Nanda what her father had done, but then hoped that perhaps she wouldn't need to address it for a few years.

As they all worked, they expressed concern over her trauma and a keen desire to hear from her own lips what had happened. She had become quite practiced of the sketchy account in a short time and so gave it, promising details later. It was late afternoon, and she was weary. She looked around at them as they worked and talked with one another and thought how much she loved them and how happy she was they were there, but the person she wanted to see the most was probably on his way to Oxford by now. Without ringing her when he landed. She had an enormous headache, her ankle throbbed, her throat hurt, and she wished everyone would be quiet.

Silence fell so suddenly, Pru was afraid she'd said that last bit aloud, but when she looked up, she saw all her guests frozen in a tableau, staring at Christopher, who stood in the doorway.

He'd been traveling for twelve hours and looked it. Robbie broke the spell with, "You're Pru's boyfriend." The room came to life again, as everyone spoke at once and moved to the door as a single entity. As Ivy grabbed both her coat and Robbie, she said, "I've put it in the simmer oven, Pru, and there's bread. It's all ready whenever you are." Fergal said, "Fire's lit, so you should have a good blaze soon." Liam patted her shoulder and said, "Well done." Cate leaned over and took Pru's clip out, arranging her hair to cover the mark on her face where Jamie had slapped her, and drew the light throw across Pru's foot to hide her bloated purple toes. Everyone spoke to Christopher on the way out. "How's your son?" "Good flight?" "She held her own with him, you know."

The door shut and they were alone. Pru smiled. "Hi," she said. Her voice, a husky whisper that morning, had started to return and now she sounded more like a fourteen-year-old boy going through puberty. Christopher didn't speak, but came to her and sat down on the sofa. He took her in his arms as if she were a delicate piece of glass.

She would not cry. She would not shed tears all over his shirt and make him feel guilty because he hadn't been there to save her. He buried his face in her hair and inhaled. She felt his breath on her shoulder like a warm breeze and heard him murmur, "My darling."

The sobs racked her body as she clung to him, and he held her tightly. Eventually, she pulled free slightly and gave him a nod to signal that it was over. She sniffed repeatedly, and Christopher reached into his jacket pocket, producing a handkerchief. She blew her nose, and he wiped the tears from her cheeks with his thumbs. That led him to push back the hair Cate had drawn forward. His face grew hard when he saw the red welt high on her cheek. His hand moved down to her sweater. Apparently, DS Hobbes had given details of her injuries. Christopher peeled back the collar to reveal the thin line where her necklace had cut into her neck, and he lifted her chin to see the blue thumbprint smudges at her throat. He clenched his jaw.

She put her hand on his arm and felt his muscles stretched tight as a rubber band about to snap. "Christopher, I'm all right."

"You are *not* all right," he fired back. He was breathing hard. "But you're better off than I imagined for all those hours."

"I'm sorry," she whispered. "I'm sorry you didn't know in time."

"The last thing I heard from David was that he had found your necklace in the walled garden, along with the Red Book and one of Davina's notes. You were nowhere to be seen."

"That's where Jamie grabbed me," she said. "I got away and ran for the house."

He took her hands in his. "And before that, I tried to ring you for hours."

All while he managed to get his injured son checked out of a hospital, to the airport, and on a plane.

She told him about her covert surveillance in the snug at the Two Bells. "I was tired and hungry — all I had for supper was two bags of crisps and a pint. And then I fell asleep and had a funny dream," she said, "about a badger."

One eyebrow shot up. "A badger?"

She could see her way out now. "Yes, a badger. He sat down on one of the boxes and told me about being a Boy Scout." She watched him as he watched her. His jaw was working. "And then Ted called time . . ."

"In your dream?"

"That might've been real, but I'm not sure. Then the badger said, 'he'll be looking for you,' and he walked out." Christopher's lips twitched. "Too bad he didn't remind me about my mobile."

Christopher dropped his face into his hands and rubbed his eyes, saying, "Oh, my God." But she could see the smile he was trying to hide. He looked at her and shook his head.

She leaned forward and paused for a moment, their lips barely touching, before kissing him. He responded in kind, reaching his arm around to the small of her back. She laid her hand against his cheek, which felt like sandpaper now at the end of a long day. "You were where you needed to be," she said.

He took her clip from the side table and handed it to her. "No need to hide that any longer. And now, I want you to tell me what happened today with Tanner."

She nodded. "Yes. Would you get us a drink first?"

"What would you like?" he asked as he stood, finally removing his coat and adding a log to the fire. "Wine?"

"Brandy," she said. "I'd like a very large . . . oh, just bring the bottle."

He returned with glasses and brandy, and perched again on the sofa. "You could sit on the chair," she said. "You'd be more comfortable."

"I am comfortable right here," he said, handing her a glass and taking a sip from his own. He rested a hand on her thigh. They both looked into the fire.

She took a drink of brandy and her throat felt good enough to tell the entire story, and so she began, describing her flight to Primrose House, Jamie's appearance, and Simon showing up to save the day.

"Simon," he marveled.

"Yes," Pru said, feeling again the amazement and joy at her brother's appearance. "He said he realized he wasn't being fair to me before. All he really needed was a little persuasion."

Christopher stopped his glass halfway to his lips. "Persuasion?"

"Birdie and Polly have been talking to him. And the letters, I know they helped."

They sat in silence, both with their own thoughts. Pru leaned back into her pillows, holding out her glass to Christopher. On her second brandy, her headache had vanished and her ankle didn't feel half bad.

Tires on the gravel prompted Pru to squeak in disappointment. "Everyone's already been here," she said.

Everyone except Tatt. Christopher opened the door, and the inspector, in tartan overcoat and deerstalker, strolled in.

"Well, Pearse, you seem to have missed out today. Not here to rescue Ms. Parke when she needed you?"

That was enough. "Christopher was bringing his son back from Dubai, where he'd been in a car crash," she said, running out of steam at the end and coughing before she took another sip of brandy. "Now just what do you want, Inspector?"

Tatt sputtered briefly, and said to Christopher, "I'm sorry to hear that. Is the boy all right?"

"He has some healing to do," Christopher replied, "but he'll be fine."

Somewhat pacified by her ability to humble Tatt, Pru asked, "Would you care to sit down?"

"No thank you," Tatt replied, straightening himself up. "I only stopped to see how you were getting on. And to tell you that it was because of the message you left DS Hobbes yesterday morning that we were on to Tanner."

Pru frowned slightly, trying to remember what she had said.

"About the pocketknife found at the murder scene," Tatt continued. "We had looked into Tanner's background already. He had no cautions, but his work history showed he'd put in several years at East Malling Research grafting apple trees. You told Hobbes that the pocketknife could be used for grafting. We questioned his co-worker in Tunbridge Wells again, and he confessed to lying about Tanner's whereabouts on the afternoon of the murder. Tanner had blackmailed him over some workplace theft, which he was more than willing to confess to if it meant seeing the end of his blackmailer. We put all that together, and well, bob's your uncle."

"It wasn't quite that simple for Pru," Christopher pointed out. "Or that easy."

"Yes, hmmm . . ." Tatt replied. "And Tanner, it turns out, was quite an archer in school."

She cut her eyes to Christopher, and lifted a finger. "I'll get to that." He regarded her but said nothing. She wasn't finished with Tatt. "What about Robbie Fox?"

Tatt gave a concessionary nod. "One of his friends at the day care center—"

"Andrew?"

"—told a story of Robin Hood taking Fox out for a bar of chocolate. It took a great deal of time to view the CCTV recordings around town, but we finally caught Tanner and the Fox boy at a newsagent off the Mount Ephraim Road, midday. On the way into the shop, Fox was wearing his red jacket. On the way out, Tanner carried it under his arm."

"And so, Robbie was not involved." Pru thought the point needed to be made.

"Evidence does not just fall from the sky, Ms. Parke," Tatt said, as if to justify the time spent investigating Robbie. He cleared his throat. "Still, I am sure your support was a great comfort to his mother."

Pru could only blink at what sounded suspiciously like a compliment.

"Well, that's me away then," Tatt said, dusting off his lapels and starting for the door. "Oh, yes, I almost forgot." He dug about in his coat pocket. "I told Hobbes I would return this to you." He held out her necklace, the two broken ends swinging morosely in the air.

One hand went to her chest and the other Pru held out, tears welling at the sight of her precious pendant. Christopher intervened, took the necklace from Tatt, and dropped it in his shirt pocket. "I'll have it repaired," he said to her.

She felt quite magnanimous toward Tatt now. "Would you care for a drink, inspector?" she asked.

She saw his eyes scan their cozy scene — glasses of brandy, flames dancing in the fireplace. She could've sworn he looked wistful.

He shook his head. "No, thank you. You have your dinner waiting — a curry, is it? And I do have a home to get to." And with that, he and his tartan coat disappeared out the door.

"A curry it is," Pru said. "I'm starving — how about you?"

CHAPTER 39

When Simon, Polly, and daughters Miranda and Peppy pulled into the cottage drive, Pru and Christopher stood waiting for them. Pru vibrated with excitement. She had invited them for Sunday lunch, they had accepted, and she had been immediately thrown into a panic about the garden and the menu. But the garden she could handle, and Ivy had taken charge of the menu.

It was one of those rare sunny March days when it might be considered almost warm. Pru could ask for nothing better. When it came time to introduce her family to Christopher, emotions overcame her, and she could barely get names out.

"Christopher, I'd like you to meet my brother, Simon" — she sniffed — "and my sister-in-law, Polly." She took a breath and cleared her throat. "And these are my nieces" — the word was almost unintelligible — "Penelope and Miranda."

They exchanged pleasantries, and Miranda patted Pru's arm. "It's all right, Aunt Pru." This prompted another outbreak. Miranda turned to Christopher. "Does she cry a great deal?"

"No, not really," Pru said, wiping her tears away. Out of the corner of her eye, she saw Christopher's eyebrows shoot up. She laughed.

* * *

Pru had been down to Hampshire twice to visit and had met both girls. The process of breaking apart and reassembling the Parke family moved like a mule — first lunging forward and then digging in its heels as they all searched for common ground. They had yet to share even the most mundane pieces of their lives. Sugar in your tea? Mash or roast? Poached or fried? It seemed no matter how they tried, there remained a vast unexplored territory, and when they approached the edge and touched on the pain of the secret years, they would all jump away and move to safer ground.

Pru told herself again and again that it wouldn't be easy or quick, but at least they all seemed determined and, even more amazing, they all got along. So far. Pru speculated that everyone was still on his or her best behavior. Who knew what it would be like when those last barriers fell? She could only hope for the best.

* * *

Drinks were followed by Sunday lunch of two roasted chickens, redolent with thyme and rosemary, accompanied by a spring risotto with asparagus and wild mushrooms. A pudding of rhubarb crumble followed by coffee finished out the meal, after which Pru conducted a tour of the gardens.

The afternoon drew to a close with — Pru hoped she wasn't imagining it — as much reluctance on Simon's part as hers. She hugged her nieces, her sister-in-law, and her brother in turn, and Christopher shook everyone's hand. While discussing with Polly her next visit to Romsey, Pru overheard Simon say to Christopher, "Again, I'm very sorry." And Christopher's reply, "No, don't worry about it. There's no need for that."

Christopher put his arm around Pru's shoulders, and they watched the Parkes drive away in Simon's mud-splattered Range Rover. They walked back to the cottage. Christopher opened the door and followed her in. When he threw the latch and turned, he couldn't move, because Pru stood directly in front of him.

"Why did Simon apologize to you?" she asked.

Christopher didn't move, only gave her one of those penetrating looks that seemed to reach deep inside her. She didn't move, either. He caught her hands in his and said, "I went to see Simon."

"You went to see him — when?" she asked with a slight frown.

He took a breath and said, "The weekend you found out he was your brother. You were devastated at hearing the news and then finding out he wanted nothing to do with you." He kneaded her hands lightly in an absentminded fashion. "I was worried about you. It wasn't fair of him to treat you that way. I knew he was shocked, but so were you, and I thought he should understand that. He should know how much this discovery meant to you."

He stopped. She waited.

Glancing around the room, and then back at Pru, he continued, "I drove down to see him that Saturday, to talk with him." He shrugged, and said with a grin, "You were right — he was angry."

A snort of laughter escaped before she slapped her hand over her mouth. "Simon gave you that black eye?"

"He needed to let off steam," Christopher said.

Her eyes grew wide. "Did you hit him back?"

"God no, I didn't hit him back," he said, almost laughing. "How would you feel if I got into a punch up with your new brother?"

She'd never had two men fight over her before even though it hadn't been for the traditional reasons.

"It hurt to see you like that — much more than Simon's fist hurt," Christopher continued. "I got up and dusted myself

271

off. Simon apologized and I left. I didn't think it would help to tell you at the time."

Pru made no reply as she attempted to sort out a jumble of thoughts and emotions. Her initial shock at Simon's anger, her love for Christopher, and his overwhelming need to take care of her — which she often paid no heed to — and the image of the two men in a fight.

"I realize that you may not like me to interfere in your family affairs, that it isn't my place—"

She stopped him with her fingertips on his lips. "You have every right. I grant you that right. I know you were doing it for me. And perhaps your visit was part of what changed Simon's mind." She reached up, rested her extended arms on his shoulders, and sighed, happy the day had been a success and happy that it was now over.

But it also meant the end of their time together, and Christopher, unable to shake loose from his responsibilities at the Met for the entire weekend, had arrived only that morning. "Will you go back this evening?"

He sighed, too, and said, "In the morning. But, I don't like this. I don't like being with you in bits and pieces."

"You might get tired of me if you saw me all the time."

"I might," he said.

She laughed. "Well, so much for fishing for a compliment."

He kissed her and said, "I don't believe I would, but I would dearly love to find out."

Together. The image wouldn't go away. "Surely we can come up with a solution."

"We'll talk about it later, when you can think of something other than the garden."

"And in the meantime," she said, "we always have weekends."

* * *

Monday morning, again. Pru watched Christopher drive off before she closed the door and collected their breakfast dishes. She was ready to leave for work when a knock came.

"Davina," she said, surprised to see her employer in person, rather than finding the usual note tucked into the door. "I was just about to head up to the garden."

Davina tilted her head slightly and smiled as she reached out and touched Pru's arm. "Pru," she said, "we have to talk."

Primrose House

30 July

Dear Pru,

Can you believe it's finally here? We'll be more than ready to greet our visitors today, and we are thrilled that, in addition to all the gardeners in England, many members of Bryan's investors group will be in attendance. I did just want to let you know of one person in particular — he's Swiss, a great friend of Bryan's, and quite influential. He is looking to move his company's headquarters to London, we are eager to make his visit today just as enjoyable as possible. A good impression could make such a difference!

Would you keep your eye out for him and perhaps give him just a little extra attention? He isn't really a gardener, but has asked if he could see . . . well, you know, where it all happened. We know that we can rely on you to make him feel like Britain is the best place for his company. He is rather tall and will probably be wearing one of those Australian bush hats — you won't be able to miss him.

Here's to success!

Best,
Davina

CHAPTER 40

Two envelopes had been stuck in Pru's door that morning with instructions written on each. One labeled "Read now" and the other with the directive "Read this evening." Pru read the first one and rolled her eyes. A Swiss investor — leave it to Davina to add one more thing to the day. She set the second note on the counter, assuming it was another plea for Pru to follow the Templetons to their next great adventure.

Bryan and Davina were leaving Primrose House. The ancient and convoluted laws that Hugo had told Pru about had stood the test of time — the Earl of Lamerton had no right to sell Primrose House, and so instead had offered a long-term lease. But the Templetons were interested in ownership, not tenancy, although Pru secretly believed that what they really liked was the process of restoration and not necessarily the finished product. So plans were already afoot for them to depart.

The earl had asked Pru to stay on, and she said that she would consider it. When she explained it all to Christopher, she kept from explaining to him that Primrose House had lost its charm for her now, and another plan had seeded itself in her mind. That, she decided, she would discuss with him the next time they were together.

* * *

For a few weeks after her accident, Pru had taken to directing activities from the balustrade terrace. Each day, Liam carried a chair out from the kitchen and she sat, using a walking stick to point and gesture. She had told them it was something else she had in common with Repton, if only temporarily. Late in his life, after a carriage accident, Repton had been confined to a wheelchair, but carried on working on site. He had even drawn a self-effacing picture of himself doing so.

But before long Pru's ankle had healed and she was back at it, as they all were — her regular crew and, after the Templetons increased her budget an eye-popping amount, many additional workers.

In April, the pond had been excavated, and they watched, over the several days that followed, the water seep in to fill the void. On the phone, she had tried to describe the scene to Christopher. "I wish I had been there," he said. "I wish you were here now," she replied.

A few days after Sunday lunch with the Parke family, Christopher had rung to say that he had been seconded — assigned to help with an investigation at another police station out of London. They were short-staffed, and as he'd done something similar before, they knew he could be trusted to do the job. It was away north in Scunthorpe.

"Lincolnshire?" Pru's voice had risen in alarm. "That's a bit harsh, isn't it?" Lincolnshire would mean no weekends together, as it would take him four hours at the very least to drive just one way. "Is this punishment? Because you've spent so much time down here with me?"

No, not punishment, he had assured her, although he hadn't sound entirely convinced himself. He would help investigate a terrible crime against a child — he knew better than to offer her details — and then stay on while they got their force back in shape after the unexpected departure of the chief superintendent. "It won't be for long." His attempt at an encouraging tone fell short of the mark. "And, when your open garden is finished, we'll make up for it."

Pru at last had conceded that she would have no time to spare for a personal life until after July, and that perhaps it wasn't the end of the world that he would temporarily be at the ends of the earth.

And so, they had gone back to separate beds, nightly phone calls, and trying to keep up each other's spirits.

When the open day approached, Christopher — still stuck in Scunthorpe and working seven days a week — had said that perhaps he could drive down early that Sunday morning.

As much as she disliked telling him no, she knew it was for the best. "Don't do it," she had said. "You don't need to. I won't have a minute to talk, and you'd have to turn right around as soon as it was all over and go back. It would be too frustrating. We'll have time later."

* * *

The last Sunday in July dawned clear and warm. In the months leading up to it, Pru had been taken on a meteorological roller coaster ride. In May, the weather had turned hot with no rain, and talk of a hosepipe ban was on everyone's lips. She was frantic — she had to water the new plants, or else everything would turn to toast. But after two weeks of unseasonable heat, the showers began. June was cool and wet, which not only kept her garden alive, but also slowed things down so that the roses had yet to go over and her late-planted alliums still held onto that moment between flower and seed. July began a bit on the cool side, but warmed up and dried out the second half, and so they could ask for nothing better.

* * *

Pru took little note of her tea and toast the morning of the open garden — she ripped the toast into tiny bits and gnawed piece after piece like a mouse. She didn't think she

277

could possibly eat anything ever again, until she walked into the kitchen at Primrose House.

No one had dared venture a guess about possible visitor numbers, but everyone had been optimistic, and so Ivy and her friends had been baking for days. Now, every inch of kitchen surface was taken up with cakes of all manner — cakes studded with currants, topped with blanched almonds, decorated with chopped candied ginger, drizzled with lemon icing.

But one cake stole Pru's attention, a Victoria sponge, its two naked layers separated by a thick cushion of fresh sliced strawberries and buttercream with a bowl of whipped cream sat nearby ready to anoint each slice. Nothing compared to English strawberries — their perfume seduced her from across the room. Pru couldn't take her eyes off the cake, and Ivy took notice.

"I don't know how that got there," Ivy said, as if the cake had stolen in the back door and was attempting to blend in with the other, more pedestrian sweets. "It'll never do for this crowd." In a wink, she had boxed up the cake and covered the bowl of whipped cream. "I'll have one of the lads run it down to your cottage."

"Oh, Ivy, the entire cake?" It was a weak protest at best. "Thank you — it'll give me something to look forward to."

* * *

A half-hour before opening time, cars began parking along the lane and people lined up, digging in their pockets and purses for the three-pound entry fee, which would go to the two charities Davina had chosen: Chaffinch's and the dog re-homing organization that had brought Mrs. Sock and Trevor together. After paying, visitors picked up copies of the leaflet that Pru had fussed over for two weeks, which consisted of a short history of Humphry Repton, a summary of the restoration, and plants in bloom. And off they went.

Pru walked the grounds nonstop in a continuous loop, ignoring the twinge in her ankle that developed on the third circuit — through the walled garden, around the gravel path to the house, along the balustrade terrace, down through the terracing to the pond, around to the front of the house, and past the oval bed. Ah, the oval bed, which had prompted so many outlandish ideas from Davina. She had finally let Pru have her own way there, and Pru had decided on a giant sequoia — still called a Wellingtonia in Britain — that stood at a young twenty feet high. She reminded herself to check back in about fifty years to see how it was doing.

She didn't think she had a second to herself the entire day. Questions came nonstop. "Did Repton design the terraces?" "Could I grow that grevillia in Shropshire?" "Have you used the blue color from Snowshill on the American chairs by the pond?"

She was quite proud of those Adirondack chairs, painted a popular vibrant blue. She stood resting her hands on the balustrade, the stone warm from the sun, and looked straight down the staircase that cut through the middle of the terraced beds, through the gap cut in the now waist-high yew walk, and onto Repton's pond with the trees mirrored in it. On the far side of the pond sat the two chairs, calling attention to themselves not only by their style — truly American — but also by their color — quite Farrow & Ball.

* * *

She could give only passing acknowledgment to family and friends. Jo, along with Cordelia, Lucy, and baby Oliver appeared, and she gave them each a hug before she was called away to explain the provenance of a few Texas roses she had found for sale at a mail-order nursery in Dorset. During one discourse in the walled garden, Pru waved her arm back toward the main gate and almost hit Simon in the face. They laughed before she introduced her brother to the group — an act that made more of an impression on Pru than it did on the visitors, but no matter.

Late in the afternoon, she noticed Liam on the terrace. He stood with one hand in his pocket and one stretched out, holding Nanda's hand as she pirouetted beneath. Cate stood near the stairs talking with Hugo. Family squabbles had been put aside by this younger generation — Cate had given Hugo her father's many boxes of notes about the area, and the reporter was writing a history of Bells Yew Green. Hugo and Ned would be listed as co-authors.

* * *

The heat took its toll on Pru. She wore a loose linen top with linen capris and fanned herself constantly with a leaflet, but she remained perpetually dripping in sweat. The dust, kicked up by cars on the lane and feet on the gravel, created thin lines of mud in the creases of her arms and neck.

She dragged herself up to the balustrade terrace once again, and Ivy appeared with a cup of tea. Pru thanked her and took a sip, but later sneaked into the kitchen and, when no one was looking, packed a glass with ice from the lemonade table and poured tepid tea over it. She hid in her old room — the former pantry, right off the kitchen — where a dozen cakes occupied the bed. In her head, she heard her mother saying, "Nothing cools you off like a good, hot cup of tea," but she was siding with her Texas dad today as she swirled the glass, chilling the contents before drinking it down in one go. She held the cold glass up to her face and rubbed it on her neck, spilling ice inside her top where it lodged in her bra and made her gasp with pleasure.

Almost everyone understood that the house was not open, but Bryan did discover an elderly couple in the upstairs hall, peering at the wallpaper and discussing William Morris, and Davina tracked down two small boys under a table in the library, playing with Bryan's collection of Dinky cars. No harm done, she said as she shooed them out. After all, that's what the toys were made for.

At five o'clock, the last stragglers were herded out of the wood, through the terraces, and from the walled garden. Davina swore that she had made five hundred copies of the leaflets, and they had run out an hour before closing. Was that possible? Pru certainly felt as if she'd talked with at least five hundred people — each one asking her about Repton, the Red Book, and which clematis was planted in the center of the walled garden beds. 'Duchess of Albany'," she replied. "It's an English selection of a Texas vine."

Ivy cleaned the kitchen in a flash and left. She had recently started a new job as head cook at Chaffinch's, and had given up her day off to help out for the open. The Templetons invited Pru to stay to dinner, but all she could think about was her quiet cottage and that Victoria sponge cake, so she begged off and headed for home.

Pru dragged herself in the door and stood for a moment in the cool, dim room contemplating which would come first — a wedge of cake or a large whisky. There was a knock.

"Pru? It's just us."

She opened the door to Liam and Cate.

"We thought we'd better tell you," Liam began, looking apologetic, "there's someone still in the walled garden."

"Oh no, Liam," Pru whined. She couldn't face even one more visitor. "Can you please tell them the garden's closed?"

"Sorry, Pru, we haven't the time," Cate said. "Mrs. Sock has invited us for tea, and we promised we'd be back by now. We've got to run."

"Yes, sure, fine," she said, and sighed heavily. "I'll go. Give Nanda my love."

They hurried out to Liam's car on the lane, as Pru walked over to the walled garden. A rivulet of sweat trickled down her spine. The gate was open just enough to slip through, and when she did, she saw Christopher leaning over to smell 'Highway 290 Pink Buttons' — a Texas rose with no fragrance whatsoever.

She laughed as her fatigue vanished and she sprinted to meet him. No words, just kisses, until finally she took a breath and said, without a speck of conviction, "You shouldn't have come all this way."

That ghost of a smile played about his lips. "I had no intention of missing it, and I've had a fine tour of the garden."

She leaned back in his arms. "How long have you been here?"

"An hour or so. I watched you from afar. I saw you talking with some tall fellow wearing an Aussie bush hat." She snorted. "I couldn't get near you; you were in such demand."

"The day seemed to go well," Pru said, with a little shrug. She touched Christopher's face. "I can't believe this. I'm so happy to see you. Although, look at me. It's been such a hot day; I'm dripping in sweat."

He pulled her close. "I thought I did that to you."

She giggled. "Oh, but you do." He tugged at her shirt in back, pulling it up to expose a band of skin that cooled immediately when the air touched it. She closed her eyes and sighed, then opened them again. "When do you have to go back?"

"Not tonight."

She was in heaven.

"Is everyone gone?" he asked.

"Yes," she whispered. "We're all alone." He pulled her shirt up farther, as her hand slipped down his leg.

"Hellooo?"

They jumped apart, and Pru whirled around to see two ladies in floral dresses and wide-brimmed straw hats peering through the gate into the garden.

"I'm sorry," Pru said, approaching them and stifling a laugh. "The garden is closed now."

"Is it?" One turned to the other. "You were right, Ellen. Now isn't that too bad?"

Pru came within five feet of them and was knocked back by the smell of gin, which was like a force field around the two women.

"We stopped for lunch at a hotel on the other side of Staplehurst," Ellen said to Pru, "and I'm afraid the time got away from us. We'll try another day." She took her companion's arm, and said, "Come along, Charlotte." She looked over Pru's shoulder into the garden. "It looks lovely."

"Could I call a taxi for you?" Pru asked, thinking that fueled-by-gin wasn't the best way to drive home.

Charlotte waved her away. "No, dear, there's no worry, Ellen's husband drove us, and he's had nothing stronger than orange squash." Pru looked past them and saw a gray-haired man with hunched shoulders sitting behind the wheel of a sedan.

"Well, goodbye then," Pru said. "Take care." She pushed the heavy wooden gate to, and leaned on it. Christopher had come up behind her. She heard the women chatting and car doors closing. "We'll just give them a minute to leave," she said. "And then, I'll get a shower."

He leaned against her. "I could help with that."

She caught her breath. "Yes, please. And after that" — could the day get any better? — "I have a Victoria sponge."

* * *

"I've decided to tell Lord Hamilton no, I won't remain as head gardener. I don't really fancy staying on after all this, and Bryan and Davina have found another undertaking." Pru had nabbed an overlooked strawberry off the plate on the nightstand, pulled on a T-shirt, and now stood at the open bedroom window, looking out on the row of oaks and hawthorn, beyond which lay the walled garden. She put her hand to the base of her throat, and felt the outline of her fan pendant, now restored to its proper place.

"Where will they go now?" Christopher got out of bed to stand beside her, and they caught a bit of evening breeze, his hand resting on her waist.

"They've bought a derelict house and estate in Wales — someplace I can neither spell nor pronounce. They've asked if I'll go and re-create the garden. They're being quite insistent. 'It'll be a seven-day-a-week post at first, Pru, but we know

283

you can do it' and 'We'll make it worth your while' and 'It's a bit more overgrown than it was here.'" She shook her head. "They do love big ventures."

"Wales," he said, as if to himself. "What did you tell them?"

She turned and studied his face without speaking for a moment, the corner of her mouth turning up. "I told them 'No, thank you.' I told them I had someplace else to be."

"Not here. Not Wales. And where is that?" He met her smile with his own.

"Well, I'm not leaving the country, if that's what you're asking. At least, not without you." She looked out the window again. "I'll go up to London. I'm sure I could get a few of my old clients back. I'll be a jobbing gardener again," she said, catching his hand.

"You don't have to do that."

"I know I don't have to. I want to. It'll give us time. You won't have to be torn between work and wherever I am, and I can start looking for another full-time post. Something in London. Perhaps Chiswick House will have an opening."

"What I mean is that you don't have to do that for me." He turned her around to face him. "Beginning the first of September, I have six months off."

Her eyes widened, and she squeezed his arms. "They're giving you time off — it's official?"

"It's taken a couple of months to get everything approved, and I didn't want to say anything until I was sure." He rested his head against hers. "I had planned on moving down here, but now that won't be necessary."

She stopped to consider the reality of their situation. "This means we'll be free."

"We'll be together," Christopher said. "I'll take you away. Where shall we go?"

They were quiet for a moment, lost in happy thoughts as they studied each other. Pru ran her finger down his chest. "Hmmm. Six months of freedom and no income." She grinned as giddiness overcame her. "But waking up every day with you." She snapped her fingers. "I've got it. We'll sell your car and buy a used caravan that my Mini can pull. We'll go down to the coast and set up camp in a layby. What do you think?"

He laughed and said, "We could move in with my sister Claire in Plymouth."

"Oh God," Pru said, "wouldn't she just love that?" She kissed him. "At this moment, even a caravan sounds perfect — an escape. See now." She walked out to the kitchen, and picked up the unopened "Read later" envelope from Davina on the counter. "It's another plea to go with them to Wales, I'm sure of it. She keeps trying — it doesn't seem to matter how many times I say 'no.' "

She pulled the letter out of the envelope, and a second piece of paper fluttered to the floor. Christopher glanced at the contents over her shoulder, then retrieved the paper from under the table, holding it up for her to see that is was a check.

Pru burst out laughing. "We may be able to upgrade that caravan."

Primrose House

30 July

Dear Pru,

Words cannot express our gratitude for your vision and hard work during the restoration of the gardens at Primrose House, your firm conviction and unswerving bravery during such trying times, and how sad we are that we must now pass it along to someone else.

If we cannot persuade you to take up the head gardener post in Wales, we hope that you and Christopher will be able to take some well-deserved time off, and toward that end we want to provide you with what might possibly be a few months' salary at an established garden.

A cheque is enclosed. Take it with our kindest regards and our hope that you both enjoy a quiet respite.

We took another look at the Red Book before returning it to Lord Hamilton, and we see that you accomplished the very essence of what Humphry Repton hoped to when he wrote:

The garden would be rather a circumstance of cheerfulness than of complaint; and the Place assume all the importance which the style and character of the mansion requires. Primrose House would be changed from a large red house by the side of a high road, to a Gentleman-like residence in the midst of a park.

Best,
Davina

THE END

AUTHOR'S NOTE

More than one hundred of Humphry Repton's Red Books exist today, and they are a delight to behold. Many remain in private hands, but some are available for public viewing. The Morgan Library & Museum will give you a virtual look at his attention to detail when presenting his landscape design to potential clients (www.themorgan.org/collections/works/repton). At the Royal Horticultural Society Lindley Library, I held the real thing — Repton's 1792 plan for Warsley Park in Huntingdonshire (part of Cambridgeshire). I could only marvel at Repton's watercolor renderings and fine handwriting, to say nothing of his ability to sell his ideas — I would certainly have hired him to make a garden. The Red Book of Primrose House is an amalgamation of text and thoughts from those sources.

Continued thanks in the Potting Shed mystery series go to my superb Alibi editor Dana Edwin Isaacson and agent Colleen Mohyde. Thanks to my sister, Carolyn Lutz, who likes each book even better than the last, and to my British resource, good friend and fellow writer Victoria Summerley. Every writer should be in a critique group; I owe many thanks to mine: Kara Pomeroy, Louise Creighton, Deb Slivinsky, and Joan Shott.

ADDITIONAL NOTE

Many thanks to Joffe Books, publishing director Kate Lyall Grant, and to my agent Christina Hogrebe (Jane Rotrosen Agency) for re-publishing my Potting Shed series!

THE JOFFE BOOKS STORY

We began in 2014 when Jasper agreed to publish his mum's much-rejected romance novel and it became a bestseller.

Since then we've grown into the largest independent publisher in the UK. We're extremely proud to publish some of the very best writers in the world, including Joy Ellis, Faith Martin, Caro Ramsay, Helen Forrester, Simon Brett and Robert Goddard. Everyone at Joffe Books loves reading and we never forget that it all begins with the magic of an author telling a story.

We are proud to publish talented first-time authors, as well as established writers whose books we love introducing to a new generation of readers.

We have been shortlisted for Independent Publisher of the Year at the British Book Awards three times, in 2020, 2021 and 2022, and for the Diversity and Inclusivity Award at the Independent Publishing Awards in 2022.

We built this company with your help, and we love to hear from you, so please email us about absolutely anything bookish at feedback@joffebooks.com

If you want to receive free books every Friday and hear about all our new releases, join our mailing list: www.joffebooks.com/contact

And when you tell your friends about us, just remember: it's pronounced Joffe as in coffee or toffee!